THE MAVERICK

Center Point
Large Print

Also by Bennett Foster and available from
Center Point Large Print:

Rider of the Rifle Rock
Cow Thief Trail

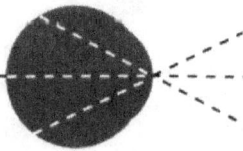

**This Large Print Book carries the
Seal of Approval of N.A.V.H.**

THE MAVERICK

Bennett Foster

CENTER POINT LARGE PRINT
THORNDIKE, MAINE

To
RALPH JONES

Chapter 1

Five good horses trotted ahead of Ray Verity, and between his legs was Spooks, the best horse on the Walking V. Ray's old saddle sported a new cinch and three new strings. The rope that rubbed against his leg was new, and his battered hat was jauntily cocked against the sun. For the first time in his nineteen years Ray Verity was going to follow a roundup wagon, going to represent the Walking V with the 10 Bow roundup crew.

Ray had deviled Wayne into letting him go. The oldest of the Verity brothers had surrendered to Ray's arguments only when the twins, Carl and Evan, added their weight. That morning Wayne, Carl, and Evan had seen him off before they rode away to their own labor of gathering Walking V steers in the Wagonwheel roughs. They stood beside the corral, grinning and calling jocund advice to Ray, each of them knowing just how the boy felt: proud as Satan and just a little scared. Now, with the 10 Bow wagon and Diamond Lake a quarter of a mile away, the pride was gone, but the uneasiness pushed Ray's heart to a pounding measure that kept pace with the trotting horses.

Ray knew that when a man repped with a wagon he was under fire. He spoke for his whole outfit, his acts, his rigging, his voice standing not for himself alone but for his outfit. For eight or nine days Ray Verity would be watched by critical eyes. The 10 Bow outfit was cow-country aristocracy, and Dutch Koogler, who ran the wagon, was a cowman second only to Miles Tenbow himself. Ray hoped that he would measure up, but he was scared.

The quarter mile ended, and Ray loped ahead to circle his horses. Dropping a lazy loop on Brownie's head and leading the horse up close to the wagon, the boy dismounted and unlashed his bed. Then, freeing Brownie, he picked up his horses again and drove them out to where the cavy grazed, letting them drift easily and with no disturbance into the bunch of horses. Lifting his hand in half salute to the wrangler, Ray rode back.

The 10 Bow maintained a camp at Diamond Lake, and the wagon was pulled up between the camp house and the corrals. Stumpy Harris, the cook, was peeling potatoes and he hardly raised his eyes as Ray, dismounting, hobbled Spooks' black-stockinged legs. It was not until the boy, striding purposefully to the fire, said, "Good mornin'," that the cook checked his potato peeling.

"Mornin'," Harris answered shortly.

Ray eyed a coffeepot hanging from the rack over the coals of the fire. His next move, assuming a nonchalance he did not feel, should be to help himself to coffee and then offer to help the cook. He hesitated. "I come over to rep for the Walkin' V," the boy announced.

Harris grunted. Ray, having stated his mission, walked over to the endgate of the wagon and bent down to take a cup from a box. He straightened and moved toward the coffeepot.

"Lay off the coffee," Harris rasped.

Surprised, Ray turned to look at the scowling cook. Very slowly the boy came back and replaced the tin cup in its box. He had never heard of a man's being refused coffee at a roundup camp; it had never occurred to him that he, his brothers, anyone, would not be welcome to a cup of coffee. Harris was again busy with the potatoes.

Walking over to his bed, Ray sat down. He watched the cook build up the fire and put Dutch ovens on to heat; he looked out to where the cavy grazed. Turning his head toward the west, he saw the dust of drives coming into the roundup ground and stood up so that his view was better.

The cattle came on, the taller, bobbing dots that were the riders showing behind them. A good half mile away from the wagon the first drives came together, and a man detaching himself from the growing mass of cattle loped toward the wagon.

As the rider came up Ray recognized Dutch Koogler. Koogler spoke to Stumpy. "Has Mr. Tenbow been out?"

"Come in right after you started," Harris answered. "He said he was goin' down to the Willow Springs an' that he'd be back for dinner."

Koogler nodded and turned to Ray. "What you doin' here?" he asked curtly.

"Wayne sent me over to rep for us," Ray answered.

Koogler frowned. "I thought Wayne or one of the twins would come," he said. "I wanted to tell Wayne."

"Tell him what?" A certain tone in Koogler's voice alarmed Ray.

"I'll let Tenbow tell you," Koogler answered briefly. "He'll be here in a little while." With no more explanation the 10 Bow wagon boss rode toward the cattle. Ray resumed his seat on the bed. Harris busied himself about the fire.

Ten minutes crawled past. The cook spoke suddenly. "Here comes Tenbow."

Tenbow came in from the east, a tall, lathy man, riding a tall horse. He stopped close by the wagon, lifting in his saddle to look out toward the cattle. Ray walked out and stopped beside the horse. "I come over to rep for the Walkin' V," the boy announced, his voice a little hoarse. "Mr. Koogler was in a minute ago. He said you had somethin' to tell me."

The eyes in Tenbow's iron-hard face were gray and cold as mountain granite. "Why didn't yore brother come over?"

"I talked Wayne into lettin' me rep."

Scowling, Tenbow thoughtfully stroked his close-cropped gray mustache. "I wish yore brother had come," he said. "I'd rather tell him. The Wagonwheel outfits are blackballed on the flats this year. We've decided not to have any of their reps with our wagons."

"You blackballed the Wagonwheel men last year," Ray said steadily, "but Wayne went with your wagon when you worked this country."

"That was last year." Tenbow stared levelly at the boy. "This year yo're included. Tell yore brother that."

Ray's lips were tight, almost white with compression. "I'll tell him," he managed to say. Turning abruptly, he walked out to where his hobbled horse grazed. Men were coming in from the herd, slouched in their saddles, taking their ease after the morning's circles, and the wrangler was bunching the cavy.

By the time the men from the herd reached camp the wrangler had the horses started in. Ray saw Dutch Koogler ride up and speak to Tenbow, saw Tenbow shake his head, hesitate, and then nod assent. The wrangler penned the horses expertly. Ray rode over to the corral.

He was inside the corral, ready to catch Brownie, when Koogler walked up to the fence. "Tenbow says to stay to dinner, kid." The foreman's voice was kind.

11

Ray did not look at Koogler. "Tell him to go to hell," the boy choked. "I don't eat with nobody that blackballs the Veritys!" The loop flipped out from his hand and settled over Brownie's wise head.

"That's yore privilege," Koogler drawled.

While he packed his bed on Brownie and got the rest of his string from the corral Ray could feel eyes upon him. Except for the men holding the cattle, the 10 Bow outfit was all in camp. The cheerful clink of knife and fork on tin plates told of a meal in progress, and voices drawled comment.

"Regular nester outfit," Ray heard Duke Greentree say. "Look at that saddle."

The back of the boy's neck reddened, but he did not turn. He started Spooks toward his horses, and these, sensing that they were going home, offered no objection. Only Brownie looked back to see if Ray was coming, and then, taking the lead as befitted his age and wisdom, struck a trot toward the north.

Four miles north of Diamond Lake, Ray Verity turned his horses west. This was against orders, but the anger in the boy's mind and the hunger in his belly overrode duty. A mile across the rolling country he came in sight of another camp. Here, too, were men who worked cattle but in a different manner and with different equipment. There was no wagon at this camp, but packsaddles were strewn about, and a bunch of cattle, under day herd, grazed off to the north. Ray, riding in, received greetings from men who stood up to welcome him.

"Hiyuh, Ray. What you doin' over here?" "Hello, kid. You come to work with us?" "Where's Wayne?"

Ray let his horses drift and got down. Here were the men from the Wagonwheel roughs, the little ranchers and their hands who, like Tenbow, were gathering beef. Tom Marvin of the Flying W, Smiley Colfax of the Slash L, Shorty Hinds and his brother Max, Earl Latiker, biggest cowman of the rough country: all gathered round.

"Hello," Ray answered the greetings. "No, I didn't come to work with you. I'm on my way home an' I stopped for dinner."

"I'll rustle you somethin'," Max Hinds offered.

"So you didn't come to work with us an' yo're on yore way home," Latiker drawled. "I thought you might be goin' to work with Tenbow's wagon, kid."

In Ray Verity the anger broke and flared into speech. "I was. I went over there. Tenbow told me the Walkin' V was blackballed, damn him!"

Silence held for just an instant, and then Smiley Colfax drawled, "Yo're in good company, Ray. That makes it unanimous. Every man in the Wagonwheel is blackballed now."

"Come an' get it, Ray," Max Hinds yelled from

beside the fire. Ray picked up a plate and filled it.

With the plate balanced on his crossed legs Ray stayed his healthy hunger. The others, politely elaborate in avoiding the subject uppermost in the boy's mind, resumed their talk. Tom Marvin, on one side of Ray, spoke to Smiley Colfax, sitting opposite him.

"I got two mavericks this mornin'. Duke Greentree an' Acey Ducey had 'em, an' I dropped in ahead about a mile an' found a slick-eared heifer an' a steer just waitin' for me."

"That's better than I did," Colfax answered. "I didn't see a thing." He turned to Ray, the perpetual grin that gave him his name exposing two gold teeth. "You'd better stick with us, kid. You got yore horses an' bed. We're goin' to work the 10 Bow gather this evenin', an' you might pick up somethin' besides a few Walkin' Vs."

Ray chewed tough beef. He was tempted mightily. These men from the Wagonwheel roughs followed an easy method of working cattle. The 10 Bows rounded up a country, put a herd together, and cut it for their own steers and those of the Drag 9 and the Bar K, the other big outfits on the Pie River Flats. Then they gave the cattle a shove back into the country that had been rounded up. It was then the greasy sack outfit took over. They bunched the released cattle and worked them again for their own brands, so avoiding the onerous business of riding circle. It was handy and almost as easy as though these small cowmen were with the 10 Bow wagon representing themselves. The only inconvenience or added expense was that of maintaining a camp and paying a cook and wrangler.

"I'd better not," Ray said. "I've got to tell Wayne what happened."

"Suit yoreself," Colfax drawled. "But you might pick up a maverick or two if you come along."

That was another thing that the pool riders did. Tom Marvin had done it that morning. When the 10 Bows made their circle the men from the Wagonwheel distributed themselves along the line of the drives. They watched the drives as the cattle drifted along, and when they saw a maverick they cut in well ahead of the circle riders and lifted out the slick. A little fire and a hot running iron and the maverick was a maverick no longer but was stamped with the brand of the man who had caught him.

"I'd better not," Ray said again. Rising, he took his plate and cup over to the wreck pan and washed them. While he was putting away the dishes Latiker got up.

"Might as well get started, boys," Latiker said.

The camp stirred to activity. Men tightened cinches on saddled horses and swung up, some with the lithe muscles and the ease of youth, some stiffly. Ray mounted Spooks, and Latiker, riding close, asked, "Are you comin' with us, Ray?"

"I'd better go on home," Ray answered.

A small, derisive smile flickered about Latiker's lips. Tall as Miles Tenbow, younger, with something of the hardness that the older man possessed, Earl Latiker was the boss of this crew. "Suit yoreself," he said, just as Colfax had done.

Ray loped out to his grazing horses. As he looked back he could see Latiker leading his men toward the south, leaving the camp deserted save for Max Hinds, the cook. Scowling, Ray started on north. He should, right now, be riding with those others, going out to bunch cattle and work them for the Walking V. And if he found a maverick and branded it, then what? What was wrong with that?

Everybody mavericked. Even old Miles Tenbow—if the tales were true—had swung a long and hungry loop not so many years ago. The state of Wyoming now claimed all unbranded cattle as its own; the Stock Association had worked and got the law passed. But sentences written in the statute books didn't change things in the grass country, didn't make a thing that was right and lawful five years ago unlawful now. Not much.

Ray had made three miles when a cow

appearing atop the rolling rise to his left stopped and looked at the horses and the rider. A big calf came up beside the cow. Leaving the horses, Ray rode up the slope. The calf was big enough to be a yearling but still followed its mother, and it wore neither brand nor earmark. On the cow's left hip the 10 Bow was plain. Temptation tugged at Ray Verity. That calf was plenty big enough to be weaned, should have been weaned long ago. Only the cow had not come fresh and . . . Anger added itself to temptation. The 10 Bow had blackballed the Verity brothers. Anybody that mavericked, anybody that had a reputation or was under the suspicion of mavericking, was blackballed on the Flats. Ray reached down for his latigo and pulled his cinch tight. Spooks trembled excitedly, knowing what was coming, as Ray took down his rope. The cow lumbered away and the calf tried to dodge, but the rope shot out and the loop fell true. Dropping down from Spooks, who kept the catch rope tight, Ray ran forward. Two minutes' rapid, panting work and the calf was tied. Ray looked around for something that would burn. He'd show old Miles Tenbow, show him plenty. He'd give that cow a good long push, and he'd drive the calf ahead of him to the roughs. Next year there would be another Walking V steer, and to hell with the Pie River outfits and the Stock Association and all the rest. He'd show them!

The cabin, set in a cove at the east side of

Verity Gap, was dark when Ray rode in. Light blossomed in its windows as he penned his horses and unsaddled, and when he reached the house and pushed open the door Carl and Evan and Wayne were in the kitchen waiting for him.

They were big men, these Verity brothers, tall and heavy and dark, oddly at contrast with Ray. Three pairs of eyes held a question, but it was Wayne who voiced it. "What's wrong, Ray?"

Slight, blond, with quick supple muscles, Ray Verity was as different from his brothers as spring from winter. Wayne, the oldest, was forty-five; the twins were forty, and Ray was nineteen.

Ray's blue eyes met Wayne's steadily. "Tenbow has blackballed us," he announced, and only because they knew him could the brothers realize the anger that flamed in the boy. "He told me that there would be no reps from the Wagonwheel with his wagon this year. I came home."

Evan cursed slowly. Carl said nothing but looked from Ray to Wayne.

"I stopped at the Pool Camp on the way home," Ray drawled, "and had dinner. We can work with them. Latiker an' Smiley Colfax both wanted me to stay."

Still Wayne did not speak. Carl growled: "Wouldn't Tenbow feed you?"

"He offered to, an' I wouldn't eat."

Silence for a moment. "Wayne," Evan said.

"I'll ride over an' talk to Tenbow in the

18

mornin'." Wayne Verity's voice was slow and level. "Are you hungry, Ray?"

Ray did not answer, but Carl, rising, walked over to the stove and removed plates from the warming oven. "Come on, kid," Carl said. "You're always hungry."

"I'll go with you in the mornin', Wayne," Evan announced. "Carl an' me both."

Wayne did not look at the twin. "No," he said. "I'll talk to Tenbow. You eat, kid, then we'll turn in."

In the morning Wayne rode off toward the south. Evan and Carl and Ray, a day's work ahead of them, watched their oldest brother go and then left the corral. As always when Wayne was gone, Evan took charge. He was older than Carl by perhaps half an hour. "We'll work the Notch," Evan announced. "We ought to be back by noon."

The Notch was close. Evan, like Carl and Ray, wanted to be at the ranch when Wayne returned from his talk with Tenbow. Ray spat out the thing that Carl and Evan were thinking as he stepped up on his horse. "I hope Wayne tells Tenbow aplenty."

Riding away from the corrals, the three Veritys passed the little hoosegow in which the Walking V steers already gathered were being held. A bunch of steers were against the fence, and Ray, with savage satisfaction, made an

19

announcement. "There'll be one more next year. I picked up a big maverick yesterday."

Carl and Evan looked at him. Evan said: "Remember what Wayne told us, Ray."

"I remember all right," Ray snapped. "But if Tenbow an' them are goin' to blackball us anyhow, what difference does a maverick make?"

Neither of the twins answered. Evan checked his horse. "You go up this side, Ray," he directed. "Start at the top an' come down. Give Carl an' me a little time to get ahead of you."

The Notch lay behind Verity Gap. Running northeast, it reached toward the tall ridges of the Whetrock Hills. Climbing the southern ridge, Ray paused at the top and looked back and down. All the country lay spread out below him. The giant reaches of the flats were to his left as he faced the west, and the rumpled, broken country of the Wagonwheel roughs below and to his right. The rough country ran for eighty miles, a basin surrounded by the broken rim, hemmed in by hills, cut and twisted and watered by little streams. Beyond it, farther north, was the Kingling River and the Sioux Agency, a place of hearsay as far as Ray was concerned, for he had never been there. Immediately below the ridge was the gap, twelve miles across, a gentle slope that led from the flat country to the rough. West, beyond the gap, the cap rock fell away, sheer and precipitous, and the Whetrocks blocked the east.

Years ago, before Wayne was born, John Verity had brought his bride into the gap and built his cabin. Verity Gap, the border line between the rough country and the smooth country, the boundary between the big outfits on the Pie River Flats and the little men who ran cattle in the Wagonwheel. Ray's horse swelled and let the wind go out of him, and Ray, turning from the scene below, went on up the ridge.

At two o'clock the twins and Ray were back in the gap with a few Walking V steers. Dropping the steers in the hoosegow, they went on to the cabin. Wayne had returned, and when all four brothers were assembled in the kitchen he reported the results of his ride. "I saw Tenbow. Ray had it right. We're blackballed on the Flats."

"Are we goin' to work with Latiker then?" Evan asked.

Wayne shrugged. "I don't know," he answered. "Tenbow told me why we were blackballed."

"What did he say?"

"He said that our west spring is the only water between the river and the Wagonwheel that hasn't got a camp on it. An' he said that it's bein' used. He says that as long as we leave that water open he'll keep the blackball on us."

"What business is it of his what we do with our water?" Ray flared.

Wayne's voice was heavy as he answered. "It ain't just maverickin' no more, Ray. Tenbow has been losin' little bunches of branded cattle, an' he thinks they're goin' into the Wagonwheel. He says that whoever is rustlin' from him has got to use the gap an' our water."

Silence followed the announcement. Evan stirred uneasily. Ray watched Wayne. Suddenly the boy spoke. "So we're supposed to play policeman for Tenbow. We're supposed to keep our friends from travelin' through Verity Gap. Tenbow mavericked. He was as bad as any of 'em, but now that he's got a big outfit he wants to stop it. I'll bet he cut manys the big calf away from its mother an' put his iron on it. It was all right for him to take a slick, but it's wrong for us."

Evan, catching Wayne's eye, glanced at Ray and jerked his head toward the door. Wayne caught the meaning of the gesture. "You'd better go out an' get some water, Ray," he drawled. "We've got to wash before we eat. We'll settle what we're goin' to do at the table."

Reluctantly Ray got up and, taking the water bucket, banged out of the house. The door had hardly closed before Evan spoke. "Ray mavericked one yesterday, Wayne. He said so this mornin'."

Wayne's voice was heavy as he answered Evan's announcement. "That kind of settles it. Ray's gettin' a wild hair in him. If we work with Latiker an' them he'll get wilder."

"So?" Evan said.

"So we'll close the west water hole."

The twins looked at each other and then at Wayne. "Latiker an' Colfax an' the rest of the men in the Wagonwheel are friends of ours, Wayne," Evan reminded. "You know how they're goin' to take it?"

"I know." Wayne Verity's face set in stern, harsh lines. "We'll get cussed, an' there'll be trouble, but we've got to do it. I won't let Ray run wild."

Evan and Carl nodded, and Wayne finished his thought: "We can't be border-liners. We've got to hook on with one bunch or the other."

Chapter 2

There is money to spend when the beef is sold. In little towns such as Gunhammer, ranchers come in to pay their long-standing bills, and the riders, with their wages burning their pockets, release their pent desires. Wayne Verity, with Smiley Colfax and Earl Latiker, were gathered in the back of Clough Weathers' store, and neither bills nor pleasure occupied their minds at the moment.

"I don't take it kindly, Wayne," Latiker stated. "I don't take it kindly at all. You say that we're not to use yore west tank comin' into or out of the gap. We've always used it. Why close the gap now?"

"I'm not closin' the gap, Earl," Wayne explained. "That ain't the idea. You're welcome to use it. All I say is that I want you to use the water at the house an' not at the west end."

"But why?" Colfax exposed his gold teeth, but the grin was not pleasant. "What's the idea? You ain't short of water at the west end, are you?"

"No." Wayne shook his head. "We ain't exactly short. I'll tell you. Tenbow blackballed us this year. I sent Ray over to work with his crew, an' he sent the kid back home. When I went to see him about it he jumped me. He said that he was losin' cattle an' he thought they were goin' into the Wagonwheel. If you boys use the water at the house I can give you a clean bill of health, that's all."

"Yo're goin' to cut cattle for Tenbow then!" Colfax snapped. "Are you on his pay roll, Wayne?"

Clough Weathers looked from Colfax to Wayne and then to Latiker. He was interested in this conversation. The 10 Bow, the Drag 9, and the Bar K, all the big outfits on the Pie River Flats, ran commissaries and bought their supplies wholesale. But, lacking the money, the men in the Wagonwheel could not do that. It was with them that Weathers did the bulk of his business, and his livelihood depended upon their wants and their good will.

"You boys have always got along," Weathers placated. "You ain't goin' to fall out over some little thing now, are you?"

Wayne shook his head. His voice was pleasant, but his words were very definite. "We ain't goin' to fall out. All I ask is to have the west water hole left alone. There's plenty of water at the house, an' it's just as short to come by there."

"Suppose," Latiker drawled, "that we don't see things yore way, Wayne? Suppose we keep on usin' the west end? Then what?"

"Why, then"—Wayne turned to Latiker—"I expect that I'd have to fence the gap an' put a camp at the west end. Tenbow would loan me the money for the fence. Likely he'd split the expense of puttin' a rider on it. I don't want to do that. I don't want to tie up with anybody."

Wayne paused. Latiker and Colfax were looking at each other.

Weathers said, "What's it all about, Wayne? What's got into you? It ain't Tenbow. You never tied up with him much."

"It's Ray," Wayne answered the merchant. "He's sore at Tenbow because we were black-balled. He's pretty young an' he wants to be wild. I won't have it. The kid's got to keep on the level."

"Meanin' that we're not on the level?" Colfax asked, danger in his voice. "Is that it? Yo're hintin' around, Wayne. Why not come out with it?" Smiley Colfax was not the amiable man that his perpetual grin would indicate.

"Wait a minute, Smiley." Earl Latiker soothed the smiling man. "We've always been friends with the Veritys. We always got along. That's Wayne's water, an' I reckon he can do what he likes with it."

"I don't like to have a man hint that I'm rustlin'," Colfax growled, "an' I don't like it when a friend of mine throws in with a fellow that's blackballed me. That's what yo're doin', Wayne. Throwin' in with Tenbow."

"That's the way it lays, Smiley," Wayne said

tightly. "I'm not accusin' anybody of anything. But I don't want my west water hole used."

Latiker laughed, easing the tension. "You'll get over it," he predicted. "Ray's been into somethin', Smiley, an' that's why Wayne's stirred up. What's the kid been into, Wayne? Maverickin'?"

"He's sore because Tenbow blackballed him," Wayne answered, rising to Latiker's good humor. "Ray wants to get even. He'll get over it." The oldest of the Verity brothers grinned. "All Ray needs to do is grow up, an' he's on the way. Today's his birthday, an' we're buyin' him a new saddle. He's twenty years old."

"I still don't see—" Colfax began.

"Oh, drop it, Smiley," Latiker said wearily. "We'll lay off the west hole, Wayne."

Relief softened Wayne's face. "You're takin' it mighty good, Earl," he said. "I didn't want to do it, but with Ray an' all . . ." He paused awkwardly. "I guess I'd better go down an' pay for that saddle," he resumed. "The twins are down there now. Come by an' visit with us, boys. You come out, Mr. Weathers." Turning, Wayne went to the door of the office.

When he was gone Latiker, Colfax, and the merchant looked at each other.

"I guess that's that," Latiker said. "You'll go by the Verity cabin from now on, Smiley."

"That damned little Ray," Colfax grated.

"Why not that damned Tenbow?" Latiker

27

drawled. "Who'd ever thought that Wayne Verity would throw in with him?"

"This ain't goin' to make any difference with you an' the Veritys, is it?" Weathers asked, concern in his voice. Trouble in the Wagonwheel meant a lessening of his business.

"Not a bit." Latiker grinned at the merchant. "We'll just go twelve miles out of our way, that's all. Wayne's seein' spooks, an' bein' blackballed has kind of upset him. None of Tenbow's cattle are goin' through the gap. Wayne'll find it out an' be ashamed of himself. Come on, Smiley. We'll see you later, Weathers." Latiker walked to the office door, and Smiley Colfax, still showing his gold teeth, followed him.

At the saddle shop Wayne found the twins watching the saddle maker put the last touches on a new saddle.

"It's all done, Wayne," Evan announced. "Want me to get Ray?"

"Go ahead," Wayne ordered. "Get him up here. I'll pay for the saddle." He reached into his pocket as the twins went out.

There was jubilation in the saddlery when Carl and Evan returned with their brother. Ray looked at the new saddle, his eyes wide, and then turned to Wayne. "Mine?" he asked unbelievingly.

"All yours, kid," Wayne answered, grinning.

"Gee!" Ray put his hands on the polished

leather of his new possession, lifted it, turned it from side to side, and then carefully replacing the saddle on its wooden horse, started for the door.

"Where you goin', kid?" Evan asked.

"To get Spooks," Ray threw back over his shoulder and disappeared at a run.

Wayne and Evan and Carl helped Ray put the new saddle on Spooks. They, in company with others, stood outside the saddle shop and watched the boy mount. The saddle squeaked, but that sound of new leather was a song in Ray's ears. He sat on Spooks while Evan, on one side, and Carl, on the other, adjusted the stirrups and then, impatient, turned Spooks and rode down the street and back to where his grinning brothers stood.

"Just as easy," Ray crowed. "She sure fits me good. An' did you see how she sets down on Spooks? I'll never sore-back a horse with this rig."

"Glad you like it, kid," Wayne drawled. "It's a mighty nice-lookin' saddle."

Ray brought Spooks around. All his boyish joy was in the yell he voiced as he kicked with his heels. Spooks caught the spirit of the occasion and jumped his full length, Ray sitting the horse as though he and the saddle were one solid piece. Down the street he rode, full tilt. Then horse and yelling boy rounded a corner and were out of sight. Wayne Verity turned to Carl and Evan, grinning broadly. "I'll just buy a drink on that," he offered. "Come on."

The Pastime Saloon was darker than the street as the Verity brothers entered. Men stood along the bar talking, slaking their thirsts with an occasional drink. Wayne made a place for himself, and the twins lined up beside him. The bartender ascertained their wants and set out a bottle and glasses. Tom Marvin, standing close to Wayne, asked a question.

"What's all the excitement outside?"

"Ray," Wayne answered, shoving the bottle over to Marvin. "It's his birthday, an' we bought him a new saddle. Have a drink with us, Tom."

"I don't care if I do." Marvin poured liquor into his glass. "You bought the kid a new saddle, huh?"

"An' a dandy." Wayne took back the bottle, refilled his own glass, and shoved the bottle along to the twins. "The kid had somethin' comin' to him."

Behind the bar, hung from pegs in the wall, were the guns and belts that law and custom prescribed should be checked when their owners came to town. Beyond Tom Marvin, toward the back of the room, was a little clump of 10 Bow men, Duke Greentree and Acey Ducey in their center. The saloon was well filled, and a card game was in progress in the back room. Wayne, suddenly inspired by an idea, lifted his voice.

"Step up an' have a drink on the Walkin' V," he called. "We've sold our steers an' it's the kid's birthday. I'm buyin'."

There was movement all along the bar as men answered the invitation. The two bartenders, grinning at a man who bought drinks for the house, moved along taking and filling orders.

Tom Marvin lifted his glass. "Here's a happy birthday to the kid," he called. "Drink up."

Empty glasses thumped back on the bar top. A babble of talk broke out. Down the bar Acey Ducey was having trouble with Duke Greentree. A 10 Bow hand, leaning forward, spoke to the bartender. "We're takin' Duke home," he said. "I'll check out his gun."

The bartender reached back and reluctantly took a gun belt from a peg. Everybody in the country knew Duke Greentree, who held down the Diamond Lake camp for the 10 Bow. And everybody knew that when Duke was drunk he was ugly, but they coddled Duke along. Able Greentree, Duke's father, was a highly respected citizen in town, and it was more on the father's account than Duke's that his quarrelsomeness was tolerated.

"Mebbe you'd better leave the gun here," the bartender said.

"We're goin' to take him home," the 10 Bow man stated. "We ain't goin' to give him his gun."

The bartender passed over belt and weapon.

Duke had quieted in Acey Ducey's grip. "I'll go home," he said thickly. "Aw right. I'll go home." The 10 Bow party started for the door.

They were abreast of Wayne Verity when Greentree broke free. Jerking from Acey Ducey's grasp, he whirled to confront the Walking V men. "I could buy saddles, too, an' drinks for the house if I rustled cattle," he snarled. "There's easy money in it!"

Space cleared about the Veritys as though by magic. Wayne and Carl and Evan were left standing alone at the bar. Acey Ducey tried to grasp Duke's arms, but Greentree threw him off. "He's drunk," Acey Ducey said swiftly. "Just plain drunk, Verity."

"I ain't so drunk I don't know what I'm sayin'," Greentree rasped. "Think I don't know? Think I can't read brands?"

"You'd better get him out, Acey," Wayne said levelly. "He's pretty drunk, an' you'd better take him home."

Acey Ducey made another ineffectual attempt to catch Duke Greentree's arms. The 10 Bow hand with him looped the gun belt over his arm and tried to help Acey Ducey. There were three or four more 10 Bow men in the room, and they shoved forward but apparently were unwilling to try to stop Duke.

"I ain't goin' home," Duke rasped, eluding Acey Ducey. "Not till I get these cow thieves told. There was a big calf follerin' a 10 Bow cow over north of Diamond Lake this fall. I knowed the calf an' I knowed the cow. The calf ain't follerin' her now. I found him over on the rim wearin' a Walkin' V. He wasn't no maverick. You stole him, Verity!"

"That," Wayne Verity said quietly, "is a lie, Duke. The Walkin' V don't steal cattle. You may be drunk, but I'll hold you to what you've said."

Acey Ducey and the cowboy with the gun belt closed in determinedly. Duke Greentree struggled. Then suddenly he had the gun from the dangling scabbard, and the 10 Bow hand jumped back. Acey Ducey made a futile attempt for the weapon and was knocked aside. It was Wayne Verity, closing in swiftly, who reached for the gun and seized it. Greentree was a big man, almost as big as Wayne. The two came together, the gun between them. There followed a swift, brief struggle, a muffled explosion, then suddenly Duke Greentree went limp. Wayne, stepping back with the gun in his hand, stared unbelievingly at the fallen body. For an instant there was no sound in the Pastime Saloon. Then a 10 Bow man yelled: "By God, he's killed Duke. Give me my gun!"

Wayne backed against the bar, Greentree's Colt in his hand. Evan jumped to the bar top, dropped on the other side, and with a sweep of his big arm possessed himself of the weapons on the pegs.

Carl backed up beside Wayne, took the gun that Evan thrust out to him, and brought it level. At the door a man yelled and dived for the outside. The 10 Bow rider, full of liquor, was loudly demanding his Colt, and Acey Ducey, wide-eyed, straightened up from beside Duke Greentree. "Duke's dead," he said, as though he did not believe his own words.

"You saw it," Wayne Verity rasped hoarsely. "You saw it, Acey."

Acey Ducey did not answer. Duke Greentree had been Acey Ducey's partner. They had shared their blankets, their last scraps of tobacco, had taken the rough and the smooth together. Acey Ducey reached into his shirt and brought out a short-barreled, nickel-plated hide-out gun that glinted evilly in the dusky light of the Pastime. Acey's gun came up, but before it reached a level Evan Verity, behind the bar, fired twice, the explosions thunderous in the crowded barroom. Acey whirled half around and pitched down across his partner's legs. Boots pounded in the Pastime as men ran, some for the front door, some for the back. A bartender, apron flapping, vaulted the bar, jammed shoulders with another man in the doorway, crowded him down, and pitched out into the street. The fallen man crawled out, and the three Verity brothers were left alone, no one to contest their possession of the barroom.

Out in the street Ray Verity, riding his new

saddle and putting Spooks through his paces, heard the sound of shots. He saw men come tumbling out the door of the Pastime Saloon, stumble and fall, get up, and bunch together at the corners of the building. A man came running down the street yelling: "Where's Jorbet? Where's Jorbet?"

Ray swung Spooks in front of the running man, stopping him. "What happened?" Ray demanded, bending in the saddle. "What was the shootin'?"

The man who wanted the city marshal did not recognize his interrogator. His eyes were wide with the fright of what he had seen. "The Veritys," he yelled, not lowering his voice at all. "They killed Duke Greentree. Where's Jorbet?"

Ray jumped Spooks ahead. Straight up the street boy and horse and new saddle clattered through the crowd at the east corner of the saloon, sending men scrambling out of their path. In front of the Pastime's door Ray turned Spooks on a dime. Bent low in the saddle, his head barely cleared the door top as the swinging shutters banged back. Spooks stopped, nostrils dilated, and Ray dropped down to the floor. The Verity brothers were together in the Pastime barroom, and outside Gunhammer seethed and boiled.

Chapter 3

There were almost as many versions of the killings as there had been men in the Pastime. The 10 Bow men, joining together, had one story that suited them: Acey Ducey and Duke Greentree had never had a chance. Some of the townsmen withdrew, removing themselves from the trouble; but others, friends of Duke's or his father's friends, joined the 10 Bow. So, too, did those Drag 9 and Bar K riders who were in town. These made a preponderance of the crowd. The Wagonwheel men, outnumbered badly, drew together, forming one small, sullen group composed of Earl Latiker, Colfax, Tom Marvin, and Max Hinds. Shorty Hinds hurried from the wagon yard to join them and hear Marvin's story.

If Virgil Jorbet, city marshal and deputy sheriff, had arrived promptly he might have circumvented further trouble, but before Jorbet came the situation was completely out of hand. A little bunch of 10 Bow hands, brave with whisky and reinforced by two Drag 9 riders and a few of Greentree's tough friends, tried to take the Pastime. They made the mistake of shooting before they charged and as a result met with a withering blast of fire at the saloon's door. A Drag 9 man was wounded slightly, and a townsman had the toe of his shoe shot off before the attacking force retired in bad order.

The Verity brothers occupied a strong position. They dragged loose tables across the doors, tied Spooks where he could do no damage, and took stock of the situation. Among the four there were seven guns and plenty of ammunition, and they did not have to sell out cheaply. Wayne saw exactly how matters stood.

"It's the 10 Bow an' some more," he announced, turning to his brothers after peering out a window. "They're drunk an' ugly. We'll stick here." Wayne's face was dark with determination. He had killed a man in self-defense, and Evan had killed another. There was a crowd outside, an ugly, belligerent, half-drunk mob. The Veritys had to hold the Pastime until reinforcements arrived if they wanted to keep on living. If they tried to go out they would be killed. That was the way matters stood when Jorbet, arriving at last, called for the Veritys to surrender.

"You get that mob outside to go an' we'll come out." Wayne parleyed with Jorbet. "We'll surrender if you do that, but we won't walk out to be killed."

Jorbet shouted again that he would protect the Veritys, but Wayne had no very high opinion of Jorbet, either as an officer or man. "You couldn't protect yourself," he countered. "Get that crowd to leave, an' we'll surrender."

The marshal turned to the 10 Bow men and those who had joined them but met an equal resistance. The 10 Bow men and their adherents were armed; they had been drinking, and they surrounded the Pastime Saloon. They would not budge. This was the situation that Miles Tenbow and Dutch Koogler encountered as they came riding into Gunhammer shortly after sunset.

The 10 Bow owner and his wagon boss saw the empty street and the little knots of men that hovered in the shadows of the buildings. Gunhammer was dark, the only illumination an occasional gun flash as some man on the outside vented his spite against the Pastime and its occupants. Tenbow and his foreman dismounted before Weathers' store and were almost instantly joined by Jorbet, who explained what had happened.

"The Veritys killed Greentree an' Acey Ducey. They've forted up in the Pastime. I tried to arrest 'em, Mr. Tenbow, but they won't come out. There's a bunch of yore men outside, an' they tried to charge the saloon, but they got throwed back. The Veritys won't surrender. I told 'em I'd protect 'em, but they won't give up."

Dutch Koogler snorted scornfully. He, like Wayne Verity, had no great faith in any protection that Jorbet might offer. Miles Tenbow looked levelly at the officer. "How'd the shootin' come up?" he demanded.

"Greentree an' Wayne Verity got to quarrelin'. Verity jumped Duke an' killed him, an' Acey tried to kill Verity. One of the twins shot Acey."

"Had Duke been drinkin'?"

"I don't think so. He—"

The owner of the Pastime Saloon, who had been behind the bar when the trouble broke, came up in time to hear Jorbet's answer. The saloonkeeper, wild with anxiety because of the damage to his property, interrupted the marshal's speech. The saloon man had contended with much from Duke Greentree and his friends in the past, and now he was thoroughly incensed.

"Duke was drunk, Mr. Tenbow," he said bluntly. "He'd been in my place about an hour an' he was drunk when he came in. I saw the whole thing."

"Tell me!" Tenbow commanded.

"Duke was drunk," the saloonkeeper said again and continued with the story. It was a fair account, slightly biased, perhaps, because he was talking to the owner of the 10 Bow. "An' that's the way it happened," he concluded. "Get 'em out of there, Mr. Tenbow. Call yore boys off. They'll listen to you. They're shootin' up my place an' now they're talkin' about burnin' it."

Miles Tenbow waited to hear no more. Tall and straight, he strode along the empty street until he reached the front of the Pastime.

"10 Bow!" he shouted. "This way, 10 Bow!"

Men began to straggle from their places of concealment. Miles Tenbow stared at them through the dusk. "Yo're all done with this foolishness!" he declared. "Yo're through." Then turning toward the Pastime, he called again. "Verity? This is Miles Tenbow talkin'. Surrender!"

An instant's pause, and then Wayne Verity said from the door of the Pastime: "We won't come out to be killed, Tenbow."

"You won't be killed. Lay down yore guns an' come out. Yo're under my protection."

In the saloon Wayne turned back from the door and spoke to his brothers. "You heard Tenbow?"

The twins grunted. Ray snarled: "I don't trust him no more than I do Jorbet. Don't give in to 'em, Wayne!"

"Tenbow means what he says," Wayne answered. "He'll protect us." He was watching the boy as he spoke, his eyes deep and somber. Here in the Pastime Saloon the Veritys might well make their last stand. There was no delusion in Wayne's mind. They could hold the Pastime for a while but not forever. Lead and fire, hard shooting and violent men would drive them out. They would kill more men before they were themselves killed. For himself Wayne did not care. He had always taken things as they came, played the cards that were dealt him. But Ray . . .

"We'll lay down our guns an' come out, Tenbow," Wayne called. "We surrender. Put down yore guns, boys. We're goin' out."

Miles Tenbow, in the street, heard the rasp of heavy objects as they were dragged away from the door. Jorbet, coming up to join the cowman, asked: "Where'll we take 'em, Mr. Tenbow?"

Tenbow did not heed his words. One by one men came from the saloon door and walked deliberately out to where Tenbow stood.

"We left our guns inside," Wayne said as he stopped.

In the crowd of men across the street a murmur rose, a growled, sullen sound that was more a threat than any words. Tenbow stared at Wayne. "You've killed two of my men," he said tightly. "You surrendered to me, an' I'll protect you. I'll see that you have a fair trial, but that's all. Come on."

Turning, not looking at the crowd, he led the way down the street, Wayne and his brothers following, Koogler and Jorbet forming an after-guard. Looking back, Ray saw the crowd mill and move toward the Pastime.

Gunhammer had no jail. There was a strong room in the front end of Weathers' warehouse, and it was there that Tenbow took the Verity brothers for safety. Equipped with a lamp, Ray and Wayne and Carl and Evan went into the strong room while Tenbow, with Weathers and Jorbet and Koogler, stopped outside. "I'll stay here," Tenbow said. "I promised you protection, an' you'll get it." He swung the door closed, and

41

the bar fell into its socket with a sullen thud. From outside the Veritys could dimly hear sounds of movement and Tenbow's voice, but the words were not distinguishable.

Wayne sat down against the wall. The twins, together as always, sat beside Wayne. Only Ray, catlike, paced back and forth. "We should have stuck it out," he flared. "They'd never have got us."

"We'd have been killed before mornin'," Wayne answered heavily. "Tenbow gave us an out, an' I took it." He dropped his square chin on his chest and stared at the floor. Ray looked at the twins and, like Wayne, they would not meet his eyes. He resumed his restless pacing.

"An' now what happens?" Ray demanded, stopping again. "What do we do now?"

"Wait," Wayne said. "I—Kid, did you maverick a 10 Bow calf? Duke Greentree claimed that we'd stole one."

Ray stood stock-still, then crossed over and sat down beside Wayne. Outside, along Gunhammer's street, lights glowed in buildings and men lined the bars and talked; and in the back room of the barbershop where the bodies had been taken Able Greentree, old and worn and white-faced, sat beside his son and stared into space.

Virgil Jorbet's first mistake that night had been in not being on hand before the 10 Bow attacked the Pastime. His second error was in not closing Gunhammer tight. He should have closed his town, should have gone along the street from saloon to store to saddle shop, to barber and butcher and every other business and closed them. Now in the saloons and in the stores and the saddlery and the barbershop men met to talk. Bottles passed across the bars and from hand to hand.

"Old Able's just sittin' there lookin' at nothin'."

"Verity didn't give Duke a chance. Jumped him an' shot him."

"Acey wasn't goin' to shoot. He just tried to stop Verity."

"The damned rustlers. Duke caught onto 'em, an' they killed him."

So the talk went. Little groups of men came together and murmured, low-voiced, 10 Bow and Drag 9 riders, townsmen, friends of Able Greentree.

"We ought to take 'em out of there an' hang 'em, the dirty murderers!"

"Hangin's too good for 'em."

"To hell with Tenbow! It was his men that they killed! What's he doin', protectin' the Veritys?"

At midnight Jorbet and Weathers came to where Miles Tenbow and Dutch Koogler sat outside the strong room. Jorbet's face was ashen, and his eyes were wide. Weathers was sullenly determined.

"They're talkin' lynchin', Mr. Tenbow," the marshal blurted. "Some of 'em went to Giant's an' got a rope. We can't stop 'em."

"You've got to get the Veritys out of here," Weathers announced. "I ain't goin' to have my place wrecked. You got to get 'em out."

Tenbow looked at his foreman, and Koogler nodded. The sullen murmur from the street was penetrating to the warehouse.

"We can take 'em into Fort Neville," Jorbet said eagerly, "an' turn 'em over to the sheriff."

"That ain't a bad idea," Koogler seconded slowly. "We could slip 'em out. Get a hack from the livery an' drive it up in the alley an' load 'em in. Nobody'd see us."

Miles Tenbow stood up suddenly. "Weathers," he ordered, "you go down to the livery an' get a hack. Get Charlie Nerril to drive it. Nerril won't talk. Bring it up the alley. Dutch, you go with 'em. You, too, Jorbet. You'd better get another man that you can trust. I'm goin' out an' stop this foolishness."

"I'll get the hack," Weathers promised and hurried off. Jorbet hesitated an instant and then turned. "I'm goin' to get my handcuffs from the house," he announced, and he, too, departed.

Tenbow looked at Koogler. "You stay here, Dutch," he ordered, and then he, too, was gone.

Weathers, en route to the livery barn, hurried past the crowd that milled in front of the

Pastime. Farther along the street stood a little knot of silent men who were taking no part in the demonstration. One of these moved as he approached, stepping out to intercept him.

"Now what?" Smiley Colfax questioned. "The boys are gettin' pretty nasty."

These were neighbors of the Verity brothers, men from the Wagonwheel. "They're goin' to take them to Fort Neville," Weathers said hurriedly. "I'm goin' to get a hack. Tenbow wants another man to go along. One of you better do it."

"Did you hear that, Earl?" Colfax demanded.

"I heard it," Latiker answered.

"I've got to get that hack," Weathers announced. He wheeled away from the Wagonwheel men and went on.

The Verity brothers heard the scrape of the bar's being lifted from the door and stood up. The door swung open, and Koogler, with Colfax and Jorbet following him, came into the strong room.

"Pretty mean outside, boys," Koogler drawled. "Gettin' mighty nasty. We figure that we'd better move you."

"Where's Tenbow?" Wayne demanded.

"He's out tryin' to quiet 'em. We're goin' to take you to Fort Neville. It'll be safer there. We got a hack outside."

Wayne nodded slowly. Jorbet, his voice

officious, gave a command. "Hold out yore hands, Verity. We ain't goin' to take any chances of losin' you on the way." Metal glinted in the officer's hands.

"You don't need to handcuff us," Wayne objected. "We won't try to make a break."

"I ain't takin' any chances," Jorbet answered. "You killed two men tonight, you Veritys did. Hold out yore hands. There!"

Metal clinked as the handcuff closed around Wayne's wrist. Ray Verity was bunched, catlike, ready to fight.

"No use, kid," Wayne said wearily. "Let him do it." Metal clinked again, and Ray was manacled to his brother. The twins offered no resistance. Wayne had submitted, and that was enough.

"Now come along," Jorbet ordered. "Blow out that lamp, Dutch. We don't want nobody to see us goin' out."

The hack was in the alley, a buckboard with canvas-covered bows. Charlie Nerril occupied the seat, and the twins climbed in and then Wayne and Ray, taking places on the cross seats behind Nerril. Jorbet got up beside the driver, and there was a squeak of leather as Koogler and Colfax mounted their saddle horses. Jorbet said: "All right, Charlie. Let's go."

From the street beyond the alley came the sullen murmur of men who meet together to make a crowd, an ugly, murderous growling.

46

Ray's shoulder touched Wayne's, and the boy shivered.

"Take it easy, kid," Wayne whispered. "We're all right. Just take it easy."

They had no trouble getting out of town. All the crowd was centered on the main street, and by swinging straight north Nerril left the street behind. Outside the town he turned his team west and made a half circle around Gunhammer. Half a mile beyond the farthest building they struck the Fort Neville road.

Fort Neville, the county seat, was fifty-five miles from Gunhammer; the Pie River ford was eighteen miles along the way, and beyond the ford was the 10 Bow headquarters. Once the party was clear of town Jorbet, Koogler, and Nerril began to talk.

"Just push yore horses right along, Charlie," Koogler directed. "We can change horses at the 10 Bow."

"I figured on that," Nerril answered.

In the hack the Verity brothers were silent. Now and again Ray's shoulder rubbed Wayne's. Once Evan said, "Let's shift, Carl. I'm tired of holdin' my hand this way." Jorbet, turning in the seat, asked questions, demanding Wayne's story of the happenings in the Pastime.

"I'll tell Frank Arnold when we get to Fort Neville," Wayne answered shortly. "No use in tellin' it twice." Frank Arnold was the sheriff.

"I could help you some with Frank," Jorbet volunteered. "I've heard about four different stories, Wayne."

"You'll hear mine in Fort Neville."

Jorbet shrugged. "All right," he agreed. "If you don't want to talk about it you won't." He faced around and spoke to Nerril again.

The hack was a good eight miles along the road when Dutch Koogler voiced an exclamation. "Somebody followin' us. Did you see 'em, Smiley?"

"I ain't seen anybody," Colfax answered.

"I'd of swore I saw a bunch come over the ridge," Koogler growled. "I had 'em skylighted. Stop a minute, Charlie."

Nerril pulled the team to a halt. Every man listened intently. Faint in the distance came the even beat of hoofs against hard ground.

"Somebody comin', all right," Koogler grated. "Whip up that team, Nerril!"

The hack rolled ahead, the horses breaking from a walk into a sharp trot. The road climbed up, and Smiley Colfax called to Koogler across the top of the hack. "Likely it's Tenbow. He might be goin' to join us."

"Tenbow was goin' to stay an' keep things quiet," Koogler called back. "Whip up that team, Charlie. Use yore whip."

Under the whip the team stretched out into a run. The hack rocked and lurched. Wayne, gripping the grab iron with his free left hand, leaned back toward the twins. "They never intended for us to get to Fort Neville," he rasped. "It was a stall."

"Tenbow, damn him!" Evan's voice answered. "He promised us protection."

Outside the hack Koogler yelled: "There's a whole bunch! See 'em against the sky line?"

Wayne leaned close to Ray. "They ain't goin' to take us," he rasped in Ray's ear. "Not without a fight. Tenbow lied. He double-crossed us. When I say go throw yore left arm up an' drop it over Jorbet's head. He's got a gun!"

He did not wait for Ray's assent but leaned back toward the twins. "We're goin' to make a break for it," his whisper rasped. "Back the kid an' me when we make our play."

"What are you doin'?" Jorbet half turned on the seat. "What's goin' on back there? By glory, I'll—"

The officer's words were broken short. Over the pounding of the team's hoofs and the rattle of the hack another sound came clear and distinct, the thunder of horses running. Koogler yelled: "By God, they've got us." A gun bellowed, and a bullet ripped into the canvas cover. Another yell sounded. "Pull up, Nerril. We want the Veritys an', by God, we'll take 'em!"

"Now!" Wayne Verity rasped and flung his manacled hand at Jorbet's head.

49

The hack lurched, and Charlie Nerril yelled at the horses. Dutch Koogler's shouted oath was cut short. Ray, moving with Wayne, felt the handcuff jerk tight against his wrist. Jorbet squawked like a frightened cat and came back toward the two Veritys as the handcuff chain caught his Adam's apple. The twins, swarming up over Ray to get to Nerril, momentarily blocked his vision. Then the team swung from the road, and the hack, striking a boulder, bounced high and pitched over on its side. Wayne yelled, a formless, fiercely jubilant shout. Ray hit the ground, his brother, Jorbet, and the twins piling up on top of him. Buried beneath the pile of bodies, he cleared an arm and shoved. Then he was free, save for the handcuff that bound him close to Wayne, and guns were flashing in the darkness all about. He heard Evan's yell, "Damn you! Damn you!" Beside Ray a gun roared an answer to the cannonade that splintered wood from the bed of the hack, that ripped through the canvas, sending dirt and gravel spurting up about them. One of the twins had also possessed himself of a weapon.

Beside Ray, Wayne fired once, then again, deliberately. A man screamed. Someone shouted: "They got guns! The Veritys got guns!" Momentarily the firing checked.

"Kid!" Wayne said hoarsely.

Jorbet was gone. Charlie Nerril was gone. The four Veritys crouched behind the overturned hack. The team had snapped the tongue and run.

"I'm all right, Wayne," Ray answered.

"Evan?"

"Here. Carl's hit."

"They'll try in a minute," Wayne rasped. "Make 'em pay for it."

"Nerril had a gun," Evan growled. "I got it. They—"

Something thudded down beside the hack. A man gave a little bubbling sigh. "Carl!" Wild anxiety in Wayne's voice. There was no answer. Then Evan spoke.

"He's dead. Carl's dead."

There was no time for Wayne to answer, no time for anything. The brief interlude was over. Again in the darkness beyond the overturned hack guns flamed. Ray felt Wayne's arm jerk against the handcuff, heard the crash of Wayne's gun and Evan's weapon as the fusillade was answered. Then the firing checked again.

"Evan! Evan!"

They waited fractionally. Wayne pulled on the handcuff, and Ray moved. Wayne's voice was dead, lifeless with defeat. "Evan too." The twins were gone. Ray could not realize that those big, laughing men who, with Wayne, had always looked after him were dead.

"Wayne . . ."

"I'm hit, kid," Wayne rasped. "Bad. I've got Evan's gun."

"Give me one!"

"No. Listen, kid. I'm goin' to get you loose. Crawl off. Don't go home. Hide. Get away from this country. Don't ever come back to it."

"Wayne . . ."

Ray could dimly see what his brother was doing. Wayne had lifted his arm that bore the handcuff. Now his left hand, holding a gun, came up deliberately. Beyond the hack there was the rasp of excited voices as the attackers discussed their next move. Wayne's gun came on up. "One for me an' one for them, an' maybe one in Evan's gun," Wayne panted. The gun exploded, the sound muffled. Ray felt the shock through the handcuff on his wrist. Involuntarily he jerked his arm away. It was free! An empty handcuff clattered against its fellow locked on Ray's arm.

"Ah . . . God!" Wayne gasped.

"Wayne! You—"

"Go on, kid. Go on. They're comin'!"

Again the guns beyond the wagon roared their hate. Wayne, staggering up, rounded the end of the hack. He fired once more, flame ringing his gun, and then went down. From the attackers came a wildly exultant shout, and the firing checked. Ray rose to his full height. He could not see Wayne beyond the hack, and the twins were a dark mass at his feet. Something struck him, knocking him back and down. He rolled, his side numb, and crawled forward. The shooting stopped entirely. There was a horse running close by. High and clear and utterly recognizable, a man yelled, "10 Bow! 10 Bow men!" That was old Miles Tenbow himself. Dirt crumbled under Ray's hands, and he pitched forward, sliding down the bank of a wash, striking the bottom with a thud. He lay there a moment, hearing the turmoil above him.

A man shouted: "Here's three of 'em. Where's the kid? Get that damned kid!" Ray Verity lifted himself up on his hands and knees and began to crawl.

Chapter 4

Mat Yoeman lived by himself and counted it a blessing. For ten years he had occupied a canyon on the east side of the Whetrocks, answering to no one for what he did or said. When he came into the country he drove a little bunch of mares and two good studs, and these he turned loose on the lower benches of the hills. Now he branded the Ace of Spades on the left hips of all the colts that he could catch. The Whetrocks were his bank and the horses his checking account. Whenever Mat ran short of cash he rounded up a few geldings and sold them and, if they did not bring enough to supply his needs, went back for more horses.

With November at hand and winter threatening, Mat decided to go to Gunhammer. He was nearly out of supplies, particularly powder with which to kill his winter meat, and, too, he was due to visit in town. Not that Mat planned to stay long. Forty minutes in Gunhammer would be ample satisfaction for his solitary spirit. He spent three days catching the exact horses he wanted to sell, took Bear Dance, his own pet saddle horse, and Custer, a big sorrel gelding, and started out. His first day's leisurely riding brought him to the bank of the Pie River where he made camp.

In the morning, rising with the sun, Mat went to the river to wash. Army training and Sioux habits conflicted in the old man, but he was cleanly. He finished scrubbing his face from which his Sioux blood brothers had painfully removed the beard and was arranging the braids of his long yellow hair when he spotted something odd across the river. Mat fastened the doeskin thong tightly about a braid and stared. Across the stream a wash came down, and at the end of the wash, almost at the riverbank, a man lay sprawled, arms thrown forward, as though reaching for the water. Mat flung his braids back over his shoulders with a flirt of his head and went back to camp to catch a horse. Within ten minutes his big gelding splashed out of the water on the southern bank of the Pie.

Mat Yoeman knew every man in the country. He had sold horses in the Wagonwheel, in Gunhammer, and in Fort Neville, and to the ranchmen on the flats. Dismounting, he turned over his discovery and looked down into Ray Verity's face. The boy was breathing faintly through his mouth; his glazed eyes were half open, and on his shirt was a bloody splotch.

"Glory!" Mat exclaimed, using his strongest expletive. "By glory!"

The situation called for immediate action. Leading Bear Dance as close to the body as the animal would come, Mat used his rope to tie up a hind foot of the horse and heaved Ray to its back. Mat was sixty years old, but he had scouted for Custer and shod horses for Benteen's pack train, and the boy's light body came up easily and was tied across the saddle.

Mat disliked the prospect of wading the November cold water, but it had to be faced. Holding the gelding's reins, Mat plunged in and wallowed across the little stream, climbing out on the northern bank, wet to his waist.

A fire and hot water were next in order. Cow chips made the fire, and a blackened kettle held the water. Mat squatted beside Ray to open his shirt and undershirt.

The boy had been shot hard but not too seriously, Mat decided when he saw the wound. The bullet had plowed through under the arm, cracking a rib and cutting an ugly raw furrow half around the body. It was, Mat thought, loss of blood that had stopped the boy, and if his hands and knees were any indication, Ray had taken a lot of stopping. The Levi's he wore were in shreds about the knees, and both knees and hands were raw from contact with rocks and brush. Mat got up from his examination and went to his meager pack which held a clean cloth and a chunk of salt pork as well as a roll of doeskin. The kettle of water was steaming when Mat returned to the boy and, kneeling, went to work.

Ray did not stir under the old man's ministrations. Mat rolled him from side to side as his work demanded, and the boy remained utterly limp. When the wound had been bandaged and Mat had done what he could for the battered hands and knees, Ray still breathed shallowly through his mouth, and his eyes were still glazed. Mat brought his own bedding, two blankets and a tanned cowhide, and covered the boy. Then, satisfied that he had done what he could, he prepared his breakfast.

While he ate jerky and drank river water Mat considered the situation. He had a badly injured man to look after and he was camped right out in the big middle of the Pie River Flats. Gunhammer was not too far away, and there were people in Gunhammer who would take Ray Verity off his hands. There lay the trouble. There were lots of people in Gunhammer, and they would ask fool questions and demand answers and be a nuisance in general. Besides, thought Mat, when a man is hurt he belongs at home where his folks can look after him. Casting up accounts, Mat decided against the town. The logical place for Ray was with his brothers at Verity Gap, and that was forty miles away. It would not be any harder to take Ray forty miles than eighteen. To be sure the 10 Bow was nearer than either Gunhammer or Verity Gap, but to get to the 10 Bow Mat would have to go upstream and cross the river. Mat swallowed the last of his jerky and stood up.

His experience with the Sioux stood him in good stead now. A hundred yards upstream he cut green willows with his ax and, dragging them back, combined the willows, doeskin strings, and the cowhide to make a travois.

All of Mat's horses, excepting his saddle horse and Custer, were broncs. Mat caught Custer and rigged a harness for the travois while the big horse turned his head to watch the proceeding. Custer was gentle and would stand for a great deal. When the travois was rigged Mat led the sorrel around to accustom him to his unusual burden and then loaded Ray. With the boy wrapped and tied securely with his saddle rope, Mat set about loading the remains of his pack upon the travois, tucking them in; then he caught his own horse and mounted. The travois dragged easily behind Custer, the spring of the willow trunks easing it over the rough places. Man and horse and boy and travois went straight north, and behind them the geldings that Mat had brought down to sell stared curiously at the departing caravan.

Every thirty minutes or so Mat Yoeman stopped to examine Ray and to see that the lashings were in place. The boy remained in a coma, although that was not Mat's word for it. Like many another of his breed and time, Mat talked to himself. Now as he and Bear Dance, followed by Custer and the travois, covered country, Mat indulged in a soliloquy.

"Somethin' bad," he said. "Mighty bad. Young buck like him oughtn't to be in a mess like this. He's walkin' with God now. By'n by he'll come back." Bear Dance worked his ears as he always did when Mat talked and daintily skirted the beginning of a wash.

Mat reached Diamond Lake at noon. The 10 Bow camp beside the lake was deserted, and the old man stopped the travois where a motte of trees made skeleton shadows with their leafless branches. Ray was babbling in delirium, and his pallid cheeks were flushed. Feeling the boy's hot head, Mat was not pleased. He had, he thought, made a mistake. Perhaps he should have taken the boy to Gunhammer. But this was no time for regrets, for certainly Mat could not turn back now. Verity Gap was nearer than Gunhammer. Mat did what he could to ease the fever and listened to Ray's muttered calls for Wayne. After a time the boy relapsed into his coma, staring up at Mat with dull, lifeless eyes.

At five o'clock, with the Whetrocks close upon his right, Mat came to the edge of the gap and struck the wagon road that the Veritys had used when they went to town. He followed it, keeping out of the road, so that the travois would not jar in the ruts. The roof of the Verity cabin appeared, and relief flooded Mat Yoeman.

No one answered Mat's call; no one moved through the November dusk. The cabin was deserted. Dismounting, Mat opened the door and went inside. If the Veritys were not at home, then he must stay with Ray until one of the brothers returned. Mat was already planning what he would do. He could stay here through the night and in the morning would ride back, pick up his horses, and resume his interrupted trip to Gunhammer. He made a bed ready and, going out, untied the lashings and carried Ray inside. Ray muttered as Mat put him on the bed but seemed to rest more easily.

There was nothing that could be done immediately for the boy, and Mat went out. He put Custer and Bear Dance in the corral, unsaddled and removed the travois, and carried his rifle up to the house. The wood box behind the stove was empty, and while Mat was replenishing the supply he saw a little party of horsemen coming down from the mouth of the gap, riding through the steely twilight. It was, Mat thought, about time that the Veritys got home to look after their brother. He carried in his wood.

When he went back to the door the horsemen were near enough for recognition. They were not the Veritys. The men in the lead were Smiley Colfax and Earl Latiker, and behind them were Shorty and Max Hinds and Tom Marvin. They stopped their horses ten feet from the cabin door and looked down at Mat.

"What are you doin' here, Yoeman?" Latiker queried.

"Waitin' for the Veritys." Mat let it go at that. A man who talked too much precipitated trouble, and Ray Verity had been shot; by whom Mat did not know.

Colfax laughed, a harsh bark of sound. There was a bandage around his head that made his hat ride awkwardly askew. "You'll wait a long time," Colfax rasped. "The Veritys are in hell by now, I reckon."

"Yeah?" Mat drawled.

"Yeah. Wayne an' the twins were killed last night about ten miles from the Fort Neville Crossin'. Ray got loose, but he was hit. Either he'll die or somebody will pick him up. If you want the Veritys you won't find 'em here."

"How'd it happen?" Max asked quietly.

Latiker dismounted. Colfax and the other three followed his example as Latiker squatted down in front of his horse. "It started in Gunhammer," he drawled. "In the Pastime Saloon. Duke Greentree accused Wayne of stealin' cattle, an' Wayne killed him. One of the twins killed Acey Ducey an' run the crowd out of the Pastime. There was hell in Gunhammer last night."

"How'd Wayne an' the twins get on the Fort Neville road?" Mat asked. "Did they make a run for it?"

"No," Latiker said, and his voice drawled on,

relating the tale while Mat Yoeman listened intently. "An' that was how it happened," Latiker concluded. "Ray got away. Wayne shot off his own wrist so that the kid could jerk the handcuff loose. Ray won't get far. He was hit. They found his tracks an' some blood, an' they'll pick him up."

"Who'll pick him up?"

"The posse that's out after him."

Just for a moment Mat studied the men in front of him. "A kind of fool thing, if you ask me," he said. "Tryin' to spirit the Veritys out of town an' lettin' everybody know where they were takin' 'em an' when. It was the 10 Bow that jumped the hack, you said?"

"The 10 Bow an' some others. Everybody was roused up about Duke an' Acey bein' killed."

Latiker got up as he said that, and Colfax, who, like Latiker, had squatted while the talk went on, also arose. "We figured that we'd get our supper here," Colfax remarked. "Wayne an' them won't be usin' their grub from now on." Colfax moved toward the door.

Old Mat Yoeman reached a hand back and possessed himself of his rifle. The gun was a long-barreled Winchester .38-.55 and carried eleven shells, eleven sure hits when Mat used the gun. He brought it out, and his calloused thumb pulled the hammer back.

"How'd you get yore head hurt, Smiley?" he

demanded. "Killin' the Verity boys?" Mat Yoeman trusted no one, not even himself at times.

"Why, damn you," Colfax rasped. "I was with 'em. I was helpin' take the Veritys to Fort Neville."

"So?" Mat said gently. "An' the rest of you was pitchin' horseshoes, I reckon. You wouldn't have time to side a neighbor in a tight. You look like a passel of skunks to me. Eat yore suppers at home. Light out!"

"Say—" Colfax began.

"I done said. Light out!"

Looking into Mat's gray eyes was like looking into the twin barrels of a shotgun with both hammers cocked. The old man was tough, just as tough as he looked. Smiley Colfax lifted his hand to his gun and then dropped it clear as the rifle barrel turned in his direction. Latiker hesitated and then, perhaps because in the last few hours he had had his fill of violence, turned to his horse.

"Come on, boys," he said. "It ain't worth killin' him over."

"You mean," Mat corrected, "it ain't worth *bein'* killed over."

Latiker mounted. Colfax' horse circled and circled before the smiling man gained his saddle. "This settles you in the Wagonwheel, Yoeman," Colfax snarled. "You'll never sell another horse in this country."

"I'm pa'ticular who buys my horses," Mat answered.

The Wagonwheel men turned their horses, every one of them looking back as they rode away. They all saw Mat Yoeman standing in the door of the Verity cabin, his rifle across his arm. When the riders had disappeared into the dusk Mat went into the cabin and stopped beside Ray's bed to look down at the boy.

Ray stirred restlessly. "Wayne," he muttered.

"Pore boy," Mat Yoeman said. "Pore kid." He stood a moment there, then, turning abruptly, left the bedside. "We'll go in the mornin'," Mat announced, voicing his thoughts. "Can't go tonight. The country's too rough to take him over tonight. I reckon I'll let them horses go. Nobody'll bother 'em. Mebbe there's some flour an' stuff here, an' mebbe there's some powder."

Three times during the night Mat was up with the boy. He found a little whisky and gave it to Ray, the worst thing he could have done, as it proved, for after the drink Ray raved for half an hour, reliving the fight and the tragedy beside the hack, shouting hoarsely for Wayne and the twins. With the first faint light of morning Mat was up, making preparations for their leaving. The improvised travois of the day before was reinforced and strengthened and padded with bedding. Custer's harness was made stronger, and when finally Mat finished his work by saddling Bear Dance the equipment was in as good condition as he could make it.

When Mat carried the boy out of the cabin Ray fought weakly. Apparently he realized that he was leaving his home and he struggled to remain. Mat was at some pains not to hurt his charge, and after Ray had been placed on the travois he opened the boy's shirt and inspected the bandages. The wound had bled but little, and Mat was satisfied.

The travois was loaded now with other things than Ray Verity. Mat took what he needed from the supplies on hand at the Walking V: flour, salt pork, coffee, some sugar, baking powder, and matches. He found clothing, some that belonged to Ray, some that the twins and Wayne had owned, but the sizes made sorting simple. There was also a sheet of lead and almost half a canister of powder which Mat added to his load.

There were, of course, things that Mat did not take, heavy objects such as beds and chairs. And there were other personal effects that he saw no use for: a woman's shawl that lay over the back of a rocker and a mirror on the mantelpiece in the front room. If Ray Verity had been able, had he known what Mat was doing, the shawl and the mirror would have been the first things added to the travois load, for they had been his mother's and were treasures. But Ray lay with unseeing eyes, occasionally moaning, muttering Wayne's name, or calling in a whisper for Carl or Evan.

"I reckon that's it," Mat said when he was through. He stood and cast a final searching glance about the kitchen. "He won't never come back," the old man continued, "not even if he lives. Mebbe I'll kill him takin' him home with me, but it's better than goin' to Gunhammer. The dirty, murderin' devils!" Deliberately Mat turned from the cabin's interior and, striding out, mounted Bear Dance and picked up Custer's lead rope.

Down into the gap they went, past the hoosegow pasture that had contained the steers, and then, turning to the left, into the opening of the Notch. The trail mounted steadily. Occasionally Mat was forced to dismount and clear a space with his ax so that the travois could go through. It was slow and heavy work, but by noon they had reached the top and the way was easier.

Now they went down, following a long slope, weaving in and out among big pines. Gray clouds overhead presaged snow, and Mat glanced at them uneasily. But the storm held off, and well after dark Bear Dance and Custer turned along a familiar trail that led into a cove well hidden among the many slopes and canyons. Bear Dance stopped at a gate in an aspen pole fence, and Mat Yoeman, dismounting to open the gate, spoke for the first time in hours.

"By glory," said Mat Yoeman. "We made it!"

Chapter 5

A man works best on his own stomping grounds. Mat Yoeman's cabin on the east side of the Whetrocks was where he belonged, and Mat, installing Ray Verity in his own bunk, settled down to work. He was satisfied that the boy's wound would heal—it was already showing signs of mending—but Ray's mind presented a far different problem. Ray had undergone a serious shock, a strain bad enough that he might, logically, have broken under it. There was nothing that Mat could do but care for Ray's bodily needs, feed him when he could make the boy eat, and keep his own counsel. He was rejoiced when, two days after their arrival at the cabin, Ray looked at him with hurt, pain-racked eyes and asked a lucid question:

"How did I get here?"

"I brung you." Mat came over to the bunk. "I found you an' I brung you home. You take it easy an' I'll get you somethin' to eat."

"I don't want anythin' to eat." Ray's voice was weak. "I want to know about—Wayne an' the twins."

Mat would not meet Ray's eyes. "They're dead." The old man turned his head away. "Killed, kid."

The silence was so long that Mat ventured a look. Ray was far away, his eyes blank with thought. "I remember," he said. "We were—"

"Don't you talk about it!" Mat commanded briskly. "Take yore time. I'm goin' to get you some soup, an' yo're goin' to eat it whether you want to or not." He bustled off briskly. When he returned Ray drank the hot broth.

"Thanks," he said gratefully when he had finished, "for everythin'."

That was the beginning. During that whole day Ray was wakeful, dozing only occasionally, but he did not talk. When Mat went to bed Ray answered the old man's "Good night," but he did not sleep. He lay on the bunk, looking up at the blackness about him and thinking, an endless chain of recollection circling in his mind. Mat turned over restlessly, and Ray spoke.

"Mat?"

"Yeah?"

"I killed them. Wayne an' Carl an' Evan."

Mat got out of bed and pulled on his pants. He put fresh wood in the fireplace, and the flame blazed up. "No," Mat answered. "It wasn't you, Ray."

"I killed 'em." The boy's voice was implacable in his self-accusation. "I cut a calf away from a 10 Bow cow an' branded it. That was what Duke jumped Wayne about. That's what started it all."

"Go on an' talk, kid, if it'll make you feel

better." Mat came over and sat down on the edge of Ray's bunk. The fire snapped, adding warmth and light to the cabin. "Get it off yore chest."

A pause and then Ray went on: "That night while we were waitin' in Weathers' place Wayne asked me if I'd mavericked a 10 Bow calf. He knew I had. The twins knew it. I killed my brothers, Mat."

"Kid"—Mat's voice was very soft—"tell me about it. Talk it out."

"They'd bought me a new saddle," Ray began, "for my birthday." The story went on from there. Mat Yoeman, his yellow braids gleaming in the firelight, listened.

"An' then Wayne said he'd get me loose. He said for me to get away, to pull out an' never go home. He shot his wrist so the handcuff would come off, an' then he jumped up an' ran around the hack, an' they killed him. I got hit then. It knocked me down an' I crawled. I heard Tenbow yellin' for his men, an' I heard 'em holler to get me. I kept crawlin'. I crawled an' sneaked an' crawled an' I don't remember any more, Mat."

The boy beside him was struggling for sanity. There was a waver in his voice, an odd inflection that Mat Yoeman had never heard. "You didn't kill yore brothers, Ray," he reassured.

There was a long wait. Then Ray said: "Tenbow! He'd promised to protect us. He was there. He knew we were goin' to be moved."

Mat could not tell what was going on behind Ray's burning eyes. He kept still, trusting silence.

"Tenbow!" Ray said again. The waver was gone from his voice, and there was strength in it.

"Kid—" Mat began.

"It was him, Mat! It was Tenbow that killed Wayne an' Carl an' Evan!" Ray struggled up until he sat erect. In the firelight his eyes were wide and glittering.

"Lie down, Ray," Mat ordered. "You lie back down. You lost a lot of blood. You got to lie down an' rest so you'll get well." Mat put his hand against Ray and pushed gently. Relief filled him as Ray offered no resistance but obediently lay down again.

For a long time Mat continued to sit on the edge of the bunk, motionless. Then tentatively he spoke, low-voiced. "Ray?" There was no answer. When Mat placed his hand on Ray's chest he felt a rhythmic rise and fall. Ray Verity was asleep, the strength drained out of him, the doubt and self-reproach in his mind replaced by hatred and bitter resolve.

Sometimes in the days that followed Mat Yoeman wondered what he should do. He went about his business, getting in his winter meat, bringing in firewood to add to his already sufficient supply, working with a few horses that he had penned in the corral behind the cabin.

Daily Ray Verity regained strength. The blood he had lost was being replaced, and his cracked rib was healing as his wound closed. But Mat, coming in out of the weather, was sometimes shocked by Ray's eyes. They were not a boy's eyes, nor were they the eyes of a normal man. There was always a glitter in them, a fire that burned behind their blue surface.

There was no more talk about the tragedy. Ray did not mention the fight in Gunhammer or on the Fort Neville road. Mat, too, kept clear of the subject. Occasionally when they talked Ray spoke of Wayne or Carl or Evan naturally, as though the brothers were still living. Neither Ray nor Mat mentioned Miles Tenbow.

Ray was up now, moving about, taking some of the work from Mat, growing stronger every day. He went out to the corral and sat there while Mat worked with the three young horses that he was gentling. The weather stayed good with only one light snow. The tops of the Whetrocks were white, but the snow melted off the slopes except in the shade. At the end of three weeks Ray was almost as strong as ever, his body healed.

In the first week of December Mat decided that he would shoe horses. He had a forge in a shed near by the corral and a good set of blacksmith tools. Even though there had been no snow, winter was on hand and bad weather could be expected at any time. When they ate breakfast in the morning Mat made brisk announcement of his decision.

"I'm goin' to shoe Bear Dance an' Custer. Mebbe a couple more. Want to come down an' help, Ray?"

"As soon as I get the place cleaned up," Ray answered. "You go ahead, Mat."

Breakfast over, Mat donned coat and cap and went out. Ray washed the dishes, brought in wood, swept the cabin's floor, and made the beds. Then he, too, dressed for the outside, putting on a sheepskin coat that Mat had brought up from the gap and adding an old fur cap, one of Mat's that fit him.

Mat was in the corral with Bear Dance, Custer, and two young horses. He had built a fire in the forge, and smoke trickled from the chimney of the shed. As Ray came down Mat put a rope on Bear Dance and led him out.

"Danged-fool horse," Mat commented. "I can do anythin' to him but shoe him. We'll have to throw an' tie him before we get shoes on them hind feet." He heaved his saddle up on the gelding's back.

They led Bear Dance, fretting and anticipating trouble, down to the forge. There, with much grunting, Mat got a rope around the black's right front foot and tied it up to the saddle horn. It is easier to shoe the front feet of a touchy horse that way, and Ray offered no comment. Mat brought his farrier's kit out of the shed, eased up to Bear Dance, and set to work.

The old man was a skilled smith. He pulled off the shoe, looked at it critically, and tossed it aside. Then with nippers and rasp and farrier's knife he pared down and cleaned out the hoof and fitted the shoe. Ray saw that the old man had turned long heel calks on the shoe and welded a calk to the toe. Mat nailed the shoe on, making dry comment to Bear Dance as the horse flinched from the hammer blows. Then he rasped a notch above each nail, twisted them off, and clenched them.

"There," he drawled as he let the black's foot down to the ground. "That's one. They's just three more."

The other front foot was no harder to shoe than the first had been. Ray helped in tying it up and asked a question as Mat fitted the shoe. "Them front calks are apt to make him stumble, ain't they?"

"They will if yo're workin' horses or cattle," Mat answered. "Bear Dance travels kind of high, an' he's clear-footed, so they ain't so bad on him. An' I'm goin' to use him for travelin'. I ain't goin' to run nothin' on him."

With the front feet shod, Mat took the saddle off Bear Dance, and Ray, helping again, threw the horse. They tied the two front feet and one hind foot, and Mat fitted the first hind shoe. Bear

Dance objected strenuously to being thrown, but there was nothing that he could do about it. That shoe on, they turned the horse over, retied his legs, and worked on the other hind foot.

"Now, by glory"—Mat panted as he let the horse up—"see if you can slip with them on you!"

"Wayne always shod our horses," Ray made slow comment. "We never put front calks on 'em. One time Evan wanted front calks on Brownie, an' Wayne put 'em on. Brownie fell an' pretty near broke Evan's neck."

"Let's get Custer," Mat ordered, freeing Bear Dance. "We won't have to throw him. He's gentle. But he interferes, an' I have to make his shoes."

Ray took Bear Dance to the corral and brought Custer back while Mat busied himself at the forge, his hammer clanging rhythmically.

"Horses," Mat stated didactically as he worked on the sorrel, "are just like folks. You wouldn't wear a boot that didn't fit, would you? Well, a horse ought to have his shoes made just like you'd have boots made. I've seen smiths heat up a shoe an' clap it on an' let it burn the hoof down. I whupped a man for doin' that one time. I used to shoe Custer's pack train, mules an' horses both. Benteen wouldn't let nobody but me work on 'em. Said that the pack train was the most important part of a army. He always figgered that if men wasn't fed an' didn't have ca'tridges they couldn't fight. He was right too."

"You were with Benteen, weren't you?" Ray queried. "At Little Big Horn?"

"I was there." Mat paused, halfway to the sorrel. "Yeah, I was there from the time the Sioux jumped us till Terry come an' relieved the column."

Like every other Wyoming boy of his age, Ray had been raised on the Battle of the Little Big Horn. He had heard it talked by men who were active when the fight occurred, friends of Custer's, others who claimed knowledge of the intimate details. "You—" he began, momentarily forgetting his own trouble.

"I don't like to talk about it," Mat interrupted. "I was there in the middle of the thing. I know what happened an' I know how it happened, but I don't know why."

He paused for a moment and then continued: "There's some that blame Custer for jumpin' into a fight an' not obeyin' Terry's orders. They say he should of waited for the infantry. If he had the Sioux would of walked off an' left him. Then there's folks that blame Benteen. They say he should have supported Custer. If he had I wouldn't be here talkin' to you. We'd of all been killed. Custer's dead, an' Benteen's drinkin' himself to death, I've heard. There ain't no use of tryin' to put the blame on nobody. What all these fellers overlook is that Crazy Horse is smart. A lot of 'em think Sittin' Bull was the one, but it was Crazy Horse. I know. I'd ought to."

More was to come, and Ray waited expectantly.

"Crazy Horse!" Mat said. "Shucks! I lived right in his camp. He was smarter'n Custer or Benteen or any of 'em. I knew that."

"You lived in Crazy Horse's camp?"

Mat eyed Ray oddly. "I married a Sioux gal one time," he said shortly. "Come on, let's shoe this horse."

By dinnertime Custer had new shoes, and Ray and Mat were both sweating. They went into the cabin where Mat sat down while Ray stirred up a meal. After dinner they shod the other two horses that Mat had up, and when night came both of them knew that they had done a day's work. That night, sitting in front of the fireplace, Mat made another announcement. "I'm goin' into town tomorrow."

"Gunhammer?" Ray asked quickly.

Mat shook his head. "Fort Neville," he answered. "First off I'm goin' down to pick up some horses I dropped when I found you. They ain't no use of lettin' 'em drift an' havin' somebody else take 'em. Then I'll go to the fort an' sell 'em an' get some stuff we're needin'. Take the two of us together an' we use quite a little."

Ray stared moodily at the blaze in the fireplace which afforded the only light. Mat could not read and had no use for a lamp. Suddenly the boy looked up and caught Mat watching him. "I've been spongin' on you a long time," Ray said.

"I wouldn't go to say 'spongin'," Mat objected. "Yo're welcome here."

"I'm plenty able to travel." Ray did not heed Mat's interjection. "An' I've got to travel. I've got things to do."

Mat had been waiting for this. "Such as?" he drawled.

"You know what I've got to do!" Ray's eyes glittered.

"Yo're thinkin' about Tenbow," Mat said. "You'd better go a little slow, Ray. You'd better be thinkin' straight."

Ray laughed bitterly. "I ain't been doin' much else but think. That's all I've been good for."

"Miles Tenbow," Mat said, "has always been pretty highly thought of, Ray. I've knowed him ever since I moved into the Whetrocks. I sold him lots of horses, an' he's always been fair. Mebbe there's somethin' about this you don't know."

"I know," Ray said, "that Wayne surrendered to Tenbow an' that Tenbow promised him protection. I know that it was Tenbow's man, Koogler, that went with us when they moved us an' that Tenbow wasn't there. Koogler said that Gunhammer was gettin' pretty ugly an' that Tenbow was out tryin' to quiet 'em down. He was out gettin' a bunch together to kill us; that's

77

what he was doin'. If it wasn't that, how come him to be with the men that jumped us? I tell you I heard him yell. I'd know his voice anyplace. An' it was Tenbow that blackballed us last fall too!"

Mat shook his head. "It looks kind of bad," he drawled. "It shorely does. But, Ray, you can't afford to go off half cocked. There ain't really nothin' against you. It was Wayne an' the twins that done the shootin'. Nobody's after you."

Ray was moodily silent. Mat tried another tack. "Let me scout around an' listen to what I can hear. I'll find out who it was that got that bunch together."

"You'll find out that it was Tenbow. He was the only one that knew we was to be moved, except them that went along with us."

Mat reflected for a moment. "Who else was along?" he asked. "You named Koogler."

"Charlie Nerril an' Jorbet an' Smiley Colfax," Ray answered. "That was the lot of 'em."

"Mmmm." Mat remembered the rag around Colfax' head. "Look, Ray," he drawled. "You stay here till I get back from town, will you? You ain't got a saddle to ride, an' I'd feel a lot better if I knew you was on the place. Kind of stick around, huh?"

"I'll stay till you get back," Ray agreed after a moment's thought. "I owe you plenty, Mat, an' if you want it that way I'll do it. But don't try to tell me that Miles Tenbow wasn't the man that got Wayne an' the twins killed."

"I ain't goin' to try to tell you nothin'," Mat answered dryly. "Let's go to bed."

Mat was slow in making his departure the next morning. He stalled around, fixing this thing and that, killing time. He was not sure that he should go and leave Ray alone. But a man can't cook bacon without slicing meat, and finally Mat stepped up on Bear Dance and rode out. When he was gone Ray walked back into the cabin.

The boy had no idea of how long Mat would be gone. First the old man would go down to the river and try to locate the horses he had left when he found Ray Verity. He might or might not succeed in doing that. Then he would go to Fort Neville and be there for a time. Ray had a week, perhaps two weeks, to spend by himself.

He stayed close to the cabin for the rest of the day, doing little of anything, loafing, thinking. In the evening he fed Custer and the other horse that Mat was keeping up and closed the corral gate on them. That night he lay awake a long time.

December days were short. Ray was up before light came. He cooked and ate and waited impatiently for day to break. With the first tinge of gray he went down to the corral.

Mat was riding the only saddle the Ace of Spades possessed, but there was an old bridle in the forge shed. Ray bridled Custer and rigged a surcingle on the sorrel, using an old strap and a cinch from Mat's packsaddle. He padded Custer's back with a tanned buck hide and then turned the other horse out of the corral and, leaving the gate open, mounted Custer. Wayne had said not to go home, to leave the country, never to return. Ray Verity was going home, back to Verity Gap.

He rode Custer west up the slopes of the Whetrocks, striking for the top of the Notch. What had taken hours for Mat Yoeman, leading a horse that pulled a travois, Ray covered in half the time. The sun was high and covered by gray clouds when he topped out between the peaks that made the Notch and began the descent. As he rode he automatically looked for cattle and saw none. At three o'clock he was on the ridge from which, not so long ago, he had watched the country below. It was still there, spread out, brown and barren. Ray rode on down. He left the mouth of the Notch and turned south. Here was the hoosegow pasture fence and here the gate. The road was plain where, for years, John Verity and then his sons had hauled hay. But the end of the road was changed. Where a tight four-room cabin, a barn and corrals and sheds had stood now were blackened ruins. Fire had swept the homestead. For a long time Ray sat on Custer, looking, hard-eyed, at the remains of what had once been his home. Then slowly he turned the horse.

He did not go back toward the Notch but rode on out across the gap. He saw no cattle, found none. Someone had made a clean sweep of the stock that usually grazed here. The sun slid down and the brief December twilight came, and Ray Verity, at the western side of the gap that bore his name, reined in once more. There, by the west water hole, a shack had been built, a little affair of logs and rock. There were horses watering at the tank, and as Ray rode close they lifted their heads to look at him. He read the brands. The 10 Bow showed plain on bay and black and sorrel shoulders. Custer snorted and turned his head. A man was coming in from the south, riding leisurely. The rider saw the visitor at the tank, and his horse's pace increased. Ray Verity did not wait. He turned Custer away and kicked with his heels, and the big sorrel, astonished, jumped and, catching the calks of his new shoes, stumbled and almost fell. Ray pulled the horse up, and Custer regained his feet and lengthened his stride into a run. From behind Ray the rider's voice came faintly:

"Hey! Hey there!" Ray did not look back as Custer traveled west.

Chapter 6

Custer was big and stout and had been fed on oat hay cut when the grain was in the dough stage. Ray Verity did not weigh over a hundred and forty pounds, for his long illness had gaunted him. The fact that Custer did not pack a saddle was an added benefit. The night was cold and crisply clear, and there was a little frosty moon. Riding toward Gunhammer along the road that he had followed with Wayne and the twins, Ray could look up at the moon and watch the sparkle of the stars while Custer's big black hoofs kept a steady cadence, never breaking or faltering. Riding was purely automatic and needed no thought, and Ray's mind was clear for other things.

At midnight Gunhammer lay ghostly in the dying moonlight, the bulk of the unlighted buildings looming darker than the black shadows they cast. At the edge of the town Ray paused. There were certain things he wanted in Gunhammer, and he had to decide how best to attain them. He had many acquaintances in the town: girls that he had known in school, and boys, too, young town bucks that worked in the stores and that were either envious or supercilious toward a ranch-raised boy, and older men and women, the parents of his schoolmates. Whom could he trust? Only one answer occurred. The Veritys had always bought their supplies from Clough Weathers. Weathers carried them from year to year upon his books, and when Ray attended school in town Wayne's word had always been: "If you need anything go down to Weathers'. He'll let you have it an' charge it to me." Clough Weathers was the answer. Ray rode on into town.

He took his way along a dark alley and up a street until, behind a big square house, he left Custer. Advancing cautiously, he skirted the house. The doors were closed, but there was a window open on the lower floor. On one occasion Ray had failed to find Weathers at the store and had gone to the house. He visited with Weathers inside and remembered now how the man, propped up in bed, had smiled at him and scribbled an order with a pencil. The open window was in Weathers' room, and Ray, advancing gingerly, reached the opening and stood on tiptoe.

"Mr. Weathers! Mr. Weathers!" He waited, and the words seemed to echo although he had barely raised his voice above a whisper. Inside the room a man sighed, turned, and began to snore.

"Mr. Weathers! Mr. Weathers!"

"Clough!" A woman spoke sharply. "There's someone calling. Wake up, Clough!"

"Huh? What's that? What's that, Martha?"

"There's someone at the window!"

Ray retreated hastily. There was a stirring inside the room, the sound of heavy padding steps, and then the sash slammed up. Weathers' nightcap-covered head was thrust out, and he stared to right and left. From the shadow Ray spoke softly.

"It's Ray Verity, Mr. Weathers."

"Who is it, Clough?" Martha Weathers demanded.

"Nothing. It's nothing, Martha." Weathers pulled his head back into the room. "Just some disturbance outside. I'll go and see."

Again came the heavy padding steps. Ray left the side of the house and hurried to the porch in front. There, crouched in the shadow, he waited, listening to the click of a key and the rattle of a doorknob as the door was opened. "Mr. Weathers?" he said softly.

"Is that Ray Verity?" Weathers demanded.

"I'm here by the porch."

Weathers padded across the planks and stopped. "What are you doing here?" he demanded. "Why did you come to me? I had no hand in killing your brothers!"

The man was frightened. His perception made keen by his own position, Ray read the fear in the merchant's voice.

"I know that," he said. "I've got to have some help."

"How can I help you?" Weathers seemed reassured.

"I left a horse an' saddle in town," Ray answered. "Where are they?"

"Why—the horse is at the livery barn." The merchant paused an instant. "Are you going down there, Ray?"

"I'm goin' to get Spooks an' my saddle. Will you let me into the store? There's some things I need."

Weathers appeared to consider. "I'm your friend, Ray," he said heavily. "I'll do whatever I can for you. Wait for me." Again the man's steps padded across the porch, and the front door closed.

Ray crouched beside the porch. The moonlight was faint, but he could see the steps plainly enough and the black shadow reaching from them toward him. It was taking Weathers a long time. He heard voices in the house. The door opened and Weathers said, "Ray?"

"I'm here," Ray answered and slipped along the porch into the shadow of the steps. Weathers was shod now. He came across the porch to the rail and peered over it, and Ray, looking back, caught a glint of moonlight on metal. Along his neck the boy's uncut hair stiffened and bristled with his fright. Weathers, the man he had supposed to be a friend, held a gun.

"Ray," Weathers said. "Don't be scared, boy. Where are you?"

Ray did not answer. He crouched, all spring steel, beside the steps. Weathers left the rail and came along the porch, heavy-footed. "Ray!" he said again.

He took the first step, and his foot was poised for the second. Ray's hand shot out, gripped, and pulled swiftly. Overbalanced, the heavy man went down, pitching forward, arms outflung to break his fall. He struck the gravel of the path, and Ray, like a cat, was on him, reaching for the gun. He caught the cold metal, wrenched it free, and thrust the muzzle into the merchant's back. Weathers stopped struggling and lay very still.

"Clough, are you all right?" the woman called from the house.

"Answer her!" Ray hissed and prodded with the gun.

"I'm all right, Martha," Weathers said heavily. "I stumbled on the step."

There was a momentary pause, and then the woman said doubtfully: "Oh. Did you hurt yourself?"

"Does she know I'm here?" Ray demanded in a whisper.

Weathers nodded. The gun pressure on his spine had not relaxed an instant. The gun was a .38-.40 Colt, a presentation double-action Army and Frontier model, with carved ivory grips and fancifully engraved. Clough Weathers knew well that if Ray Verity pulled the trigger about two hundred grains of lead would shatter the man's spine and mingle with his inner workings.

"Tell her that I've gone. Tell her yo're goin' downtown to get Jorbet!"

"He's gone, my dear," Weathers said shakily. "I'm going downtown to get Jorbet."

"Be careful, Clough," Mrs. Weathers said. "Those awful Veritys!"

She had not come to the door then. Ray was thankful. He pushed slightly with the gun. "All right." His whisper grated. "I'll be right behind you. Start!"

"For heaven's sake, be careful," Weathers muttered. "That's a double-action gun."

"Yo're the one to be careful," Ray rasped. "Start walkin'."

He made Clough Weathers go around the house to where Custer waited. Already the outlaw was showing in Ray Verity, and he was beginning to use a wisdom and an instinct that would take him along his trail. A wild animal could have been no more alert and ready than the boy, and a seasoned lawbreaker would have known no more clearly that he must not be separated from his horse. Leading Custer and keeping Weathers ahead of him, Ray directed his captive toward the town.

At the door of the store Ray dropped Custer's reins across the hitch rail and ordered Weathers to open. There was some delay while the frightened man fumbled for his keys. Clough Weathers was no more cowardly than any other man, but he knew that he was up against a hair-triggered youngster and he was afraid. The door swung open, and man and boy entered the building.

Difficulty now presented itself. The store was dark, and Ray could neither see what he wanted nor watch Weathers. Boldness was necessary.

"Light up," Ray ordered. "Get a lamp lit."

Weathers fumbled for a match, struck it, and lighted a lamp on the counter. The yellow flame flickered, and Ray, pushing with the gun, shoved Weathers away so that he could reach out and lower the wick.

"You meant to take me," he accused bitterly. "What have I ever done to you? What law have I broke?"

"Your brothers—" Weathers again tried to justify himself.

"My brothers are dead. All I done was to get away from a bunch that meant to kill me."

"You were arrested," the merchant spluttered. "You were with your brothers in the Pastime."

"We ain't goin' to argue," Ray snarled. "I'm goin' to break the law now, all right. I want a Winchester out of yore case, an' ammunition for it an' for this gun." He gestured with the Colt as he spoke. Weathers could see the lamplight glitter from the bright engraving.

"Back over there," Ray snapped. "Put yore hands up."

Weathers backed as directed and raised his hands.

"This dirty little town helped kill my brothers." Ray's voice was very cold, and his lips were a thin uncompromising line. "If you make a bust I'll kill you. Now be quiet." Deliberately he edged around the counter, keeping his eyes on the man.

Clough Weathers shivered. He had never, in all his life, seen such glittering, cruel eyes as those of the boy that confronted him. The merchant realized that his living hung by a thread, that this boy was ready and wanted to kill.

"If I lay down," he quavered, "I couldn't see what you were doing. I couldn't do anything."

For an instant Ray reflected on that suggestion and then accepted it. "Lay down on yore face then!" he commanded.

Weathers lay down. He kept his arms up, sprawled out ahead of him, and was very still. He could hear the boy move, hear the thump of articles being placed on the counter.

"That's about it," Ray rasped. "What caliber is this gun?"

"A .38-.40."

There was another thump. "Get up," Ray ordered.

Slowly Weathers scrambled to his feet. He saw a pile of articles on the counter: a rifle lay there, ammunition piled beside it, a new belt and holster, a heavy Mackinaw coat. Ray was frowning thoughtfully. "I need a saddle," he said. "I don't know what to do with you, Weathers. I ain't goin' to turn you loose."

"I—" Weathers stammered. "Wayne owed me a little bill for some stuff he'd bought. I've got your saddle in the back room. I didn't mean to harm you, Ray. I didn't have nothin' to do with your brothers bein' killed. Why don't you just lock me up?"

"Where?"

"I could open my strong room."

A grin flashed across the boy's face, utterly grim, utterly hard. "Where you kept Wayne an' Carl an' Evan before you took 'em out to kill 'em? All right." Ray reached out and picked up the lamp. Clough Weathers, relieved that his suggestion had been accepted, led the way. With Weathers in the strong room, Ray dropped the bar, put the padlock in the hasp, and closed it. High excitement filled him as he crossed from the warehouse to the store. He picked up his saddle from where it lay beside vinegar barrels and stacked sacks of flour and carried it along the length of the store, thrusting the Colt into his belt so that he would have both hands free. Leaving the lamp on the counter beside his plunder, he took the saddle and a new pad out to the street. Custer stood patiently while Ray removed the surcingle and replaced it with the saddle.

Recklessness filled the boy. He had broken over, was outside the law now. He didn't care.

Back in the store again he rolled his gathered plunder in the new Mackinaw. The gun belt he buckled around his waist under his old coat and pushed Weathers' Colt down into the stiff new holster. He looked around to see if there was anything else he wanted and spied the candy case. Wayne had always frowned on candy, always said that buying candy was a waste of money, for Wayne had no taste for sweets. Ray filled the pockets of his coat with peppermints and striped sticks of sweetness. Then, leaving the lamp burning, he picked up the Mackinaw and went out to tie it on his saddle. He was tugging the last knot tight when he heard a sound and looked up. A woman's voice shrilled: "There's a light in the store. Please hurry, Mr. Jorbet."

Ray jerked at the saddle string to tighten the knot, put the reins over Custer's neck, and, holding his new rifle, swung up. Hearing approaching footsteps, he waited fractionally, then, reining Custer around, he gained the middle of the street.

A woman huddled into a man's overcoat and a man rounded the corner of the store and stopped stock-still. Then the woman screamed, and the man lifted his arm and shouted.

"Verity!"

Flame bloomed at the end of the upflung arm,

and lead smacked viciously past Ray's head. Glass shattered in the building across the street.

Jerking up the rifle, Ray cocked it and pulled the trigger. His reward was a click. He had forgotten to load the gun. He transferred the rifle to his left hand even as he reined Custer and kicked with his heels. Custer was tired, but the shot had frightened him. He broke into a heavy lope, almost stumbling as the front calks in his shoes caught. Then Ray half turned in his saddle and had the Colt out. Jorbet fired a second shot, wild as the first. Ray brought up the Colt to chop it down, hesitated because he saw the woman, then pulled the trigger. The double-action gun went off, its muzzle pointed toward the sky. In the dwellings back of Gunhammer's main street lights were beginning to blossom. Above the Exchange Saloon and back of Giant's store lamps showed their yellow glow. A man carrying a feeble lantern ran out from the livery barn into the street still dimly lighted by the dying moon.

Custer's hoofs pounded on hard ground, and Ray Verity's voice rose in a yell, high and shrill and derisive. Again and again the Colt in his hand thundered, and glass shattered in windows, and a woman screamed, her voice as shrill and continuous as a steam whistle. Then the gun was empty and the last building was behind and Custer was running heavily across open country, following a road.

The elation and excitement drained out of the boy as he pulled the horse down from run to easier lope. He fumbled in the pocket of his coat and there, among sticky candy, he found loose shells. He tied the rifle by a saddle string and used both hands to hold the Colt and work the ejector, shoving out the empty shells and reloading. Custer slowed from lope to trot, to lope again as Ray kicked his ribs. Looking back, the boy could see Gunhammer, dotted with lights now. He had caused some excitement in Gunhammer, plenty of excitement. Thinking of Clough Weathers and his treachery, the boy scowled.

"I'd ought to killed him," Ray growled. "He meant to get me. He'd of killed me if he'd had the chance."

Custer's big hoofs pounded the hard dirt of the road, and Ray shoved the newly loaded gun into his holster.

"Damn him," he growled, still thinking of Weathers. "I will, the next chance I get!"

Back in Gunhammer, Mrs. Weathers continued to scream for her husband as she searched through the store. Men, half dressed, nightshirts tucked hastily into trousers, shotguns, rifles, pistols in their hands, converged on the place. At the livery barn the hostler who slept in the grain room assured Charlie Nerril that everything was all right, and the two of them, leaving the barn open, joined the gathering crowd just in time to

93

hear Virgil Jorbet say, "It was Ray Verity. He shot at me twice, an' I'll bet he didn't miss me that far." With slightly spread hands Jorbet designated perhaps two inches. "He's killed Weathers," the marshal continued. "I know he has. We'll find him in the store someplace, layin' behind a counter."

Nerril pushed past the marshal and entered the store. He was a hard, bold man, this Charlie Nerril who owned the livery barn, and at one time had ridden for the 10 Bow. "Let's find him then," Nerril flung back over his shoulder.

The crowd poured in through the store's open door. Mrs. Weathers had ceased her screaming and was beside the counter now, moaning monotonously and wringing her hands.

Nerril went on through the store. The back door was open, and muffled thuddings issued from the warehouse. The liveryman raised a yell, and the crowd came back to join him. A sledge hammer brought from stock smashed the padlock, and Clough Weathers came out of the strong room, disheveled and mad. He pushed his wife away when she threw her arms about his neck, and his voice was lifted in anger. "That Verity kid. Damn him! He held me up. He got away with my ivory-handled Colt!"

Questions poured on Weathers as he forced a passage through the crowd intent on entering the store and seeing what damage had been done.

Charlie Nerril shrugged and with his hostler walked around the building. On Gunhammer's street the liveryman stopped and looked off toward the east.

"That kid," Charlie Nerril drawled, not to the hostler beside him, not to the men who were congregated in front of the store, but to himself, "that Verity kid! He's gone plumb bronc. Not that I blame him much. Let's go back to the barn, Joe."

Five miles east of Gunhammer, Ray Verity headed a tired horse for the river.

Chapter 7

The studs that Mat Yoeman had turned loose in the hills were thoroughbreds, and Custer carried a heavy strain of hot blood. He would go until he dropped, for there was no give-up in him. But good as Custer was, he played out. From Mat Yoeman's cabin in the Whetrocks to Verity Gap was twenty-seven miles, and from the gap to Gunhammer was forty-two. Custer had come about seventy miles, and now Ray was calling for more distance. It simply was not there.

Ray knew that he would either have to change horses or rest Custer. It would be simpler and safer to give Custer some rest, and, accordingly, some eight miles from Gunhammer Ray left the road and turned straight south. The Pie River cut through a piece of broken country, rough and more or less deserted, and that was the place Ray Verity sought. He could hide, rest his horse, and perfect the plan that was forming in his mind.

Custer slowed to a walk. The moon was gone and the stars were dim, but Ray knew that the river was close by. He worked down into a barren, broken country beset by brush, and then when the river gurgled almost at Custer's feet he dismounted. Morning dawned to find the boy curled under his two coats, the loaded rifle beside him, and Custer grazing wearily on the coarse brown grass that grew along the river. The sky was overcast, and a little wind moaned through the oak brush, rattling the dry leaves, breaking their tenuous hold and sending them scurrying.

All that day boy and horse rested. Custer watered at the river and went back to his grazing. Ray huddled in his coat, for it was cold and he dared not build a fire. He munched candy, glad that he had thought to bring it, and as evening came on he shot a rabbit which, after dark, he toasted over a tiny fire and wolfed down, half raw.

Snow fell that night, but the wind grew stronger and the snow did not last. Ray kept the fire going, sleeping in snatches, rousing to put more brush on the blaze and warm himself. With the first faint light he saddled the sorrel and left his hideout, hunting a river crossing. As the sun rose Ray tied Custer in willow growth and, carrying the rifle, moved away from the river. He climbed a little bluff and, pausing at its sheer front, looked down. The 10 Bow headquarters were below him, the big house, the bunkhouse, the corrals and hay barn and sheds spread out in a panorama. Smoke rose lazily from the chimneys. The 10 Bow was up, but the day's business had not yet begun. Ray Verity lay down on the edge of the bluff and shoved out the rifle before him. He estimated the distance and, coldly deliberate, lifted the rear sight a notch. Then, patient as a rattlesnake beside a game trail, he waited.

The sun rose higher, veiled in gray, a molten ball masked behind the clouds. Down below men stirred to life. The wrangler came out of the bunkhouse, saddled a horse in the corral, and loped away to return presently with the cavy. There were perhaps twenty head of horses in front of the wrangler, but that meant nothing. Naturally he would bring in the whole bunch from the horse pasture. For a time after the horses were in there was no activity. Then a man came from the big house and two more issued from the bunkhouse, and all three converged at the corral. Ray was pleased. He had thought that there would be a bigger winter crew at the 10 Bow, four or five men at least, but there were only two. He could see Miles Tenbow, his tall figure unmistakable at the two hundred yards' distance, giving orders. Ray lifted the rifle and looked over the sights. Tenbow was masked by the muzzle end.

Reluctantly Ray lowered the gun. It wasn't time yet. He could afford to wait. Those two riders would leave presently, and Tenbow would be alone.

The thing he planned, Ray told himself as he waited, was no worse than what Tenbow had done. Tenbow had deliberately lied to Wayne, promising him protection that he did not intend to give. And Tenbow had led the men who attacked the hack and killed the Verity brothers. What was wrong in dry-gulching a man like that?

The riders were in the pen, saddling their horses. They came out and rode away, one going along the river, the other striking south from the ranch. Soon they were dots in the distance, fading out of sight.

Ray lay quiet, watching Tenbow. Tenbow had a horse saddled but did not ride off at once. Instead he went into the barn and stayed for quite a time. Ray's fingers were numb with the cold, and he blew on them to warm them. Tenbow came out and stood beside the barn door. Slowly the boy raised the rifle again. It was a good gun and would shoot true. Ray had killed a cottontail at a hundred yards. Surely twice that distance was not too far to shoot a man. He brought the gun up slowly to his shoulder and cuddled his cheek against the stock. His thumb brought the hammer back, and his eyes squinted over the sights. He held a little coarse, the bead of the front sight halfway showing in the notch of the buckhorn rear sight, and Tenbow's head plain above the bead. Tenbow stood still, a perfect target, and the gun was motionless, frozen in place. Then the muzzle wavered, lowered, rested on the earth, and Ray Verity, freeing his right hand, dashed it across his eyes. He was a coward, he told himself, a weakling. He couldn't shoot. He could not summon that last ounce of resolve, that last bit of cold-blooded resolution that would tighten his finger on the trigger and send the man who had killed his brothers to hell where he belonged. He was just no good, no good at all!

Down below Tenbow stepped away from the barn and walked forward. Someone was coming from the house. Not the cook, certainly, for the cook would be busy in the kitchen cleaning up after breakfast. Ray squinted at this new arrival. He knew her. Hannie Koogler, Dutch Koogler's daughter, kept house for her father and Miles Tenbow in the 10 Bow headquarters. What was she doing down at the corral? Why hadn't she made her appearance when her father was there? One of those riders must have been Dutch Koogler.

Tenbow stood talking to the girl, and then they both entered the corral. Ray could see the horses mill as one was roped. He saw the girl lead the horse over to the gate. A little spit of snow struck Ray's face, icy and stinging. Absently he wiped the snow away. Hannie Koogler had saddled, and she and Tenbow were leaving the corral together. Relief filled Ray Verity. He couldn't shoot, not now. He could not kill Miles Tenbow, not while Hannie Koogler rode beside him. Hannie and the owner of the 10 Bow disappeared behind the barn. When they reappeared they were a full three hundred yards from where Ray Verity waited. He watched them until they dropped out of sight over a rise of ground, then Ray slid back from the edge of the bluff, stood up, and went downhill. He reached the thicket that held Custer and, untying the sorrel, mounted. Hannie Koogler wouldn't ride far with Tenbow. She would come back to the ranch, and that would leave Tenbow alone. It was better this way, much better than lying on a bluff top to dry-gulch a man. This way he could intercept Tenbow, could ride out and throw a gun on him and let him know why he was dying and who was killing him. That, Ray Verity told himself, was why he hadn't fired back on the bluff; that was why he had not pulled the trigger. He wanted Tenbow to know who was killing him.

The rifle resting across the saddle, Ray rode Custer out of the river bottom. The big horse heaved himself up over the bank, and brush tugged at Ray's Mackinaw. As the boy went north snow began to fall in small flurries with intermittent pauses. Winding his way through the round-topped brown hills that flanked the Pie River, Ray rounded a point and, squarely facing him, was Hannie Koogler.

Ray had danced with Hannie in Gunhammer. She was a big girl, plain-featured and pleasant, her Dutch ancestry evident in her flaxen hair and smooth peach-tinted cheeks. Hannie's lips made a little round red O of surprise, and her blue eyes were wide.

"Ray!" she exclaimed. "Ray Verity!"

Ray did not answer at once. He stared at Hannie and watched the expression in her eyes change from one of astonishment to pity. Impulsively the girl urged her horse forward. "Why, Ray!" she exclaimed once more.

"Yeah," Ray grated. "I'm Ray Verity all right. What did you think I was?"

"But—" Hannie checked whatever it had been that she intended to say. "I—" she stammered. "You frightened me, coming around the turn like that. I went with Mr. Tenbow this morning. I've been at home and I wanted to see Dad, and Mr. Tenbow was going over. Then it began to snow, and he said I'd better go home."

"Yore dad ain't at headquarters?" Ray's eyes were narrow.

"No. He's—What are you doing over here, Ray? What do you want at the 10 Bow?"

"What I want ain't at the 10 Bow," Ray answered grimly. "I've wasted enough time." He lifted the reins preparatory to riding on.

Intuition prompted the girl. She swung her horse across the trail in front of Custer, and the sorrel stopped. "You came to kill Mr. Tenbow!" the girl accused. "That's why you're here. That's why you are carrying that rifle!"

"An' why wouldn't I?" Ray flared. "Miles Tenbow got my brothers killed. Why wouldn't I settle with him?"

"No, Ray!" Hannie urged her horse again, bringing it up beside Custer so that she faced Ray, not three feet from him. "You can't do that, Ray. Mr. Tenbow didn't kill your brothers. Dad told me. Mr. Tenbow was in town, and he learned that a bunch had gone out to follow you. He hurried as fast as he could, but he wasn't in time."

"That's what Tenbow says," Ray refuted scornfully. "Of course he'd lie. I heard him yell for his 10 Bow hands, siccin' 'em onto us just like we was wolves. Don't try to tell me, Hannie. I know what happened!"

The girl could read the futility of argument in Ray's face. Still she tried once more. "Then why did Mr. Tenbow fire every man that rode after the hack?" she demanded. "It's left him shorthanded. Dad's having to hold down a camp until we get some men. Why did Mr. Tenbow do that?"

"Don't ask me why Tenbow does things," Ray flared. "I can't tell you. Why did he want my brothers killed? Answer me that!"

"He didn't. He didn't want anyone killed. He— Oh, what's the use? I can't talk to you. You won't believe me! Why don't you talk to Dad? He can tell you the truth!"

Shaken despite himself because of the girl's vehemence, Ray did not answer immediately. Hannie Koogler was very much in earnest, and her reference to her father had been a happy stroke. Everyone in the Pie River country respected and liked Dutch Koogler, and Wayne had sworn by the 10 Bow foreman. Ray could recall that on his arrival at the 10 Bow wagon it had been Koogler who talked to Tenbow,

103

who had protested letting a hungry boy ride off without his dinner. But he remembered, too, that Koogler had accompanied the hack.

"Where is yore dad?" Ray asked abruptly.

"He's in camp in Verity Gap," Hannie answered eagerly and instantly saw that she had said something wrong. Ray's eyes thinned to slits, and his lips made a harsh line. "In Verity Gap, huh?" he drawled. "Helpin' Tenbow steal our country. It was them that burned our place an' took the cattle out of the gap, too, wasn't it? Yeah. I'd do well to talk to yore dad."

He pushed Custer past Hannie's horse as he said the last words. The girl brought her mount around. "You've got to listen to me, Ray," she pleaded. "Please. Please!"

Custer did not stop. Hannie Koogler kicked her horse, and the surprised animal jumped half a length and lit running. She went past Ray and Custer as though they were standing still. "You'll not kill Mr. Tenbow," the girl screamed. "I won't let you. I'll tell him you're—"

Hannie Koogler's bay horse was no match for Custer. The sorrel's stride overhauled the bay and brought Ray up level. He reached out for the reins, and the girl struck at him wildly. Bay and sorrel stopped.

For a moment Ray Verity debated. Then he pulled Custer around, bringing the girl's bay with him. "I'm goin' to take you home," he rasped,

104

looking over his shoulder. "Where you belong. Right now!" Leading the bay horse, he started back toward the 10 Bow.

Snow was falling straight down when Ray Verity led Hannie Koogler's bay up to the 10 Bow corrals. The girl slipped down from her saddle, and Ray, dismounting, opened the corral gate. Hannie stood by, her eyes angry as Ray pulled the saddle from her horse.

"And now what are you going to do?" she demanded as Ray placed the saddle under the shed.

"Now," Ray answered deliberately, "I'm goin' to take these horses an' pull out. I'm not goin' to have you carryin' word to Tenbow that I'm comin'."

"You're still going to hunt Mr. Tenbow after what I've told you?"

"I'm still goin' to hunt him."

There was an instant's pause. The 10 Bow horses were over against the far fence of the corral. Custer stood waiting, his head drooped.

"You won't believe anybody," the girl accused bitterly. "Oh, Ray, why can't you have some sense? Why won't you believe me when I tell you that Mr. Tenbow didn't mean for your brothers to be killed?"

Without answering Ray mounted Custer and rode across the corral, his rifle dangling from the saddle strings where he had tied it to free his hands. Hannie Koogler stood in the gate to block the way, but Ray, bringing the horses along the fence, raised a yell, and the girl jumped back as the 10 Bow cavy thundered down on her. At the gate Ray checked fractionally, and the horses, breaking free, headed for the horse pasture. Hannie's eyes were tortured and almost black with anger, and the cook was running down from the kitchen to ascertain the cause of all this commotion.

"I hate you, Ray Verity!" the girl screamed. "I hate you!"

The rifle banged against Ray's leg as Custer swung to turn the horses. Ray did not look back at the girl at all.

At first Ray meant simply to run off the 10 Bow horses, to give them a push so that neither Hannie nor the cook could catch one. Not that he believed that either the cook or the girl could beat him to Verity Gap, but he did not want to take any chances. Then, when he had taken the horses past the pasture gate, another idea occurred to him. Why not just take them with him? Why not drive them to Verity Gap and through it, into the Wagonwheel roughs beyond? He had business in the gap, a grim accounting to take, but if he came out of that he would need a stake in new country. And it was fitting and proper that the 10 Bow furnish that stake. There were men on the north

106

end of the Wagonwheel, men who traded over in Montana and who knew the ropes. They would take these 10 Bow horses off his hands and pay him well. The idea pleased Ray Verity, and he drove the horses along.

It was a long way to the gap, a good long ride. The day would be finished by the time he reached the opening into the Wagonwheel. Mentally Ray outlined his route. He would take the west side of Diamond Lake, so avoiding the 10 Bow camp there and any possibility that he might be seen.

The rifle struck his leg again and, scowling, Ray untied it. He wished that he had been more thoughtful in Weathers' store. He might have taken a rifle scabbard as well as spurs and some other things that he had overlooked. The 10 Bow horses trotted along, and Custer kept after them. The snow fell now in great flakes that settled on Ray's coat and melted on his face. It was not so cold as it had been that morning, and the wind was gone.

Time crawled by with the miles. The snow was deepening on the ground, falling from a leaden, lifeless sky. There was snow on the backs of the horses, their body heat not melting it as fast as it fell. Custer's shoes crunched briskly into the whiteness, and occasionally he shook his head to free it from snow. They must, Ray thought, be past Diamond Lake now. They had come far enough. He looked to right and left and could tell nothing. The country was blotted out by a curtain of snow. All that he could see was the little bunch of horses that he drove ahead.

Gradually the temper of the storm changed. Bitter cold crept in, and the wind began, little puffs at first that whirled the falling flakes, and then settling into a monotonous whine. The snowflakes were smaller and no longer soft. Wind-driven, they stung as they struck the boy's face, and he hunched himself deeper into his coat collar and turned down the tabs of his cap for protection as the moaning of the wind changed to a howl of attack.

Custer began to act the fool and refused to quarter across the wind, wanting to turn his back to it. Ray straightened the horse and looked ahead. The 10 Bow horses were not where they should have been. They were gone with only snow to replace them. Ray let Custer go down-wind, hoping to pick up the horses again.

He did not find them. The snow seemed to increase in volume and closed down all about him so that he rode in a little white-walled room, just he and Custer, all alone. His legs, covered by denim, were already numb, and his feet had no feeling. The cold crept in through his coat and, more insidious than the cold, fear began to creep into Ray Verity's mind. He was lost somewhere on the Pie River Flats, somewhere in a scope of country that was two hundred miles long by a hundred broad. Custer was plugging along, quartering across the wind. The wind was Ray's only hope of salvation. It had come from the west. If he kept it on his left cheek he must travel north and so strike Verity Gap or the rim west of the gap. If he could get to the gap he would find shelter.

The cold had gripped the boy completely now so that he ached and was numb with it. He checked Custer, and the big horse turned tail to the storm. Ray got his right foot out of the stirrup and somehow slid from the saddle. The rifle impeded his dismounting, and he let it drop. His hands were too void of feeling even to try to tie the gun to the saddle. On the ground he leaned against Custer for a moment and then, wrapping the reins around his arm, his hands so stiff that he could not bend them, started ahead, still quartering across the wind.

Movement restored Ray's congealed circulation, and with the blood pumping strong again his mind cleared. He stamped his feet and swung his arms, feeling the exquisite pain as warmth seeped into them. The wind was not so bad now, and Ray realized that he must be under a ridge, behind one of those long low folds of ground that wrinkled the flats. But he had no idea of what ridge. Custer, following, kept turning to the left. He was on Ray's heels, and when Ray hesitated the sorrel rammed his head against the boy's back. If he turned left Ray would be going squarely into the wind. Why was Custer turning? A horse will drift with a storm unless . . .

Ray turned so that he faced the storm. "I'll take a chance on you," he told the horse. "I'll risk it, Custer." Maybe the wind *had* shifted. Maybe it was blowing from the north. Maybe Custer was right and shelter lay ahead, straight into the storm.

They plodded on. Snow slipped under Ray's boots, and he stumbled. His legs were playing out. If he walked he kept warm, but how long can a man walk when the wind whips him with a tearing lash and pushes him back, when with every step he takes his feet slide? If he rode the piercing cold would strike again, and, too, Ray doubted that he could mount the big sorrel.

"It's got to be pretty soon," the boy muttered. "It's got to be."

He staggered on, climbing a long rise. At the top the wind struck with renewed vigor, stopping him in his tracks. The gust died and he was able to move again, downhill now. Every step was forced, every movement an effort. There was rock under the snow, slippery and treacherous. A larger rock was just ahead and, numbly, Ray Verity turned a trifle to avoid it. Abreast of that long, low-lying rock he stopped, and Custer's nose bumped his back. It was no rock at all. Ray stared unbelievingly at booted feet. He took a staggering step and then another and, bending stiffly, Ray caught at a man's shoulders and pulled and tugged. A face looked up at him, long, lean, strong-featured, the eyes closed. The boy let go his hold and straightened up. There at his feet lay Miles Tenbow. Miles Tenbow who had blackballed the Veritys, who had betrayed the Veritys, who had brought death to Wayne and Carl and Evan, and whom Ray had sworn to kill!

A smear of blood stained the side of Tenbow's long face. He had been hurt, but he was breathing still. The cold had gripped Miles Tenbow, and it seemed to Ray that the man was asleep, peacefully resting there. Men had frozen to death in Wyoming storms before this, had been caught in the open and, unable to find shelter, gone until they could go no farther, lain down, slept, and died. Here was Miles Tenbow, and all that Ray Verity had to do was to go, to stagger away, to travel the quarter of a mile or the half a mile that he had left in him. Then he, too, could lie down and let sleep come and accept the pleasant warming lethargy that the cold would bring. It would be good. He could go to sleep and join Wayne and the twins, and they would all be together once again and he would be happy because Miles Tenbow was dead. All he had to do was go! Deliberately Ray turned and, fighting the wind, walked away from Tenbow.

Chapter 8

Two steps were all Ray took. He hesitated, turned, and came back and stood looking down at Tenbow. Then suddenly fury possessed the boy. Here was the man he had ridden to kill, the man he had steeled himself to murder, lying pleasantly asleep while cold struck in and stole his life away. Tenbow was cheating, stealing from Ray Verity, defrauding him. Anger stifled the boy's weariness and the bitter, numbing cold. He fell upon Miles Tenbow, venting all that spite and fury. He jerked Tenbow up, slapped his long, pallid face, shook him and beat him with clenched fists. As he pummeled Tenbow he drove out the ice from his own body, forgot his utter fatigue, defeated the insidious, creeping lassitude that was slowly engulfing him.

Tenbow responded. He opened his eyes, and some resilience sprang to his muscles as he returned to life. Against the wail of the wind Ray Verity's voice screamed: "Wake up, Tenbow. Get up, damn you! You can't do this to me. You can't cheat me, damn you!"

It was slow in coming, but presently there was color in Tenbow's cheeks, and he fought back sluggishly against the boy's attack. Custer, frightened at his rider's sudden fury, hung back against the reins, and Ray held the leather tighter as he lashed at Tenbow with his open hand.

"Get up. Damn you, get up! You can't die here. I'm goin' to kill you!"

It was mad, crazy, insane. Ray Verity, who had resolved to kill Miles Tenbow, fought to save his life. Miles Tenbow, half frozen, was jerked back from the pleasant warmth and lassitude into the blizzard and the cold by a madman. Tenbow staggered to his feet and remained standing, his arms dangling limply by his sides.

Ray came up when Tenbow did. Custer, aroused thoroughly now, pulled back against the reins as the boy advanced. Ray cursed the horse; he cursed Tenbow and raised his fist to strike again.

The blow was checked. Tenbow swayed on his feet and mumbled. "Horse fell. Lemme 'lone."

Ray's clenched fist opened to seize Tenbow's shoulder, and he shook the older man like a wolf tearing flesh from a hamstrung calf shakes the carcass. "Move, damn you! Move!" the boy shouted. "You can't lie down an' die. I won't let you!"

Tenbow took a sluggish step and then another, staggered, and almost fell, and only Ray's quick grasp saved him.

Fright combined with Ray's anger. Tenbow was on his feet; he was alive, but he could still cheat Ray Verity. He could fall, and all the boy's fury, all his efforts, would not lift the man again. That must not happen; it could not. Ray was obsessed with the thought. He did not reason at all, did not think of what the storm would do, of how the storm could kill them both. In Ray there was anger and fear and determination. He would not be cheated! Gripping Tenbow, supporting him, he pulled on the reins and drew the reluctant Custer close, swinging the horse so that, for a moment the sorrel's body blocked the wind.

"Get up!" Ray shrilled to Tenbow. "Get on that horse."

Tenbow looked at the boy with dull, lackluster eyes.

Ray was almost crying with rage and with futility. He lifted Tenbow's arm and put it on the saddle. The arm slid off, and Tenbow swayed. Ray struck the man again, slapping the flaccid face with his open hand. A spark came into Tenbow's eyes, a little gleam of anger.

"Get on that horse!" Ray screamed. "Damn you, you yellow coward. Get on that horse. Yo're afraid!"

"Ain't 'fraid," Tenbow muttered. "I ain't."

Again Ray lifted Miles Tenbow's arm to the saddle. Somehow the numb fingers curled and held the fork. "Get up there!" the boy shouted against the storm. "Get yore foot up!"

Bending, he lifted Tenbow's foot to the stirrup, thrusting it in. Custer stood, his head turned from the wind, waiting patiently. Cursing, rasping at

114

Tenbow, calling him a coward, striking the man, Ray worked and tugged and shoved and hauled. Somehow Tenbow got to the saddle; somehow the boy pulled his right leg across the cantle, and instinctively Tenbow sat up. He had spent the major portion of fifty years astride a horse, and straddling a saddle was more natural to him than walking.

Now with Tenbow mounted, the final terrible chapter began. Still grasping the reins with unfeeling hands, Ray headed straight into the wind, his breath coming in great searing, tearing gasps as the cold air tore at his tortured lungs.

Tenbow swayed back and forth, perilously balanced. Ray, bent forward, leaning into the wind, led Custer, and the big sorrel plodded steadily after the boy. They made ten yards, twenty, fifty, a hundred, and then the wind cut off as though a door had been closed against it. The snow fell and the storm raged overhead. To the right the gale howled and swept up snow to whirl it in a mad bacchanal, but about Ray Verity and Miles Tenbow and Custer there was utter calm. Custer swung to the left, and Ray, feeling the horse's pull, also turned and took five more staggering strides before he fell, pitching headlong against a plank door.

Inside the new 10 Bow camp in Verity Gap, Dutch Koogler and Tom Marvin huddled close to a sheet-iron stove. The rock-and-sod shack was tight enough, but five feet away from the redly glowing stove the air was icy. Marvin had been caught by the storm just as he reached the gap, en route home from town, and wisely had made for shelter.

"Yo're lucky, Tom," Dutch Koogler said for perhaps the tenth time. "Mighty lucky that this place is here. Suppose Tenbow hadn't put a camp in the gap? Where'd you have gone when the storm hit you? The Verity place is burned, an' there ain't any shelter except here."

Tom Marvin, like every other man in the Wagonwheel, resentful of Tenbow's calm pre-emption of Verity Gap, puffed on his pipe and frowned.

"Yeah," he drawled. "I'm pretty lucky all right. Who'd of thought that it was goin' to snow like this? She's a regular Wyoming twister, ain't she?"

"Sure is." Koogler turned his back to the stove to get that side of his body warm. "I saw her comin'. I got my horses in the shed before she hit. It's a good thing that Tenbow had some grain hauled in. A couple of days like this an' the stock that's out is goin' to be pushed to find somethin' to eat."

"We'll make out in the Wagonwheel all right," Marvin stated. "We got enough breaks so that the cattle find shelter. An' we all put up hay."

"I expect," Koogler drawled without looking

at his guest, "that the Verity cattle worked down into the roughs. I've been here two weeks now, an' I don't think I've seen more than five or six head of Walkin' Vs in the gap. They must of known that a storm was comin' an' worked down to shelter."

"Cattle are pretty wise all right," Marvin agreed. "How come Tenbow to put you in a camp, Dutch? I thought you was foreman of the 10 Bow."

"We're shorthanded," Koogler replied briefly.

Tom Marvin knew why the 10 Bow was short-handed. He knew that Miles Tenbow had fired every 10 Bow man who had been in Gunhammer on the night the Verity boys were killed. He knew, too, that Tenbow had been able to replace only about half his crew.

"Maybe this storm is kind of a good thing," Koogler drawled. "Shorthanded the way we are, we could lose some cattle winterkilled, but we might of lost more another way if it hadn't stormed." He turned so that he could watch Marvin with his bright blue eyes.

Marvin shrugged. "Funny about the Verity place bein' burned," he said, testing Koogler, prying in to see how much Koogler knew. "If that hadn't happened you wouldn't of had to put a camp over here. You could of used the old Verity place. How do you reckon it happened?"

It was Koogler's turn to shrug. "Some saddle

tramp, maybe," he answered. "Passed by an' holed up for the night and got careless with his fire."

"You don't think Ray Verity burned the place so nobody could use it?"

"Maybe."

There was a temporary lessening in the howl of the wind above the line camp. From behind the men there came a thump as though some heavy object had struck the door. "What's that?" Koogler asked sharply. "Did you hear that, Tom?"

Marvin was already moving across the little room. "Somethin' blew into the door," he said. "Lord"—he stared at the snow-filled window—"if anybody's out today—"

Koogler passed Marvin and paused at the door, his hand resting on the latch. "Nobody's out," he said. "Everybody's holed up like we are. Just the same . . ." He pulled the door open.

A man, snow-covered, pitched headlong into the room, raised himself to his hands and knees, and began to crawl. Koogler bent swiftly and caught Ray Verity's shoulder. Marvin was on the other side, and together they lifted the boy to his feet.

"Tenbow," Ray muttered. "Outside. He tried to die on me, damn him!"

Koogler released his hold and plunged out into the storm. Marvin half led, half carried the boy over to the bunk and let him down. Ray sat, bent forward, supporting himself by will and not by muscles. Koogler appeared in the door carrying a snow-rimed burden. He crossed the cabin to deposit Tenbow on the bunk beside Ray.

"Get the clothes off 'em," Koogler snapped. "I've got to get a horse into the shed." He hurried out of the door again, banging it closed behind him. Tom Marvin bent and fumbled at the buttons of Tenbow's coat.

When Koogler came back Marvin had pulled off the ranchman's coat and was working on his boots. Dutch knelt and seized Tenbow's other foot.

"Get the kid undressed," he rasped. "I'll look after the boss."

Marvin dropped a boot and turned to Ray. Ray's eyes were wide and blank, and he did not recognize the man who tugged at his coat and jerked the snow-covered cap from his head.

Working swiftly, Dutch Koogler and Tom Marvin flayed the stiff clothing from the men who had cheated the storm. They put blankets beside the stove and carried Ray and Tenbow to them. Koogler stoked the stove with fresh wood, and the fire roared in the chimney while the whole stove grew red. They chafed numb blue feet and rubbed their calloused hands over naked bodies, and while they worked they talked.

"Tenbow an' Ray Verity," Koogler marveled. "How did they ever come together?"

"Pass me that coal oil, Dutch," Marvin rasped. "Ray's feet are about froze."

Gradually the heat began to penetrate to Ray Verity. The tortures of the damned twisted his muscles and tore at his body as life came back to it. Koogler, working over Tenbow, bethought himself of the whisky bottle and mixed a slug of the liquor with hot water for both patients. Ray, by no means in as serious a condition as Tenbow, felt the whisky hit bottom like liquid fire. It warmed him and made him respond more readily to Marvin's ministrations.

"I found Tenbow down," Ray managed to say. "His horse had fallen an' he'd passed out. I got him onto Custer an' we come in."

Koogler paused a moment beside the boy and looked down with open admiration. "You done a chore," he praised and went on back to Tenbow. Ray closed his eyes. The agony was leaving his muscles, and he felt warm and relaxed.

"Couldn't let him die," the boy muttered and then, utterly exhausted, slept.

When Ray wakened gray light was seeping into the shack through the snow that covered the window. The stove was roaring briskly, and Dutch Koogler was getting breakfast. He did not look at Ray but spoke to someone else in the room. "She let up durin' the night. It's clear outside but cold as hell."

"Yeah. There ain't as much snow as I thought

there'd be." Ray recognized Tom Marvin's voice. "I'm goin' to eat with you, Dutch, an' then pull out. I've got to get home to my folks. They'll be worried."

"Think you can make it all right?" Koogler asked.

"It'll be O.K. in the roughs. Maybe some drifts, but I can buck through 'em."

"Come an' get it then," Koogler invited. "She's all ready."

Ray sank back into a pleasant lethargy.

He was roused from his sleep by the banging of the door. Turning his head, he could see the whole of the little room unoccupied save for himself and Miles Tenbow lying on the bunk. Ray himself was close to the stove, blankets over him and under him. He withdrew a hand from beneath the blankets and touched his cheek. There was no feeling. Ray sat up. Clothing hung on a line behind the stove, his underwear, shirt, trousers, and coat. He felt weak, and the room rocked dizzily for an instant before it quieted. Pulling the blankets off his legs, he looked at himself. He was utterly naked. Reaching out to a wall for support, Ray got up. He was standing shakily, dressing himself, when Dutch Koogler came back into the room. Koogler gave an exclamation and hurried across to Ray.

"You stay in bed," he ordered. "You come in

here damned near froze to death last night. What do you mean, tryin' to get up?"

"I'm goin' to get out of here," Ray rasped. "I'm all right. Let me alone." He pushed Koogler away and resumed the labor of buttoning his shirt.

Koogler stared at the boy. "You brought Tenbow in; do you know that?" he demanded.

"I know it," the boy snarled. The shirt was buttoned.

"Where'd you find him?"

"I don't know. He was down an' I stumbled onto him. I thought he was goin' to die, damn him!"

Dutch Koogler poured a cup of coffee. "Here," he directed. "Drink this. You ain't goin' anyplace, Ray. You can't make it, an' besides, yore horse is played out."

Ray swallowed the hot coffee. It put new life into him. "I ain't goin' to stay here," he rasped. "Do you think I'll stay where Tenbow is?"

"Set down an' have another cup of coffee." Koogler pushed a box forward with his foot. Ray sank down on it reluctantly. The box felt good. He was weak, and standing had been an effort.

"Why won't you stay around Tenbow? You sure saved his bacon yesterday. What have you got against him?"

"You know what I got against him. He killed my brothers!"

Dutch Koogler's blue eyes were wide. "Are

you crazy?" he demanded. "Don't you know what happened? Don't you know that Tenbow come out from town to stop that racket? Where have you been, Ray?"

"I know," Ray answered sullenly, "that a bunch jumped us an' that Wayne an' the twins were killed. I know that I heard Tenbow yell an' that he was there. I know that you were there too, Koogler. You an' Smiley an' Jorbet were supposed to protect us!"

Dutch Koogler could not meet the boy's eyes. "I was there," he said hoarsely. "Ray, you got to believe this. We never had a chance. I was knocked off my horse an' beat over the head with a Colt. I don't know what happened to Smiley an' Jorbet, but Charlie Nerril took an awful beatin'. There was a dozen men jumped us. It was black as a cow's insides, an' we never even got untracked." He looked at Ray now. "An' you boys had made a break for it too," he reminded. "Don't forget that."

"Who were they, Dutch?" Ray demanded, forgetting for the moment his hatred of Tenbow.

Dutch Koogler shook his head. "I don't know," he answered. "Bill Brown was one of 'em. I knew him all right. He was beatin' me over the head while somebody held me. I reckon Bill was sore at me anyhow. But the rest I couldn't swear to. All I know is that they come down on us."

"You got to know!" Ray got up from the box

and advanced on Koogler. "Damn you. You're like all the rest. You're lyin'. Tenbow went to town an' framed the whole thing. He got a bunch together an'—"

"Tenbow come to stop it. He's fired every man that worked for him that was in Gunhammer that night. Does that sound like Tenbow got 'em together?"

It was Ray Verity's turn to lower his eyes from Dutch Koogler's gaze. He stared at the dirt floor. "Then who?" he demanded. "Who, if it wasn't Tenbow?"

Koogler shook his head. "There was me an' Jorbet an' Weathers," he answered. "We were there. Jorbet an' Weathers went to town. Take yore pick. But it wasn't Tenbow, Ray."

Ray looked up. "I could maybe believe that if I hadn't heard Tenbow yell," the boy rasped. "I can hear him yet, callin' his dogs, hollerin' for his men. I'll give you this, Dutch: You done your best, likely, but I can't get it out of my head that Tenbow was behind it." He turned his back on Koogler, walked to the box, and, sitting down, began to pull on his boots.

"If that's the way you feel about it I won't try to stop you," Koogler said quietly. "But I say that Tenbow was tryin' to stop the thing, not eggin' it on."

Ray poised a boot before his foot. "An'," he said bitterly, "I reckon that this ain't a Tenbow camp an' that you ain't holdin' down country that belonged to the Veritys. Who makes the most out of us Veritys bein' wiped out, Dutch? I'll tell you! Tenbow!"

"Then why," Dutch Koogler rapped, "did you bring him in? Why didn't you let him lay out an' freeze?"

For a long minute Ray did not answer. Then he said slowly, "I'll be damned if I know, Dutch, except that it looked like he was cheatin' me. I'd planned to kill him myself."

He pulled on the boot, wincing as the leather rubbed against the chilblain on his heel, and, rising, reached for his coat. "I'm able to travel," Ray announced. "An' I'm goin' to travel. Don't try to stop me, Dutch."

"I ain't tryin', am I?" Koogler did not look at the boy. "There's a Walkin' V horse that's been comin' up to be fed. Take him with you when you go."

Ray pulled on his coat, found his cap, and donned it. Around his middle, outside his coat, he buckled the belt that bore Clough Weathers' Colt, and then, without a glance at Tenbow on the bunk or at Dutch Koogler beside the stove, went out.

Custer was in the corral beside the shed, and Brownie, wise old Brownie, thrust his head over the corral bars. Ray Verity saddled Brownie and put his rope on Custer. Leading the big sorrel, he started out. There was snow on the ground,

125

and clouds lined in a low bank to the north, but the sun was shining. Brownie struck a little drift and went through it, and Ray Verity rode down the long slope of the gap. He would strike the Notch Canyon on the eastern side and, using both horses alternately, he believed that he could buck a way through.

Back in the 10 Bow line camp Miles Tenbow stirred on the bunk. Opening his eyes, he looked up into Dutch Koogler's anxious face.

"How'd I get here?" Tenbow demanded weakly. "I was out an' it was snowin', I remember."

"Ray Verity brought you in," Koogler answered quietly. "You lay still, Miles. I'll bring you a cup of coffee an' tell you. We got to talk, I reckon."

Chapter 9

Mat Yoeman cut through the Notch after leaving Ray and went out of the gap into the Pie River Flats. Passing the Verity place, he saw the burned ruins and stopped to investigate them briefly, but he did not cross the gap and so missed the new 10 Bow camp at the western side. From the old Verity place Mat went straight south and by night reached the river, stopping just where he had camped when he found Ray.

The following morning Mat rode on, trying to locate the horses that he had left and, fortune favoring him, spotted four of the six Ace of Spades geldings sent with a bunch of 10 Bow summer horses that had been turned out when the fall work was finished. Mat spent the balance of the day penning the horses at the deserted Diamond Lake camp, cutting out his own horses, and getting his pack horse and camp outfit up to Diamond Lake.

The next day he started early and about five o'clock came juning into Fort Neville and penned his stock in the corral at the Star Wagon Yard, unsaddled and pulled off his pack.

The man who owned the yard was a horse trader, and Mat entered into negotiations with him. A price was offered for the four Ace of

Spades geldings and scornfully rejected. Mat went uptown to let the deal simmer awhile, visited a store and gave an order, sure that he would have the money to pay for it, and then sauntered down to the courthouse. The sheriff was an old friend, and Mat never visited Fort Neville that he did not drop in to pass the time of day. His moccasined feet made no sound as he walked along the courthouse corridor and stopped at the sheriff's door.

Frank Arnold, a wide man, inclined to run to belly, had held the sheriff's office for eight years, which was a mark of respect and efficiency. Mat cleared his throat, and Arnold looked up and grinned. "Come in, Mat," he welcomed. "How are you?"

"Pretty good." Mat entered the office and, disdaining a chair, squatted by the wall. "Goin' to be cold pretty soon. Everythin's puttin' on a heavy coat of hair, an' the squirrels stored a lot of nuts last fall. I come to town to get some stuff before winter hits."

Arnold nodded. He knew Mat well enough to tell that there was something on the old man's mind besides winter supplies. He also knew that Mat would not come out with a direct question but, Indian-like, would wait, dropping in a slow word now and then until he led up to his subject.

"That was a hell of a thing over at Gunhammer, wasn't it?" Arnold said, making conversation. He doubted if Mat had heard of the killings, for Mat stayed in the hills pretty closely.

"What was that?" Mat asked.

"You ain't heard?" Arnold did not wait for an answer but continued, repeating the story of the deaths in the Pastime Saloon and the killing of the Verity brothers.

"Mmm," Mat said. "Kind of tough. The kid got away, you said?"

"He got away."

"What you doin' about it?" Mat rubbed the side of his nose thoughtfully.

"I went over an' made an investigation," Arnold answered. "The Veritys made a break all right. They jumped my deputy an' Charlie Nerril an' made a stand. That Wayne had more guts than a brass elephant. He shot off his wrist so that his kid brother could get away. Plenty nervy."

"Yeah," Mat drawled. "What about them fellers that jumped the hack? You after them?"

Frank Arnold frowned. "I'm after 'em," he answered, "but it's goin' to take a long time. I talked to Koogler an' Colfax an' Jorbet an' Nerril. Tenbow too. The only one they could swear to was Bill Brown, an' he's left the country. It was dark, you see, an' there was a gang, all drunk an' crazy-mad. Nobody I've talked to knows anythin' or else they all lie. You can't expect a man to squeal on himself, Mat. Accordin' to what I hear, there wasn't anybody there but Koogler an' Colfax an' Nerril an' Jorbet, but I know damned well that half of Gunhammer was mixed up in it an' a lot of 10 Bow men. Tenbow fired every rider he had that was in town that night. He was plenty sore. I guess I'll just have to wait till somebody gets careless an' makes a slip."

Mat said, "Mmm," once more. "Kind of tough on young Ray."

Arnold shrugged. "He's makin' it tougher," the sheriff announced. "Weathers was in here about noon with a complaint. Young Verity come into Gunhammer last night, got Weathers out of bed, an' made him open his store. He stole Weathers' Colt, took a rifle an' some shells and a new coat, an' just about cleaned out the candy case. Mrs. Weathers got worried because her husband was gone an' went down an' got Jorbet. They got to the store, an' Ray took a shot at Jorbet an' rode out of town, shootin' the place up while he went. Weathers left at daylight to get over here. He's mad as hops. I got a warrant for Ray right here on my desk."

Mat Yoeman got up. "You'll aim to serve it, I expect?" he drawled.

"Jorbet is supposed to be out lookin' for the kid now," Arnold answered. "I'm goin' over to Gunhammer tomorrow. You say that things are pretty good in the hills, Mat?"

"They ain't so all-fired good," Mat answered. "I expect I'll pull out, Frank."

130

He padded out of the office and along the corridor. Frank Arnold, eyes wide with surprise, looked at the vacant door. "Now what do you suppose got into him?" Arnold demanded. "What do you suppose . . . ? Hmmm." The officer's eyes narrowed. He was thinking rapidly and accurately. "Mebbe . . ." Arnold said. "Mebbe that's it. I expect I'll drop in to see Mat pretty soon."

From the courthouse Mat went back to the Star Yard. There he surprised the owner by accepting the offer for the geldings, was paid, and betook himself to the store where he urged haste in filling his order. He paid for the goods, packed them on weary Bear Dance, and, putting his saddle on his pack horse, pulled out. It was dark and cold when Mat left Fort Neville, but he pushed along for several hours, traveling by moonlight. In the morning gray skies warned him that he must hurry, and before he reached the foothills snow was spitting, but he made his cabin before the storm broke in all its fury.

The cabin was deserted. Mat put his horses in the shed, fed them from his meager supply, and prepared for the siege of the storm. Impatient and anxious as he was, he knew the uselessness of trying to move when winter attacked. All the remainder of the day and through the night Mat listened to the wind howl and saw the white flakes falling. About three o'clock the storm lessened, and Mat, waking as the wind died down, grunted satisfaction. In the morning he could leave to look for Ray.

At daylight Mat went out. The cabin was sheltered, and there was a bunch of horses that had been driven in by the storm. Mat caught two, saddled one of them, and, taking the other for a lead horse, started for the Notch. He used one horse and then the other alternately to break trail, so conserving their strength and making time. The gray sky threatened, but Mat pushed along. Before noon he had reached the Notch and started down the other side. He topped out on a ridge and, looking at the country below, saw a black dot that crawled along toward him. Mat changed horses again and rode on down. He was at the mouth of Notch Canyon when he met Ray Verity. The boy was riding an old brown horse and leading Custer. He looked at Mat with haggard eyes as he rode up.

"I was bringin' Custer back," he said.

"Ray"—all Mat's anxiety was in his voice—"did you—?"

"No," Ray said. "I had Tenbow over my sights yesterday mornin' an' I couldn't squeeze the trigger. Then yesterday evenin' I stumbled right square over him in the storm. He was layin' there freezin' to death, an' all I had to do was move on an' leave him."

The boy paused. Mat's question trembled,

unspoken, on his lips. Ray's eyes were bitter. "You know what I done?" he demanded. "I taken him in to Koogler's camp in the gap. That's what I done. Damn me, I saved his no-account life! I ain't no good, Mat. I just ain't worth a damn!"

"You change horses, Ray," Mat Yoeman ordered gently. "We'll head for home. That ol' brown horse yo're ridin' is about played out. Let's get home before it snows again."

Dumbly the boy got down and loosened his cinch and, in Mat Yoeman's eyes as he watched, there was a gleam of satisfaction and contentment. Ray Verity said that he wasn't worth a damn, but Mat Yoeman harbored a far different opinion. He grinned slyly to himself as he led the way back up the canyon toward the Notch, following the trail that he had broken. Ray Verity, coming wearily along behind, could not see the older man's grin.

When they reached the Notch, Mat stopped and Ray drew abreast. "What's the matter with me, Mat?" the boy asked. "What's wrong with me?"

Mat, looking steadily at Ray's face, gave the answer. "Yo're growin' up, that's all." He took the trail again, and once more Ray followed.

About the time that Mat Yoeman met Ray Verity in Notch Canyon Dutch Koogler and Miles Tenbow rode away from the line camp. Tenbow swore that he could ride and was determined to go back to headquarters, and when Dutch went outside and looked at the weather he doubtfully agreed with his boss.

There was more snow coming, and Dutch knew that Tenbow needed to get home. There were no facilities at the camp for taking care of a sick man, and Tenbow was sick. Exposure and cold had weakened him. Dutch gave Tenbow his own saddle, packed his bed, closed up the camp, rounded up his horses, and they departed. Five miles south of the gap they found Tenbow's horse, dead. The animal had broken a leg when it fell, had gone a short distance and fallen again. Unable to get up, the horse had frozen. Dutch retrieved Tenbow's saddle and put it on a horse, glad enough to be done with riding bareback.

Neither man talked on the way home, and when they reached the 10 Bow headquarters Dutch turned Tenbow over to Hannie. Both the headquarters riders were in and had questions to ask, but Dutch hurriedly turned his horses into the corral, threw his bed down on the porch of headquarters, and went in to help his daughter. He got Tenbow undressed and into bed, and Hannie, efficient and wise, saw to Tenbow's comfort with a hot toddy, mustard plasters, and a hot foot bath.

"You act like I was a kid," Tenbow growled in protest, but accepted the attentions gratefully. Not until he was warm and comfortable and fed did he and Dutch talk, Hannie hovering anxiously in the background.

"So Verity brought me in," Tenbow drawled. "I would of expected anythin' else from him. What did he have to say, Dutch?"

"He said"—Koogler's blue eyes were steady on Tenbow's face—"that he couldn't let you die. That was when he first come in. He acted kind of mad about it, like maybe you'd tried to cheat him. Then this mornin' when I tried to get him to stay he wouldn't do it. He said he wouldn't stay around you. He'd found you layin' out, an' I reckon he had quite a time bringin' you to camp. He was played out."

Tenbow made no comment, and Dutch, taking a deep breath, plunged in. "Ray thinks that you killed his brothers. He heard you yell that night an' he thinks that you got a gang together an' jumped them. I tried to tell him different, but I didn't have much luck. He called my hand. He said that it was yore camp in Verity Gap an' that you were holdin' down country that belonged to him. An' he asked me who stood to make the most out of the Veritys bein' wiped out. He said that you did."

Tenbow thought a long time. "Maybe you were right about me not puttin' a camp over there, Dutch," he admitted. "It would look bad to the kid. Did you tell him I'd fired the men that were in town that night?"

"I told him, an' it didn't seem to make much of a dent. I'll tell you how Ray figures, Mr. Tenbow: He knows that the men his brothers killed were our riders. He thinks that you'd naturally back up yore own men. He knows that you promised his brothers protection an' that we didn't give it to 'em. He knows that there must of been a leak when we started to take the Veritys out of Gunhammer. He heard you yell when the bunch jumped the hack an' he's seen our camp in the gap an' his own place burned down. He's pretty bitter, an' I'm damned if I blame him."

Miles Tenbow's face was gray and his eyes moody. "So he thinks I killed his brothers, does he?" the older man drawled.

"That's what he said."

"An' yet he picked me up when I was freezin' to death an' took me in to camp." Tenbow shook his head wearily. "I don't figure it."

"He was here yesterday morning," Hannie said swiftly. "I met him when I came back. I think he'd come to kill you, Mr. Tenbow."

Tenbow looked at the girl and smiled faintly. He was fond of Hannie, as fond of her as he ever allowed himself to become of anyone. "So you talked to him, did you, Hannie?" he asked.

"I did," the girl answered with spirit. "I told him that he was wrong. That you'd had nothing to do with his brothers being killed."

Loyal Hannie. "Maybe," Tenbow said slowly,

"you were wrong. Maybe I did get his brothers killed. If we'd kept them where they were an' not tried to move them—" He stopped, thinking back to that night in Gunhammer. "I've let things go, Dutch," he continued, "too much. Duke an' Acey were my boys, an' they'd been killed. I don't know. A man lets things slide sometimes. An' when I put the camp in the gap I was protectin' myself. That bunch of rustlers down there will steal us blind unless somethin's done. Maybe when I can travel I'll look around. I don't give a damn what Ray Verity thinks of me, but I did promise the Veritys protection."

"I'm going to bring you another toddy," Hannie announced, "and you're going to drink it and go to sleep, Mr. Tenbow. And, Dad, you've got to put some more coal oil on Mr. Tenbow's feet. If you don't he won't be able to walk at all."

Hannie hurried out, and Tenbow looked at his foreman. "I'd like to have a crew like her, Dutch," he said slowly. "No, damn it. I'd like to have a daughter like her. Yo're lucky, Dutch."

Dutch Koogler picked up the saucer of kerosene and moved the lamp so that the light was better. "I couldn't get along without Hannie," he answered. "Stick yore foot out, Mr. Tenbow, an' I'll rub it."

Another man traveled that day. Tom Marvin left the camp in the gap and headed north. He

137

reached his own house at noon, ate a hurried meal, and, on a fresh horse, went on. At two o'clock he stopped beside Earl Latiker's corral, and Latiker and Smiley Colfax came out to him.

"Hello, Tom," Latiker greeted. "Yo're movin' around some, ain't you? I'd think that you'd be locatin' yore cattle after the storm."

"My cattle are all right," Marvin answered briefly. "I was comin' back from town yesterday when the storm hit. I holed up with Dutch Koogler in his camp. Know what happened?"

"Don't tell me that you got Koogler killed," Colfax drawled. "You didn't go an' do that, did you, Tom? I figured you'd save him for Earl an' me."

Marvin flushed. He had made some threats when Tenbow put the camp in the gap. "I'll tell you what happened," he snapped. "Ray Verity and Tenbow showed up together. Tenbow had got down in the storm an' was afoot, an' Verity brought him in."

Latiker and Colfax exchanged glances. "What did they say?" Colfax demanded.

"Nothin'. They were both played out. Dutch an' me had to get the clothes off 'em an' thaw 'em out. I left this mornin' before either of 'em was up. But they were together, Smiley."

"Mmmm." Colfax pursed his lips and squinted his eyes at Marvin. "I thought that Ray Verity would have sense enough to stay out of this country," he said. "Didn't you, Earl?"

Latiker nodded.

"He never left the country," Marvin said. "He was ridin' an Ace of Spades horse, that big sorrel that Yoeman had with him when we met him at Verity's. I'll bet you that Ray was with Mat Yoeman right then. I'll bet that's why Yoeman pulled a gun on us."

"An' I'd bet that you were right, Tom," Latiker drawled. "Well, that kind of changes the color of the horse, don't it? Tenbow an' Ray Verity together an' Verity savin' Tenbow's hide. I expect that they'll want to work the Wagonwheel for Walkin' V cattle next spring, Smiley."

Colfax' smile was tight, more a snarl than a smile. "Wantin' to an' doin' are different things," he drawled. "So Ray had an Ace of Spades horse, did he? It ain't so far to Yoeman's but that we could pay him a visit."

Latiker frowned thoughtfully. "We'll do that," he decided. "Right away."

Tom Marvin took a deep breath. "You mean—?" he asked.

"I mean"—Latiker stared at Marvin—"that we've started somethin' we've got to finish. Got to, Tom. We can't back down."

Marvin's shoulders slumped. "I reckon yo're right," he said. "But—"

"Get down an' come in, Tom," Latiker invited.

"Spend awhile. You don't have to go home right away."

Marvin got off his horse and tied the animal to the corral fence. "I knew that night we were gettin' in over our necks," he said as the three walked toward the house. "I knew it."

"We're in deep enough so that we got to swim," Colfax agreed. "Brace up, Tom. Earl's got a bottle in the house, an' we'll all take a drink."

So on the day after the storm men moved in the Whetrocks and the Wagonwheel, in Gunhammer and Fort Neville and on the Pie River Flats. Plans were made and ideas exchanged. Frank Arnold thought about Ray Verity, as did Miles Tenbow and Dutch Koogler. Mat Yoeman, unsaddling in his own corral, also considered the boy. In Gunhammer, Virgil Jorbet had Ray Verity on his mind, as did Clough Weathers, missing one Winchester rifle, a new Mackinaw coat, and a presentation Colt. And that night when Hannie Koogler said her prayers, she, too, thought of Ray and included him in her petition, remembering his savage face and his tortured, angry eyes.

At midnight, waking, Hannie heard the wind howl around the 10 Bow headquarters and, her mind clear, lay back down to sleep. At midnight Mat Yoeman roused and listened to the storm. In the morning the world was white and riven by a gale that, unchecked, blew down across the flats. For three days the storm held, and when it was over, with hardly a respite, another came. The Pie River country, the Wagonwheel, the Whetrocks, all were gripped and held. Winter had declared an armistice.

Chapter 10

Beginning in December, the cold and snow closed down. Men quit using spurs in their meager riding to obviate the pain of the cold iron's burning through their boots to their heels. A day's work called for three, four, sometimes five or six head of horses, and then they could not venture far from home. A trail broken, going out to a bunch of cattle, was drifted closed before its maker could return along it. Horses, usually self-reliant and able to paw down to grass, were caught in isolated spots, penned in by snow, and ate the manes and tails from each other in their futile search for food. Cattle lay down and died. All across the flats, in the edges of the Whetrocks, and in the Wagonwheel roughs were the pitiful snow-covered mounds that told of tremendous loss. The hay so laboriously cut was gone long before spring, and anything and everything was used for substitutes. That was the winter that the old cow died, a winter long remembered and handed down in the annals of the Wyoming cowman. And it was the winter in which Ray Verity grew up.

In Verity Gap, Ray had been the kid, the youngster that was looked after. It had always been Wayne that made the decisions, or lacking

Wayne, Carl or Evan. They had shielded Ray and sheltered him and taken the rough edge. Mat Yoeman did none of those things. Mat pulled his own weight, and he expected Ray to do something besides sit steady in the boat. The old man was iron and rawhide combined. On the coldest days he fared out, a buckskin shirt and a fur cap his barriers against the weather. He wore moccasins and disdained gloves. Once when they were cutting willows so that the horses might browse from the twigs and shredded bark, Ray found his partner swinging an ax, his buckskin shirt unlaced so that the bearlike mat of hair on his chest was exposed, and this in weather so cold that the limbs of the trees were popping.

Mat took things as they came, the rough and the smooth with equal equanimity, and he expected Ray to do the same.

Ray learned during those days. He was too busy living and keeping stock alive to brood on past troubles. Mat's horses were in the hills, and Mat was determined to bring them through. No man to lie idle and let the winter close his bank account, Mat took all the precautions and did all the things he could to save it. He cut logs and made a drag which he pulled along the ridges, so exposing the grass. He cut willows. He fought winter tooth and nail, with a ferocity that equaled the weather, and he saved a lot of stock. When a horse died Mat took it as a personal affront and redoubled his efforts. Ray, perforce, kept pace with Mat.

There were days when they could not venture out, when an excursion to the wood ricked against the cabin was a perilous adventure, and when a man going out into the weather could not see an arm's length ahead of him because of the swirling snow. But even those days were utilized. Then they worked in the cabin or in the shed that held the forge. Ray made buckskin trousers and a shirt from the hides that Mat had stored in the cabin loft. He hammered out a pair of spurs for himself, cutting the big round rowels and blowing the bellows while Mat made the shanks. He spun hair into a long rope while the firelight danced and the wind beat against the cabin door. And somewhere in December or January or February he lost the glitter in his eyes, the insane, glassy expression. In those months he grew, not just physically, but mentally as well, as he listened to Mat's slow stories of the Indian campaigns or of the days that he had spent among the Sioux. Listening and working and watching, Ray Verity learned that there were other people in the world besides Ray Verity and that there were troubles compared with which his were as a child's hurt. He heard the story of the subjugation of a race, of the passing of the buffalo and of men who, proud as Lucifer and free as the wind, were cheated, tricked, and confined.

"They used to own it all," Mat said, waving his arm in a gesture that covered half the land. "The Sioux was boss. They had the buffalo for meat an' clothes, an' they had horses to ride. What more could a man ask? Now they got to live on a little reservation an' eat beef that the govament gives 'em—when they get it. They had the whole country, an' now they got the leavin's. They was lied to an' stole from an' cheated every time they turned around, an' they fought just as hard as they knowed how. An' now they're still bein' cheated an' lied to, but they can't fight."

Ray listened to Mat.

But the boy did other things than grow and work through the winter months. Old Mat had a cunning and a stock of lore. He knew by instinct what a horse would do and where he would go to do it, and Ray acquired something of that instinct. Mat could tell with certainty where the deer would make their beds, and Ray learned that too. Mat shot his old .38-.55 without a lot of preliminary fidgeting around, and he used the long-barreled, frontier-model Colt he wore in a battered holster as though it were a part of him. He was critical of Ray's shooting.

"Lookit here, Ray," he commanded. "Stand over there an' try to hit that log."

Ray stood as directed and, showing off a little, pulled the double-action Colt and went to work. Speed was Ray's idea, and he got the gun out and smoking. But when he looked at Mat the old man shook his head.

"Too fast," Mat said. "It ain't the first shot that counts. It's the first shot that hits." And so Ray's instruction began.

He learned to save his spent shells at that first lesson and that night, using Mat's mold, cast bullets to replace those that had been shot. Mat made a powder ladle from an empty shell, and they reloaded the ammunition, a fascinating, painstaking task that appealed to the boy. And he learned to pull a gun smoothly and without hurry and to throw lead where it would count.

Three months is a long time with many, many hours that cannot be spent in sleep. Mat Yoeman filled those hours for Ray. And Ray, braiding his long brown hair with doeskin plaits as Mat braided his yellow locks, his soft beard beginning to curl on his chin, took the teaching and the work as a dry land soaks up rain.

Sometimes they talked about Wayne and the twins, and sometimes Miles Tenbow was the subject of their conversation. Mat ventured questions that, before Ray's eyes cleared, he avoided as a pestilence, and Ray answered them. He heard the story of Ray's fruitless attempt on Tenbow's life; of how, lying on the bluff, the boy had lined his sights and could not pull the trigger. He heard of Hannie Koogler and her just wrath and of the tale that Dutch had told.

There was a doubt in Ray's mind, and he expressed it. "I don't know for sure, Mat," the boy said. "At first I thought it was Tenbow. I couldn't see anything but him. He'd promised us protection an' he didn't give it to us. He's to blame for Wayne an' the twins bein' killed, but I don't think like I used to. I can't just say that Tenbow did the killin'. People like Dutch an' Hannie wouldn't stick up for him if he was that kind of a man. There were three more there, Jorbet an' Weathers an' Dutch. Jorbet an' Weathers went to town when Tenbow did. An' after the way Weathers acted—" Ray stopped. He had already told Mat the story of his raid on Gunhammer.

"Yeah," Mat said. "You got to remember, Ray, that the whole town was touchy as gunpowder that night. Just any little thing might of set it off. Mebbe Weathers or Jorbet said somethin'. An' you want to remember that Colfax come to ride with you. Somebody told Colfax to come, an' he knew what was goin' on. I never mentioned it to you before, but when I was bringin' you here I run into Smiley an' Earl Latiker an' some others at yore place. I'd stopped there with you, an' they was goin' home. Smiley had a rag around his head like he'd been hurt, an' they didn't take it kindly when I wouldn't let 'em into the house."

"Colfax an' Latiker were our neighbors," Ray said. "Them an' Marvin an' the Hinds boys.

When Tenbow blackballed us Latiker an' Colfax both invited us to work with them. You can count them out, Mat. They weren't mixed up in it. Tenbow's to blame because he didn't do what he promised he'd do, but it might not be like I thought. Maybe he didn't get the gang together. Maybe it was somethin' that Jorbet said or somethin' that Weathers let loose."

"Weathers," Mat drawled, "has got a warrant swore out against you for raidin' his store, Ray. Did you know that?"

Ray shrugged, and his eyes were slits. "I've thought about it some," he answered slowly. "I figured that he'd swear out a warrant."

"What are you goin' to do about it?"

Ray shook his head. "I don't know," he answered honestly. "Except that I ain't goin' to be arrested, Mat. Wayne gave up, an' him an' the twins were killed. I'm not goin' to be arrested, an' I ain't goin' to be put in jail. Maybe I'll be killed, but I won't be taken."

Mat thought about that for a long time. He knew just how Ray felt and how he thought, and he knew the resolution that was in the boy. Ray would not be taken; he might be killed, as he said, but he would not be taken. There was something that could be done about that warrant, Mat thought. Frank Arnold was a friend and a reasonable man too. The sheriff could see another's viewpoint. And Ray had saved Miles

Tenbow's life. Tenbow owed him something. If Weathers was paid for his loss and if Tenbow put on the pressure and the sheriff was talked to, the warrant against Ray could possibly be squashed. As soon as he could travel Mat resolved to see several people.

At the end of February the first sign of breaking winter set the cabin's eaves to dripping. Ice froze nightly, but the days were bright and the cold relented. Two more snows fell in early March, futile and ineffectual affairs compared with the fury that was passed, and then during the month's last weeks spring came. The snow thawed and went off the ridges, remaining only in the shade and on the northern slopes. When April dawned a warm rain that lasted for two days completed the victory of the season. After the rain winter was gone, and on the naked earth the havoc was exposed.

The river and creeks ran torrents. Good fords were fifteen feet under brown and rolling water, and not a bridge was left save only the railroad bridge across the Pie River. Whole hillsides, normally dry, were afloat with running water, and springs broke out in places where springs had never been. Travel was almost as obstructed as though the snow still held, but men moved about the country, nevertheless, counting the carcasses of their stock and locating their cattle, and the buzzards and crows grew fat and surfeited with plenty. Gradually the rivers fell so that almost normal traffic was resumed, and Mat Yoeman, without mentioning the matter to Ray, resolved to go visiting. The 10 Bow, Gunhammer, Fort Neville, all were on his list of calls.

About a week after the streams began to fall and while Mat was still toying with the idea of travel visitors descended on the little cove in the eastern slope of the Whetrocks. They came trailing down through the Notch—men, horses, children, women, and dogs, and in that order—first the bucks, mounted on poor rawboned ponies, then the boys herding a few more half-starved horses, and then the squaws.

"Mat!" Ray Verity yelled from in front of the cabin. "Come here!"

Mat Yoeman thrust his yellow head through the doorway. Then, stepping out deliberately, he walked to the pole fence and opened the gate.

"How, Chola?" Mat greeted, thrusting out his hand. "How, Sunheart?"

The tall Sioux in the lead smiled and took Mat's hand in his own. "How?" he answered. "How, Ahkota?"

Each brave, greeting Mat by his Sioux name, shook hands solemnly. The boys, five thin bright-eyed urchins, drove the horses down to the flat below the cabin, and the women and girls immediately went about the business of making camp. Mat called to Ray and when he came named him to the men and spoke briefly in Sioux. Ray was uneasy under the stare of expressionless black eyes. Then the tallest of the bucks held out his hand.

"That's Sunheart," Mat announced. "Shake hands with him." The order was unnecessary, for Ray had already gripped the tall brave's hand. In turn he shook hands with Man Who Walks and Black Wolf. There was more guttural conversation between Mat and the braves, and then the Sioux laughed, glancing at Ray as they did so.

"I told 'em you was my boy," Mat explained, grinning. "They want to know where you got yore brown hair."

Ray grinned too. He and Mat were partners, and there was an unspoken working agreement between them. Now Mat had claimed him to these Indians. More talk, and then the braves departed to where three tepees stood on the flats.

Mat turned to Ray. "We'll feed 'em," he said. "They been goin' pretty gaunt. How much meat we got in the meat house?"

"We've got a side of venison left," Ray answered. "An' there's a side of salt pork."

"Git 'em," Mat ordered briefly and strode toward the cabin.

When Ray brought the meat Mat had already built a fire in the yard and erected a spit over it.

The deer quarters, neatly butchered, went on the spit, and Mat sliced salt pork. While he worked he talked.

"Sunheart's my uncle," he said. "I married his niece, an' that makes him a relation, the way they figure. I got a couple of cousins in the bunch, too, an' two-three aunts. Sunheart's got two squaws, an' Man Who Walks is married to Sunheart's sister. They been up on the Spruce Agency this winter an' havin' a pretty lean time of it, I'd judge. Anyhow, they decided to go down below, to Nashota Reservation, an' try their luck down there. Sunheart's a good man, an' so are the other two."

"They're awful thin," Ray said. "The kids ain't but just skin an' bones."

"Sunheart ain't by rights an agency Injun," Mat announced. "He ain't never come in an' taken govament rations. He hangs around the edges. Don't trust the agents, I reckon."

All the side of salt pork was sliced, and Mat put it in a Dutch oven and covered it with water. "You turn the meat," he directed. "I'll stir up some bread."

It was a mighty meal that the two prepared. Before it was cooked the children from the camp on the flats were standing around the fire, their thin nostrils sniffing, their eyes wide with anticipation. Mat went down to the camp, returning with the braves. Despite their evident

152

hunger, there was some delay before eating began. The Sioux were gravely ceremonious. But once the ice was broken the food disappeared as though by magic. The women and girls did not eat with the men but drew apart, waiting for their betters to finish. When the men had gorged themselves the others took their turn, and there was nothing left once they were done. Only lean dogs quarreling over the venison bones and greasy, contented faces recalled the feast. Mat brought a long stick of black tobacco from where it was hidden under the eaves above his bunk. Buckskin pouches, beaded but lean, were produced and the tobacco sliced into these with sharp knives. Sunheart produced an ornately carved pipe and, loading it, lighted the tobacco with a coal from the fire. The pipe went around the circle of men, and then the talk began.

Ray understood no word of it but was content to sit and listen to the slow, grave gutturals and to watch the faces as first one and then another spoke. The talk chopped off, and the circle broke. The three braves went silently striding down the slope to their tepees.

Mat got up, grunted, and stretched. "Ain't much to clean up," he commented.

"They ate it all," Ray marveled.

"That's the way an Injun works," Mat explained. "They eat when they got it, an' if they ain't they do without. These fellers been doin' without. Now we'll have to eat with them. They're duty-bound to feed us."

"But," Ray said, "if they're on short rations what'll they feed us? There wasn't any grub in their packs."

Mat shrugged and walked toward the cabin. "Dog, likely," he threw back carelessly over his shoulder. "I'm kind of a big feller with 'em, an' they'll want to give us the best they got. They're proud, the Sioux are."

"Dog!" Ray expostulated. "I—"

"You'll eat it," Mat interrupted. "Yo're supposed to be my boy, an' if you don't eat what they serve you they'll be hurt. An' there ain't nothin' better than a fat dog that's well cooked. Sunheart's squaw is a master hand at stewin' dog."

Ray, following Mat, made mental reservations. Maybe fat dog was good, but the dogs that hung around the Sioux camp were not fat.

The next day Ray and Mat visited in Sunheart's tepee, and they ate dog. Ray thought he would gag before he took the first bite, but the meat was tender and good. Sunheart's squaw was, as Mat had said, a master hand at stewing dog.

There were two people in the tepee that interested Ray. One of these was a boy, Sunheart's son, whose paralyzed hand hung dead and limp at his side. "Stonehand," Mat interpreted the boy's name. Stonehand, who spoke English, came close to Ray and sat down, watching the young man with bright, interested eyes. The other was a girl, tall, supple as a young aspen, and, like the aspens, budding into womanhood. She was not pretty—no Indian woman is beautiful by the accepted standards of the whites—but she moved with an easy natural grace and, like her brother, she watched Ray. Her name was three liquid syllables that meant, Mat said, "Where the Lakes Meet."

After the meal in Sunheart's tepee Black Wolf and Man Who Walks came in silently, squatted down, and there was a ceremonial smoke. On the way back to the cabin, walking through the dusk, Mat glanced at Ray.

"Kind of made a strike with that gal, Ray," he drawled. "I seen you watchin' her. You figurin' to tie yore pony outside of Sunheart's tepee?"

"What's that?" Ray asked.

Mat laughed shortly. "I remember when I done that," he said. "I wasn't no older than you. Long Man had a daughter. I'd been livin' in the camp for six months, an' she suited me. I tied my horse outside of Long Man's tepee. She cost me twenty ponies, but I can't say I ever was sorry." The old man's voice trailed off, and Ray, knowing that Mat was far away in the past, kept respectful silence.

"No," Mat said as they reached the cabin, "I wasn't never sorry. She was a good woman,

Mary was. Her name was Shinin' Hair, but I called her Mary. I dunno. I dunno—sometimes I think . . ." They went inside, and Mat sat down on his bunk. Ray remained by the door, looking down to where the tepees made black cones on the flat.

"It's a good livin'," Mat drawled. "Free—no one to boss you . . . A good livin'."

"I want to take your rifle in the mornin'," Ray announced. "I know where there's a barren doe hangs out. I'm goin' to go get her."

"They'll like the meat an' use it," Mat drawled. "Yo're welcome to the rifle."

Chapter 11

Dutch Koogler did not go back to the camp in Verity Gap but stayed at headquarters all through the winter weather. Tenbow was slow to recover from the exposure and shock of his experience, and most of the work fell upon Dutch. The 10 Bow was shorthanded; it was hard to replace the missing men, and Tenbow himself did not want the camp occupied.

"I done wrong, mebbe," he told his foreman, "puttin' a camp there an' holdin' that country. We'll let it go awhile." Such an admission from the old man was surprising. Generally Tenbow went through with anything that he started. But Dutch carried out his orders.

The 10 Bow, like every ranch on the flats, lost heavily through the winter. When spring broke Koogler estimated at least a twenty-percent death loss, perhaps more. Tenbow, too, considered the cattle that he had lost and placed an estimate even higher than the foreman's. When the snow went off the country the rider at the Diamond Lake camp had more than his hands full and complained to Dutch that he could not do it all. The Diamond Camp man was sure that he had some cattle missing. Dutch rode the country out of the Diamond Lake, and he, too, found that there were 10 Bow cattle gone. Tenbow scowled when his foreman made the report.

"We miss the Veritys," Dutch said. "They always rode the gap an' threw back anythin' of ours that was in it. The man at Diamond Lake can't ride the gap an' do his own work too."

Tenbow did not answer for some time. He had, in the fall, considered putting a fence across the gap and arrogantly taking possession of country that was not his either by ownership or usage. That idea he now discarded. Too many of his cattle had winterkilled to spend the money that a fence would cost.

"We'll put a man down in the camp at the gap," Tenbow said suddenly.

"Who?" Dutch was blunt.

Tenbow thought again. He had to have a man in the gap that he could trust, an old head, a loyal 10 Bow man. "I expect you'll have to take it awhile, Dutch," Miles Tenbow announced, looking at his foreman. "I need you here, an' all that, but I'll have to spare you. You go down there an' work at the job. We'll catch that Wagonwheel bunch one of these days, an' when we do I'll go in there an' clean the place out. I'll take on yore ridin' an' try to get a man to put at that camp, but you hold it down for now."

Dutch grunted. If Tenbow took over Dutch Koogler's work out of headquarters he would spend about twenty out of every twenty-four

158

hours in the saddle, and Dutch was doubtful concerning Tenbow's ability. Tenbow had aged. His hair and mustache, iron-gray when winter set in, were snow-white now, and the man's face was thin and pinched. That evening, as he made preparations for his early departure, Dutch expressed his doubts to Hannie.

"I'll look after Mr. Tenbow, Dad," Hannie assured. "I don't like to have you gone though. I hope he gets a man for that camp right away."

"There's nobody he can get," Dutch answered. "There ain't a man in the country that wants work that ain't hired. I wish the Veritys was still alive an' holdin' down the gap. The old man was clear out of line when he blackballed them last fall. The Verity boys made pretty good neighbors."

Hannie considered her father's statement. Then: "Dad," she said, "couldn't you get Ray to go back to the gap? Couldn't Mr. Tenbow give him the new camp so that he would have a place to live? I've thought about him a lot since that day that he was here. He looked so—I don't know how to say it—so lost, I guess. And then when he found Mr. Tenbow and brought him in—I don't see why Ray Verity wouldn't be just the one. And, Dad, Mr. Tenbow owes Ray something."

Dutch considered the suggestion. "If Tenbow an' Ray would both do it," he said, "it would be fine. But Tenbow's hardheaded, an' the way Ray

159

feels, I doubt if he'd take anythin' off the old man. Still . . ."

"You talk to Mr. Tenbow, Dad," Hannie urged.

"I will."

Good as his word, Dutch broached the subject to Tenbow before he left the following morning. He was surprised that Tenbow heard him through. When he had finished the ranchman stared thoughtfully at his foreman's face.

"That ain't yore idea, Dutch," he accused. "Hannie thought of that."

Dutch Koogler admitted the accusation.

"I never," Tenbow said, "run the Veritys out of the gap. I got along with 'em until last fall, an' Wayne was pretty reasonable when he came to talk to me. There's Walkin' V cattle in the Wagonwheel, an' if the boy wanted to come back an' look after 'em I wouldn't try to stop him. But I want a man that I can trust in the gap right now, an' that's why I'm sendin' you."

"If Ray came back where would he stay?" Dutch asked slyly.

"He could stay at our camp for all I'd care," Tenbow answered. "I owe him somethin', I guess. But I don't think he'll come back. He made a raid in Gunhammer last fall, an' Weathers has got a warrant out for him. He'll have that to face." The ranch owner paused and considered for a moment. "Not but that somethin' could be done about the warrant," he concluded. "I'll be over to see you in a day or two, Dutch."

So dismissed, Dutch returned to Hannie and reported the conversation. Hannie smiled. "Mr. Tenbow just doesn't want to say that he was wrong about the Veritys," she said confidently. "Dad, if you see Ray you talk to him. If we could get them together . . ." She smiled flashingly.

"Ray was hangin' out at Mat Yoeman's last fall," Dutch said. "He was ridin' an Ace of Spades horse when he brought Tenbow in to camp. I might get to see him."

"Please, Dad," Hannie coaxed.

"All right, I'll try to see him then," Dutch Koogler agreed. "But it's not goin' to do any good, Hannie. He hates Tenbow."

There was a lot of merit in Hannie's suggestion, Dutch thought as he rode away. Always a kindly man, he wanted to do what he could for Ray Verity. If Tenbow worked on Clough Weathers and squashed the warrant, and if Ray came back to the gap and looked after his cattle and didn't throw in with the men in the Wagonwheel, and if everything went right . . . A whole lot of ifs, but worth trying just the same.

He reached the camp that afternoon and put his horses in the corral. The next morning he rode from west to east and, the short distance completed, debated with himself briefly, then swung down through the gap to Notch Canyon. He was going out of his way and pulling off from his job, but Dutch had resolved to visit Mat Yoeman and talk things over with Ray if he was there.

A good part of his ride was saved for him, for a mile below the Notch on the eastern slope of the Whetrocks, Koogler encountered Mat. The old man drove a few horses ahead of him, and he left them when Dutch raised a yell. They met and shook hands.

There was some preliminary conversation before Koogler broached his subject. He knew Mat well enough not to ask questions, but he also knew that Ray was staying with Mat when, as he spoke the boy's name, Mat looked at him sharply.

"What do you want with Ray?" Mat asked.

"I want to talk to him," Koogler answered. "I'm in camp in the gap now an' I'm bound to run into some Walkin' V cattle. I'd like to know what he'll want done with 'em."

"What's the other reason?" Mat demanded.

"I'd like to get him an' Tenbow together," Dutch answered frankly and went on to state the real reason for his errand.

Mat scowled when Dutch finished. "I don't think the kid would do it," he said. "He's sore at Tenbow, an' I don't blame him. I'll tell him that you want to see him though."

That was all that Dutch Koogler had asked. He and Mat parted with mutual invitations to "come over and see me," and the 10 Bow man went back through the Notch to the gap.

That night at supper Mat told Ray of having met Koogler and mentioned casually that with Koogler in the gap he was bound to see some Walking V cattle.

"You'd ought to go over there, Ray," Mat continued. "Somebody's got to look after them cattle, an' they belong to you. Why don't you drift over there tomorrow?"

Ray thought over the suggestion and agreed to it. "I'll do that," he said. "There ain't anything I've got to do here."

This statement was true. Sunheart and his families of Sioux were gone, having departed the day before; the horses were located now, and there was little to do except ride the country. Colts would not be coming for a while yet, and there was a slack in the work. Besides, now that winter was over Mat did not take work seriously.

"Will you come along, Mat?" Ray asked.

Mat shook his head. "I'm goin' to get ready to go to town tomorrow," he answered. "I got an errand that I been puttin' off, an' Sunheart an' his people comin' in the way they did kind of delayed me too. You go over by yorese'f, Ray."

"All right," Ray agreed.

"I'll likely see Sunheart on the way to town," Mat said slyly. "The way them Sioux are movin', they won't be hardly out of the hills. You want me to give yore love to that gal, Ray?"

Under his beard Ray flushed. "I wish some-times I'd gone with 'em," he answered. "If I had I wouldn't have all this business to bother about. I'd be clear of the country. Sunheart asked me to go along."

"That was because he thought you was my boy an' because he's lookin' for a husband for the gal," Mat said gravely, hiding the twinkle in his eyes by turning his head. "Yo're a right upstandin' young buck, Ray—if it wa'n't for them whiskers—an' the gal likes you."

"You can't hurrah me, Mat," Ray answered. "Not about an Indian girl."

In the morning Ray pulled out for the Notch, leaving Mat to make his preparations for the visit to town. Ray said that he would be back that night as he mounted Custer. Mat watched the boy go, affection in his eyes.

"You won't do it," he muttered. "But it ain't goin' to hurt you to talk to Dutch. Dutch is all right."

About three hours after Ray's departure Frank Arnold and Virgil Jorbet rode in to the cabin. Mat came out to meet them, a question in his eyes, and Arnold went directly to business.

"Howdy, Mat," he greeted. "We come over after Ray Verity."

"He ain't here," Mat answered.

"No use tryin' to protect him," Arnold answered.

"Last fall when he raided Gunhammer he was ridin' that big sorrel of yores. Everybody knows that horse. An' when I told you that there was a warrant out for him you pulled your freight out of town. He's here, Mat."

"No, he ain't," Mat answered with asperity. He could lie with all the cunning of an Indian and was torn with the desire to do so, but there was no use lying to Frank Arnold. The sheriff had the deadwood on Mat and Ray too.

Arnold proceeded to prove his prowess. "That ain't yore shirt on the line behind the cabin," he announced. "You ain't wore a cloth shirt in years. It's the kid's. I want him, Mat."

"He ain't here," Mat said for the third time. "He was here, but he's gone."

Mat was telling the truth. Arnold, looking down, could see the set of big tracks that Custer had left in the soft soil. Mat, of course, had reset the shoes on all his shod horses, but Custer's calks had bitten deeply.

"Just left," Arnold said. "All right, Mat, we'll pick him up. He's headed in the right direction, anyhow."

Mat Yoeman, remembering Ray's thin-slitted eyes and the boy's voice when he said, "I won't be taken," made a hasty decision. He could not possibly get around Arnold and Jorbet through the gap and to Ray in time to warn him. The next best thing was to go along with the officers.

Maybe, just maybe, he could talk Ray into giving up without a fight.

"Wait till I get a saddle on a horse, an' I'll go with you," Mat said.

"That's what we're waitin' for," Arnold answered. "You must like the kid, Mat, or you wouldn't let him hole up with you, an' I don't allow that I want you to warn him we're comin'. Go on an' saddle up an' just leave yore gun in the house. You won't need it."

Mat growled, "All right," and went to the corral.

Ray Verity took his time going up through the Notch and down the canyon. He looked for cattle and found a few, and he stopped a long time at the ruins of his old home. The good spring grass was greening up all over the country, and weeds were beginning to sprout around the burned cabin. Ray got down from Custer and walked through what had been the door and looked around. In November, on the morning of his birthday, he had stood in this room and talked to Wayne and Carl and Evan. It was a hard thing and a bitter thing that all the Veritys were gone. Even the cabin was gone. In no very happy frame of mind Ray rode on across the gap.

The day matched his mood. Clouds hung low over the Whetrocks and made a blanket for the gap, for the Wagonwheel roughs and the flats.

Occasionally a little rain fell, a splattering of fine drops that fell in intermittent showers.

Ray saw a few cows now, most of them wearing Marvin's Flying W, with an occasional Slash L cow. He noted automatically that a bunch of cattle had been trailed through the gap, just about the center. He wound back and forth, dropping down into the roughs and working clear on back to the flats. He found one lonely Walking V cow. Somebody had cleaned the gap and cleaned it thoroughly.

When finally Ray reached the 10 Bow camp at the western limit of the gap, it was past noon. Ray dismounted well away from the camp and called. There was no answer. He called again, waited, and then walked up to the cabin. The door was not latched, and Ray, looking in, saw the familiar, primitive housekeeping arrangements of Dutch Koogler. Koogler was out. Ray, not too anxious to see Dutch anyhow, remounted Custer and, having watered the sorrel at the tank, rode off. He would, he decided, make a swing down into the Wagonwheel and look for more Walking Vs.

Ray rode straight north from the tank until he had made about eight miles. He saw more cattle, Flying Ws, some Slash Ls, and some of Latiker's Rafter M cattle. No Walking Vs. Ray changed course and hit for the Notch and the canyon that led to it. He had told Mat that he would be home for supper. Custer was tired, and Ray had quite a ride to make. As he neared the mouth of the Notch Canyon he saw a little party of horsemen converging on him. One of those riders was Mat Yoeman. Ray could recognize the big black Bear Dance horse as far as he could see him. Ray grinned, thinking about Mat. The old scamp had come over into the gap anyhow, trip to town or no trip to town. The grin erased itself. Ray was close enough now to recognize the riders with Mat. They were Frank Arnold, county sheriff, and Virgil Jorbet, deputy from Gunhammer. Ray pulled Custer to a halt. The other party came along, drawing closer. Ray slid his hand back to the butt of Clough Weathers' fancy Colt, and, seeing the motion, Arnold reined in.

"Ray!" Mat called. "I—"

Arnold said something, and Mat stopped. The grizzled sheriff faced Ray again. "I've got a warrant for yore arrest, Verity," he shouted. "Drop yore hand off that gun an' surrender."

Ray did not drop his hand from his gun, and for the instant he did not answer Arnold. What was Mat doing with the sheriff? Why was Mat along? Had Mat . . . ?

"I've told you, Verity," Arnold called. "Are you goin' to give up peaceful, or do we have to take you?"

"Ray," Mat called. "It ain't nothin', boy. Give up to 'em."

168

So Mat was with them too! Determination steeled in Ray Verity. He slid the Colt out of its holster. He wasn't going to be taken. Wayne had surrendered, and Wayne and the twins were dead. Not Ray. If he was to be killed, all right, but he'd have his chance. There wouldn't be handcuffs on him.

"He's goin' to shoot," Jorbet shrilled and made a mistake. Jorbet was beyond Arnold and half hidden. He jerked his gun out and set it to smoking.

Back there in the hills Mat had said, "It ain't the first shot that counts. It's the first shot that hits." The .38-.40 in Ray's hand barked once, and Jorbet's yell rose in pitch and he fell off his horse, his voice roaring assurance that he was not dead.

Frank Arnold was shooting now, and Arnold was a lot different man from Jorbet. Arnold was no speed artist, but Arnold was accurate. Custer was fighting to run, and the lead buzzed past Ray. This was far different from shooting at a log. A log didn't shoot back. Ray sent three shots at Frank Arnold, and Arnold's horse, hit hard, went down. Custer got his head now and wheeled, loping heavily away. Ray looked back. Mat was on the ground beside Bear Dance, and Mat was waving to Ray, sending him on. Then he had been wrong about Mat. Mat wasn't with the sheriff, not in spirit at least. If Mat had really been with

Arnold and packing that old .38-.55 Ray Verity wouldn't be sitting up on Custer, cutting a wide circle around the posse. Custer struck a slant of ground, followed it, dropped into a draw, and the cluster of men were lost to sight. Where now? Ray thought. Where should he go now? There wasn't an answer.

Mat, standing beside Arnold, who was pinned under his horse, said: "He's done gone, Frank."

Arnold tried to free his leg. "Get after him," he rasped, pushing at the inert carcass that held him. "Get him, Mat."

Mat calmly walked over and sat down on the dead horse's hip. Jorbet was sitting up, pale-faced, gripping the biceps of his left arm with his right hand. Ray's slug had barked Jorbet and effectually taken the fight out of him. Jorbet moaned as though he were leaving the world. Mat looked at him scornfully.

"I ain't even got a gun, Frank," he drawled. "Remember? I left mine to home."

"Take mine," Arnold grated. "Get this damned horse off my leg, Mat. I think my leg's broke."

Mat peered thoughtfully at Arnold's leg where it disappeared beneath the body of the horse. "I don't think so," he said consolingly. "The ground's soft. Likely you wrenched her a little."

"Damn you, Mat," the sheriff swore. "Are you goin' to get this horse off me?"

"He's too much for me to lift alone," Mat

replied, unperturbed. "You know, Frank, I'm kind of disappointed in that boy. I thought I'd learnt him to shoot better'n that."

The sheriff was livid with rage. His gun had fallen just beyond the reach of his hand, but he struggled to grasp it. "Mat," he vowed, "when I get out of here I'm goin' to throw you in jail so hard you'll bust. You'll lay there till you rot. Damn you!"

"Then," Mat drawled, "mebbe I'd better not get you out." He arose deliberately and walked over to where Bear Dance stood eying proceedings.

"Mat"—there was a plea in the sheriff's voice now—"you wouldn't go off an' leave me here alone?"

"You got company," Mat pointed out. "Here's yore deputy, a'most adyin', the way he sounds."

"Mat," Frank Arnold said, "quit playin'. The kid's got away. That's what you wanted."

When the sheriff assumed just that tone it was time to obey. Mat said: "Give yore leg a jerk when I lift, Frank," and, bending, heaved on the dead horse. Arnold pulled his foot clear, and Mat helped him up.

"An' now"—the sheriff's voice was still quiet—"yore boy's wanted bad, Mat. By me, personal. This ain't just a warrant no more. I'll get him."

Mat did not answer. Arnold meant what he said. Whereas he had, prior to the meeting, been

171

simply an officer doing his duty and serving a warrant, he was now grimly and personally involved. Ray had pulled and shot. The next time Arnold would pull and shoot, and the sheriff had a reputation for not missing. Ray, the young fool, had messed things up for fair. The old man squatted down and unfastened the cinch that held Arnold's saddle to his dead horse.

"What you goin' to do now, Frank?" he drawled.

Arnold straightened from his examination of Jorbet's arm. "You ain't hurt," he said shortly to his deputy. "Shut up an' get up. Now?" He turned to Mat. "Why, now we're goin' over to the 10 Bow camp. I'm goin' to ride yore horse, Mat, because I'm crippled a little. We're goin' to get fresh horses over there an' we're goin' after Ray Verity. We're goin' to get him too. Come on."

He hobbled out to where Bear Dance stood and mounted the black. Jorbet, frightened because death had come so close, but more frightened of the sheriff, got up and caught his horse.

Mat looked sullenly at Arnold. "You an' me been friends a long time, Frank," he drawled. "But I reckon you taken yore jug to the well onct too often. I'll go with you to the camp because I got to, but I won't he'p you chase Ray. An' I tell you, he shoots a heap better than he did awhile back. That was the first time he ever shot at a man. Next time it will be different."

"Let's go," Arnold said quietly. "It's a long walk, Mat. Hand me up my saddle. I'll carry it."

It *was* a long walk. Mat trudged ahead, making a good consistent five miles an hour, covering the ground with his long, easy Indian stride. Arnold and Jorbet followed, and all the way not a man spoke.

The sun was pointing down in the west when they arrived at the 10 Bow camp. They came in rapidly, closing on the little building. A bunch of horses were in the corral, but there was no smoke rising from the chimney, nothing but the horses to show that the place was occupied.

Arnold called as they arrived and, when he received no answer, handed his saddle down to Mat and dismounted stiffly from Bear Dance. He limped toward the cabin door which hung open and stopped. His voice rasped an exclamation that caused Mat to hurry to him and made Jorbet hasten to the door. Dutch Koogler lay inside the cabin, feet toward the door, prone on his back, arms flung wide. Dutch's face was turned toward the roof, and from his body blood seeped out to make a little pool.

"Good glory!" Mat exclaimed, and Jorbet gasped. For a full long minute they stood there, the three of them in the doorway. Then Frank Arnold said: "So this was why he wouldn't give up an' took to shootin'. This is it."

"Frank—" Mat rasped and stopped as the sheriff turned to him.

"It ain't just a warrant for breakin' into a store no more, Mat," Arnold said quietly. "An' I don't want Ray Verity for resistin' arrest. No. I want him for murder!"

Chapter 12

Gunhammer had never seen a funeral like Dutch Koogler's. The church was filled an hour before the services began, and men and women, solemn-faced, congregated on the lawn. They had come from west of Gunhammer, from the Wagonwheel, from the Pie River Flats, from Fort Neville. There were even a few who, traveling for four days, had come from Cheyenne and Laramie. Word had spread out across the country, carried by riders to lonely, outlying ranches, flashing over the wires from Fort Neville, and Dutch Koogler's friends had answered it. Not his friends alone. There were many present who came because Dutch Koogler was a 10 Bow man, and they felt it politic to pay their respects. Miles Tenbow was an influence in the state, a big man in the Stock Association. Others were there because they were curious, taking a sadistic pleasure in attending the funeral of a murdered man.

The Reverend Caleb Starke, pastor of the Fort Neville Methodist Church, made the funeral oration, and Mrs. Clough Weathers and Jessie Balcomb sang "Abide with Me" and "Lead Kindly Light" before the procession, a full half mile long, wound its way up the little hill to Gunhammer's weed-grown cemetery. There, near the Verity plot where now Wayne and Carl and Evan lay beside John Verity and their mother, Dutch Koogler was buried.

After the funeral men met in little groups and talked low-voiced, and women visited together, making a social event of the occasion. There were two kinds of talk among the men, but the subject was the same: Ray Verity.

In Gunhammer's small hotel Miles Tenbow and Blithestone of the Bar K and half a dozen other big ranchmen, all members of the Stock Association, met together. Tenbow had little to say, but Blithestone, who was a vice-president of the association, did enough talking for both. It was Blithestone who sent out for Frank Arnold. The sheriff arrived, wide and gray, and faced the cattlemen.

"There's no criticism in this, Frank," Blithestone said, "but we'd like to know just what you've done to catch young Verity."

Arnold, hat in hand, looked from one face to another. These were the big men of the flats, the solid, substantial citizens, the men whose good will had put him in office.

"I followed him," Arnold said. "After we'd found Dutch I sent Jorbet to town an' I got a fresh horse an' went out. I left Mat Yoeman there with Dutch. It was pretty near sundown before we'd got to the camp. I struck straight for where we'd had our run-in with Verity an' went on from there. Dark caught me an' it began to rain, an' I turned around an' came back. The next day I got a posse together, an' we went into the Whetrocks. We went to Yoeman's place an' found the horse that Verity had been ridin' when he met us. Verity had been there an' pulled out. We combed the country. We split up an' worked the hills an' we sent a posse into the Wagonwheel. They stopped at every ranch an' worked the country out. I put out a notice on Verity from Fort Neville. I sent telegrams to the sheriffs of every county in the state. We ain't found him."

Blithestone nodded. "What about Yoeman?" he asked.

Arnold shrugged. "He says Verity didn't kill Koogler. He says it was somebody else. I was goin' to arrest him, but the district attorney says we ain't got nothin' to hold him on. Did you gentlemen have any suggestions about what I'd ought to do?"

Tenbow raised his head. He had been watching the floor during the sheriff's recital. "The coroner's jury didn't name Ray Verity," he announced. "They left an open verdict. I'd put Dutch down there to—"

"We'll get to that after a while," Blithestone interrupted. "No, we haven't any suggestions, Frank. But we've decided to place a reward on Verity. The Stock Association will pay five hundred dollars to the man who brings him in.

And we don't care how he's brought in. The five hundred is paid just the same, if he's alive or dead."

Frank Arnold took his courage in his two hands. He owed his job to these men, and their enmity might ruin him. Just the same . . . "I don't like that," the sheriff said forcefully. "I want to question Ray. I want to ask him where he was an' what he done when he come down to Koogler's camp. But I can't say that he killed Dutch. After all, like Mr. Tenbow says, Dutch was down there to watch the gap. He—"

Again Blithestone interrupted. "You *did* say that you wanted Verity for murder," he reminded. "You said that just after you'd found Koogler's body."

Mentally Arnold cursed Virgil Jorbet and his proclivity for talk. It had been Jorbet who spread the story of Arnold's statement and the swift quarrel with Mat Yoeman that followed it.

"Mebbe I said that when I was hot," Arnold drawled. "I've got a warrant for Verity now, on a charge of armed robbery. I'd like to serve it. An' Verity resisted arrest. I don't overlook that. But murder's a pretty serious thing. If the district attorney handed me that kind of a warrant for Ray I'd serve it. Still, puttin' an alive-or-dead reward on the boy . . ."

"You'll have your murder warrant all right," Blithestone assured. "It isn't just that we want to get the man that killed Koogler, Frank. This goes deeper than that. There ain't a man here who hasn't lost cattle these past few years. There's a lot of maverickin' goin' on, an' the men who maverick don't stop with takin' slicks. They're stealin' branded cattle. Tenbow put Koogler down in the gap to stop that if he could. Koogler was killed. If we let this go these rustlers will think they can do anything. They'll get worse an' worse. It could get so bad that we'd have to put a man in to stop 'em or take the business up ourselves. We've got to get young Verity. We've got to make an example of him."

"Whether," Arnold said bitterly, "he done it or not?"

Blithestone's eyes were sharp. "If you don't want this job, Frank—" he said softly and then dropped the threat unspoken.

Arnold shrugged. "I've been sheriff a long time," he answered. "I've always tried to fill the office. What warrants I get I serve."

Blithestone nodded. "We'll be behind you, don't forget," he said. "I guess that's all, Frank."

So dismissed, Frank Arnold stalked out of the hotel room. When he was gone talk broke out among its occupants. "I don't like the way he took that," Fay Grierson of the Drag 9 snapped. "He don't act to me like he was goin' to push this. I say let's get a man in. Let's get somebody who will get behind this business an' shove it."

Tenbow spoke wearily. "You don't know Frank Arnold, Fay. He's a good officer. He'll do his job. But I'm like Frank. I don't think a reward—"

Blithestone interrupted. "We know how you feel about it, Miles," he said. "We know that you feel responsible for young Verity goin' bad. Just the same, you've got to remember that it was your man he killed. You've got to think of that."

"Can I forget it?" Tenbow snapped.

"I still think," Grierson persisted, "that we'd do well to get a man in here. The law we got ain't handlin' these rustlers. Over in my country they've opened up a bunch of land for homestead, an' every damned nester that comes in there is a cow thief. Now I think . . ."

There were other meetings besides that in the hotel. In the Pastime Saloon, favorite meeting place of the Wagonwheel men, Earl Latiker and Smiley Colfax, with the Hinds boys and Tom Marvin, were forgathered. The saloon, as well as all the other business houses in Gunhammer, had been closed for the funeral, but now business was brisk. These men, all from the southern end of the Wagonwheel, stayed together and listened to the talk that went on around them.

"I don't blame Ray Verity," a tall puncher from the north end of the roughs proclaimed. "Tenbow had put a camp in Verity's country. Hell, the gap always belonged to 'em. An' it was Tenbow that got Wayne an' the twins to give up by promisin' to protect 'em. A fat lot of protection they got! Their own neighbors didn't even go to bat for 'em!" The tall man from the north end cast a jaundiced eye toward Colfax and Latiker, and his companion beside him nudged the man sharply.

"Shut up, Lanky," the second rider growled. "Yo're drunk."

"I ain't drunk an' I know what I'd-a done if I'd been here that night," Lanky snarled.

Latiker, watching Colfax' face, jerked his head toward the door. "Let's get out of here, Smiley," he said.

"Not till I get that long drink of water told," Colfax growled. "Givin' up head that way. He—"

"Let's get out," Latiker interrupted again. "Tom's drinkin' too much. Let's get him out of here before somethin' happens."

Colfax glanced at Tom Marvin. Marvin had a bottle in front of him and was pouring a drink with an unsteady hand. "All right," the smiling man agreed suddenly. "Let's go."

He advanced on Marvin while Latiker took the other side. "Let's go home, Tom," Latiker said. "We've been here long enough."

Marvin raised his glass, slopping a little liquor out of it. "Home?" he said. "Go home?"

"Sure, Tom. Let's go home."

"Ain't no use of goin' home. My wife—" Marvin stopped. Colfax had jerked his arm

181

abruptly, and the liquor from the glass spilled on the bar.

"What'd you do that for, Smiley?" Tom Marvin half wheeled to Colfax. "Wastin' good liquor thataway."

"We're goin' home; don't you remember?" Latiker asked. "Yo're all set to go, Tom."

His hand under Marvin's arm half wheeled the man. Colfax was pulling from the other side. Bewildered and on unsteady feet, Tom Marvin tracked between his friends toward the door.

The lanky man from the north end grunted scornfully. "Yellah," he sniffed. "I'd always heard that Colfax was tough."

"He's tough enough. He just ain't startin' trouble in Gunhammer," the other puncher answered.

"Just the same," the lanky man announced, raising his voice so that all in the barroom could hear him, "I don't blame Verity a bit if he did kill Koogler. He's been shoved around an' choused around, an' so have the rest of us. Them damned Pie River cowmen come clear up into my country with a posse lookin' for Verity an' nosin' around an' makin' a big talk about maverickin' an' stealin' cattle. *I* allus taken a maverick when I found one an' I ain't goin' to stop because of them." Lanky glared around the room and saw nodding heads. It seemed that the sentiment in the Pastime was with Lanky.

"Tenbow an' Blithestone wasn't so hot against maverickin' ten years ago," a grizzled old-timer stated. "They carried plenty long ropes in them days. If Ray Verity—" He stopped. The door of the Pastime swung and Mat Yoeman stood framed in the opening.

Mat had been drinking. A bearlike, compact figure of a man, his head was thrust forward and his blue eyes were small and belligerent.

"Who's talkin' about Ray?" he growled. "Is somebody in here shootin' off his wind about the kid?" Mat's old Colt in its worn holster was thrust forward, and Mat's hand toyed with the butt of the gun.

"We was just talkin' about the Pie River outfits," the old-timer said hastily. "We wasn't puttin' the kid on the pan, Mat."

"You'd better not." Mat shouldered his way forward to the bar. "Ray never killed Dutch, an' anybody that says he did is a liar!" He glared at the men about him and instinctively they shrank away. If there was a bad man to fool with in Gunhammer that day the man was Mat Yoeman.

"Whisky!" Mat growled to the bartender.

The man who owned the Pastime spoke hurriedly to a fellow townsman beside the door. "Slip out an' get Frank Arnold down here. Don't get Jorbet; bring Arnold. I already had one killin' in this place an' I don't want another!"

The townsman went out. Mat took the bottle and poured his drink.

"I'm goin' to find out who killed Dutch," he declared, holding up the glass. "I scouted for Terry. I was with Benteen at the Little Big Horn. I come into this country when the Whetrocks was holes in the ground. Who wants to count coup on me, huh? Who wants to lift my ha'r? Hiiiiii yuuuuuh!" Mat's shout went up, the long, quavering war whoop of the Sioux.

In the Pastime men looked nervously at each other. No one had ever seen Mat Yoeman on the warpath like this, but there had been tales, stories that had drifted into the country from farther north. Mat tossed the whisky down his throat.

"I'll make medicine," he declared, glaring about him. "Dutch Koogler was my friend, an' Ray's my boy. Thar'll be a medicine dance tonight." Without offering to pay for the liquor, Mat wheeled away from the bar and padded to the door. When he was gone relief filled the Pastime.

"I don't want that old wolf on my trail," Lanky said. "By gosh, I'd hate to be Frank Arnold."

Outside the Pastime, Mat paused on the sidewalk. His little eyes glared up and down the street. He held an unbelievable amount of whisky and, save to make him ugly, it had no effect. Potentially Mat was as dangerous as a loaded gun in the hands of a child. Anything would touch him off. Having surveyed the street, Mat started along it, looking for trouble, hunting someone who would speak evil of Ray Verity. So far he had had no luck in his search, but there was still plenty of time. His moccasined feet took him along the walk toward the hotel and, thrusting open the hotel door, he entered the little lobby. Two women, one sniffling into her handkerchief and the other stony-faced and red-eyed, passed him.

"Squaws," Mat grunted scornfully and moved across the room.

Just beyond the lobby was a hall, and from it a door opened into a room. Voices, properly restrained, babbled in the bedroom. Mat paused. The room was filled with women. One of them, close to the door, saw Mat and gave a tiny stifled scream. At that moment Mat Yoeman was sufficient sight to make any woman scream. As though by magic the talk stopped, and there was a sudden shifting movement. Looking through the little corridor that had formed, Mat saw Hannie Koogler sitting on the bed.

Hannie was composed. Dark circles under her eyes told of sleeplessness, and the eyes themselves were big, wide with hurt amazement at this thing that had happened to her. Her lips were drained of color and her cheeks were pale. For hours, ever since she had come to Gunhammer, all through the funeral and since, she had been constantly besieged. Well-meaning women had surrounded her, and men, awkward in their sympathy, had gone to shake her hand and mumble meaningless words. The girl was dazed. She needed solitude, needed to be alone with her hurt. But friends, with the best of intentions, had served in relays to keep her from what she needed. She looked at Mat Yoeman in the doorway, and Mat, meeting that look, shambled forward. He stopped beside the bed and reached out a hand and, trustingly, Hannie placed her own in it. Mat half turned. He glared at the silent women.

"Git out!" Mat commanded. "Git outen here!"

"Please," Hannie said. "Please go!" She clung to Mat's hand. Mrs. Weathers, close by the door, sniffed audibly.

"I must say," she snapped, "that this is a fine way to treat your friends. I must—"

"Git!" Mat snapped. "Git out!"

He remained there beside Hannie, a big bear of a man, blue eyes violent, his whole body bristling his animosity. First one woman and then another left the room. It emptied, and Mrs. Weathers, last to leave, pulled the door shut viciously. They were gone, and Mat sat down upon the bed beside Hannie Koogler.

"Now," he said gruffly, "go on an' cry if you want. You got a right to cry."

Blindly Hannie turned to him. Her arms, lifting,

pressed Mat's yellow braids against the leather of his neck, and her body shook him with her sobbing. Slowly, as though afraid, Mat lifted one pawlike hand and stroked her hair.

After a time the first paroxysm of sobbing lessened. The girl cried quietly, draining out her emotion and despair. The door opened a trifle, and Frank Arnold looked in. He saw Mat Yoeman with Hannie but was not seen himself. Arnold closed the door and thoughtfully went to the lobby. He waited there. The minutes ticked past, ten, fifteen, twenty of them. Half an hour passed. There were padding steps in the hallway, and Mat entered the lobby. He saw the sheriff and stopped.

"She's all right now," Mat said, slow-voiced. "Needed to cry, she did. Didn't need all them women around her. I scatted 'em out."

Arnold, who had been hunting Yoeman, intent to arrest him, to lock him up and prevent trouble, nodded gravely.

"She don't believe Ray done it either," Mat growled. "She knows he didn't kill her daddy."

"So . . . ?" Arnold said gently.

"So now I'm goin' to go home. I can't do Ray no good in jail. I'm goin' home an' make medicine. I'll find out who killed Dutch."

Mat wheeled away from the sheriff and padded on to the door. Frank Arnold drew in a long breath and let it go, relieved. Hannie Koogler had done something that was Arnold's job and that he doubted he could do. She had tamed Mat Yoeman. Mat would be as good as his word. He would go home and he would make medicine. And perhaps he would discover the murderer of Dutch Koogler. Doubt flickered across the sheriff's eyes. Mat did not believe that Ray had done the killing. Mat said that Hannie did not think it was Ray. Perhaps . . . Arnold shrugged. He was an officer, sworn, with a duty to perform. He had no business to trifle with beliefs or disbeliefs. It was his business to serve the warrants that came to him, to carry out the law. He looked again at the empty corridor beyond the lobby and then, wheeling, also left the hotel.

In the bedroom that had been hers for three days Hannie Koogler poured water in the basin and washed her face, freshening herself and removing the traces of her tears. She was relieved, in a better frame of mind than she had been since she had learned of her father's death. Somehow the breaking of the dam, the flood of emotion long pent up, that Mat Yoeman had released had helped the girl. She was calm now, able to confront the world, able to face a future in which there was no father to bolster her. When she had dried her face she lighted the lamp and set about putting the room to rights, finding more relief in action.

Hannie thought about Mat as she worked,

coupling him with her father and her childhood. The first pony she had ever owned had been a little Ace of Spades horse that Dutch bought for her. She could remember Mat as he delivered the horse and her curiosity concerning him, his blue eyes and his yellow braids. Then there had been the time when Mat brought her a Sioux woman's dress, beaded and decorated with dyed quills. And the necklace that Mat had given her, a string of eagle talons and bear claws combined, beautiful in its very savageness. It seemed to Hannie that she and her father had known Mat always.

She thought, too, of how just a few minutes ago Mat had spoken of Dutch and of Ray Verity. His deep, growling voice had been very low, but there was truth in it.

"They say Ray killed yore dad, Hannie. I say he didn't. Dutch was tryin' to help Ray, an' the boy knew it. Yore dad was killed. It mebbe looks like Ray, but Ray didn't do it. You got to believe me, Hannie. Somebody's got to believe in the boy."

Hannie had told Mat then that she believed him, feeling the desperate need in the man, the vital necessity for reassurance. Mat was struggling with himself, trying to prove to himself that Ray, the boy of whom he had grown so fond, was innocent of the crime. And Hannie, blindly intuitive, had reached out and spoken to fill that need, unthinking and unheeding. Now she paused momentarily in her bedmaking.

She knew, of course, the evidence that her father's death presented. She had heard the talk, had heard Ray Verity accused, and all the things that pointed to his guilt. But, standing there beside the hotel bed, she could remember Ray's face and his eyes that day she had met him north of the 10 Bow headquarters. And she remembered, too, what she had told her father. "He looks so—hunted." The tears welled up again in Hannie's eyes, and determinedly she wiped them away. Ray Verity had not killed Dutch. Not that tortured, hunted boy. He hadn't!

A knock, timid, light, sounded. Answering it, Hannie pulled open the door. Ruth Marvin stood there, blinking in the lamplight.

"Come in, Ruth," Hannie said and led the way.

Six years ago Ruth Marvin had been Hannie's teacher, a slight, pretty, fun-loving girl who knew how and loved to laugh. Three children and unending work had changed her. She was old now, worn, her face prematurely wrinkled. She followed Hannie uncertainly.

"Won't you sit down?" Hannie asked.

Ruth seated herself on the edge of the bed. "I hadn't seen you since—since it happened," she said. "I wanted to tell you how sorry I am, Hannie. I couldn't go home until I did tell you."

Hannie sat down beside her former teacher.

190

"Thank you, Ruth," she answered. "You're kind."

She could see the woman's work-worn hands nervously locked together and an ugly black-and-blue bruise on Ruth's forearm.

"You've hurt yourself," Hannie exclaimed impulsively.

Ruth Marvin glanced at the bruise and then back to Hannie. Her lips trembled. "It was Tom," she burst out. "He'd been drinking. Oh, Hannie, what will I ever do?"

Hannie's arms went out to the older woman and drew her close. Like a child, Ruth Marvin put her head against Hannie's breast. Her voice was muffled and broken by her sobs.

"He drinks all the time. He keeps a jug in the kitchen. Yesterday he slapped little Tom, and when the sheriff came he locked me up in the meat house. He said he wasn't going to have me talking. Oh, Hannie, what will I do?"

There was nothing for Hannie to say, nothing that she could say. She closed her arms more tightly about Ruth Marvin's slender shoulders.

"I was going to leave him," Ruth sobbed. "I wrote my mother to send me the money to come home. I can't bring my children up with a drunken father, can I? I've got to think of them, haven't I?"

"You've got to think of them, Ruth," Hannie answered. "Did Tom beat you?"

"He was drunk," the woman repeated. "He'd

been gone all day, and when he came home I asked him where he'd been. He told me that it was none of my business and struck me on the mouth. Oh, Hannie—"

Hannie Koogler had forgotten her own troubles as she comforted the sobbing woman. "You'll have to leave him, Ruth. You can't stay there. You've got to protect yourself and your children."

Ruth Marvin pushed back from Hannie. "But I love him, Hannie," she objected. "I remember how he was when we were first married, and before. We were so happy together. And then the children came and—it was perfect. I'd work my fingers to the bone for him, Hannie. He's not himself. It's Smiley Colfax and Earl Latiker. Since he's been going out with them he's changed. He never used to drink. He was always laughing and jolly and so good to little Tom and the girls. He—Oh, I can't bear it!"

She hid her face again. Hannie Koogler stared at the wall with troubled eyes. What could she say or do?

With an effort Ruth Marvin gathered herself. She straightened and freed herself from Hannie's arms. "What must you think of me?" she asked. "Here I've come to you with my troubles when your father has just been buried. Forgive me, Hannie. I didn't mean to break down. But it's been so dreadful these last few months. Ever since last fall."

"There's nothing to forgive, Ruth," Hannie said gently. "That's what friends are for, to tell your troubles to."

Ruth Marvin stood up. She dabbed at her eyes with a crumpled handkerchief, and anxiety supplanted the place of the tears she wiped away.

"You won't say anything, Hannie?" she beseeched. "You won't tell anyone about the trouble that Tom and I have been having?"

"I won't say anything," Hannie promised.

"And I'm sorry I broke down. Forgive me, Hannie."

"There's nothing to forgive," said Hannie Koogler. "I only wish I could help you."

Chapter 13

Ray Verity was neither glad nor sorry that he had not killed a man. He had done his level best, lining his sights and using the Colt as a single action rather than a double action, just as Mat had taught him. But the important thing was that he had got away, not how he had done it. He had not given up to Frank Arnold.

Ray had a coldly clear realization of his status. He was wanted now for the robbery of Weathers' store and also for resisting arrest. He knew Arnold's reputation and that the sheriff would take this recent happening as a personal offense. There was no place in the Pie River country or in the Whetrocks for Ray. He could not go back to Mat Yoeman's Ace of Spades; he could not go to the gap; he couldn't stay in the Wagonwheel, for Arnold would relentlessly comb those places. Oddly enough, the boy was relieved. There was now something definite to go on. He knew just where he stood.

Custer climbed up through Notch Canyon and the Notch itself. Horse and rider went down the eastern slope, following a familiar trail. At Mat Yoeman's cabin Ray dismounted. He had but a little time, and with this new clearness that blessed his thinking, he set about utilizing the period of grace. The first thing he did was to get in a bunch of horses. From these he took old Brownie and then, making a careful selection, a buckskin horse named Ribbon that he had ridden a few times and liked. Mat would not begrudge him the buckskin.

Ray saddled Ribbon and regretfully turned Custer out. He would have liked to take Custer, but the animal had been ridden plenty and was tired, and Custer was a marked horse. The description that Arnold would doubtless send out would mention the sorrel.

Ray tied his two horses in front of the cabin and began his other preparations. He collected his clothes, two blankets, two tanned hides, and a little food. He put all the ammunition that he had for the Colt in his pockets and the loops of his belt. He added a battered, blackened lard bucket, a knife that Mat had made from an old file, and Mat's hatchet, some matches, a coil of hair rope, and lashed them all in a pack on Brownie's back. With a final look around the cabin Ray closed the door and went to his horses. Mounting Ribbon, he picked up Brownie's lead rope and rode off. He went east, along the canyon that led out to the flats, and he did not look back, not once.

When night came Ray was in the lower foothills of the Whetrocks. Rain fell steadily, not hard, but remorselessly. Ray scarcely heeded it.

Outlaws traveled in rain or shine, by day or night, listening for the owl's hoot. Hunted men had no choice of time or weather.

The foothills closed around him, black shapes against a lighter sky, and sure-footed Ribbon and Brownie came right along, their feet sogging in the mud. Midnight found him out of the hills and swinging toward the south. Down there was the Nashota River and beyond it Utah and the Uinta Mountains. Colorado lay to the left, and below Colorado were New Mexico and Arizona, all cattle country, all horseback country.

Toward morning the rain ceased, and when the eastern horizon showed gray Ray looked for a place to stop. He had never before been in this country, but instinct led him downhill until he found a little creek running through the flatlands. Willows grew along the creek and offered a place of hiding. He stopped among the dripping willows and picketed his horses. Then with the night growing lighter, he rolled out his bed in an open space. Sleep was a fitful thing that would not be wooed or won. Resting by his dead fire, looking at the gray sky, Ray Verity could go back over the few short months that had brought him here.

Things can happen to a man in just a little time, and there was a chance for Ray to be philosophical, but he was not. Instead the events marched in orderly procession through his mind.

Step by step he could trace the episodes, but he did not go behind them and seek causes. Rather he acknowledged results. He could stay and kill and be killed, or he could go and, finally acting upon Wayne's advice, he was going. He could almost hear Wayne's hard voice hiding the man's desperate hurt: "Don't go home. Hide! Get away from this country! Don't ever come back to it!" There at the last, hard hit, realizing that he was finished, planning a desperate measure, Wayne had counseled him. With his last sand running out, Wayne had thought not of himself but of his youngest brother. And now Ray was doing what Wayne had commanded.

The clouds were a heavy blanket that shrouded the earth, and Ray Verity, rolling over on his belly, pillowed his head on his arms and cried, deep sobs racking his young body. Ribbon and Brownie lifted their heads and stared toward the hoarse sounds, then resumed their grazing.

The sun came up, breaking through the scattering clouds. The horses cropped sparse grass. Ray slept, finally exhausted by his efforts and the release of emotion. He wakened in the afternoon and, having moved his horses to better grazing, waited in the willows. As dusk came he was up and moving again, mounting and crossing the stream headed south.

The meandering creek also followed a southerly direction. Night came. Ahead, a long way off, little gleaming points of fire showed. Ray swung west to avoid those lights, and Ribbon worked his ears and showed his nervousness. In the creek bottom Ray could look up and silhouette the world against the sky line. Conical shapes showed, and Ribbon's nicker was answered from the darkness. A dog barked; a woman called, and Ray, swinging his horses, went riding in toward the tepees. Sunheart, tall and heavy-bellied and with an impassive face, came out to greet him, and with the brave was the boy with the crippled arm.

"How, Chola?" Sunheart's voice was deep and strong.

"How?" Ray answered.

Stonehand's face mimicked his father's, but his eyes were bright with friendship.

"Yo' come go with us?" the boy asked.

"Why not?" Ray Verity asked himself. He slid his foot out of the stirrup and swung down. "I've come to go with you," he said.

A smile broke over Stonehand's face as he spoke in Sioux. Sunheart began to grin and swept his arm in invitation as he spoke.

"Yo' eat," Stonehand said. "Yo' hungry, huh? We got meat."

Ray had not meant to travel with the Sioux. He had not even thought about Sunheart and his band when he rode out of the Whetrocks. Yet resting that night outside Sunheart's tepee, he asked the

198

question again, "Why not?" and found no answer for it.

In the morning they were up betimes, rising in the coolness with all the beauty of the new day about them. There was no rush, no haste. Food was scarce and yet all ate. There was the bustle of camp breaking, disorderly, with much cackling talk from the women, and yet the tepees came down as though by magic and the whole camp made into bundles loaded on the travois that the ponies pulled.

The men rode ahead, Sunheart and Man Who Walks first, Black Wolf and Ray following them, the women and the camp horses behind. The little bunch of ponies, loosely herded by the boys, traveled to the left, grazing along.

They followed the creek, not deviating from it, and to Ray Verity who had lived out of doors all his life, there was amazement in their journey. The Sioux lived with nature. Nothing moved, nothing happened, no matter how slight, that they did not see and that did not have a meaning. If a cottontail jumped out and back into the willows the party stopped and hunted until the rabbit was killed. A rattlesnake, sunning himself in the early morning, was deliberately skirted but not molested. Willow grouse, startled up from the creek bottom, afforded the excuse for an hour's delay, and when the party rode on there were four grouse hanging against the shoulders of the ponies. They foraged as they rode, savages living from a savage country, and at midafternoon they stopped and made camp. The squaws went to the creek for wood and water, and the men loafed in the shade of the tepees while the boys, having circled the horses, held them loosely on good grass. Nothing was hurried; no necessity pressed and demanded time; the day slipped by as smoothly as the sun slid through the sky.

Other days followed that first day, a sunny procession. When the rain came the party stopped, and while there were discomforts, no one heeded them. Wet clothing and a damp bed were all a part of living. There were days when the hunters failed to find food, and there were days of plenty. They moved as animals moved, following the season, drifting with the sun. Ray Verity was one of them.

For companionship he had the boy Stonehand and his meager English. Ray began to pick up a few words of Sioux, first the names of people and things and then the names of actions. A gesture sufficed to show size or distance. He did no work. The women assumed the tasks of making and breaking camp, of gathering wood, of caring for the fires, of bringing water. Sunheart had two squaws and the girl, Where the Lakes Meet, and the older of the squaws scowled and chattered when Ray, producing his hatchet, would have gone for wood. She took the hatchet from him and departed, returning shortly with a backload of willow and alder, while Sunheart looked on, amused. The women, too, looked after Ray's garments. He had a new shirt of buckskin to wear with his tattered overalls. Ray loafed with the men, the lords of creation, the hunters and providers. So like a cloud shadow drifting across the flats, Sunheart and his Sioux went south, and with them went Ray Verity.

In the wide, relatively untenanted scope of country they met few people. Their path was not the roads and trails, and their way did not lead them to the settlements. Twice they saw riders going about their business, and once in camp a grizzled cowman rode in to visit and ask questions. On that occasion Ray betook himself discreetly to a tepee before the cowman arrived and stayed there until he was gone. If his action was noted by the Sioux it caused no comment, at least none that came to Ray. Perhaps Sunheart and the braves looked at him a little more keenly, but that was all.

The ponies grew fatter as they moved, their winter gauntness succumbing to the good grass. They were shedding and showed sleek in their summer coats. The country was fatter too. Ray found a maverick heifer and beefed her, and the whole camp feasted. There was rejoicing that night, and they stayed on the spot to finish the remnants of the fat heifer. The next day they went on, and in the morning, free of all restraint, Ray left the men and followed the horses with the boys. Black Wolf's second son raced against Man Who Walks' boy and won the wild dash and challenged Stonehand. He was accepted promptly, and Ray watched while the two lads lined their horses at a mark and, started by a wild yell, raced away. Something prompted him to enter the fun and, giving Ribbon a touch of his heels and with a yell, he went after the boys. Ribbon had a turn of unsuspected speed. Starting almost ten yards behind Stonehand's horse, he flashed past the racer. Ray let the horse go a full quarter of a mile before he drew up, flushed and grinning, to wait for the boys. He was childishly pleased at Stonehand's wide eyes and at the way the other lads gathered around him.

The race had not passed unnoticed. That evening when camp was made Sunheart came up to Ray. The Sioux was leading a horse, a bay with the short coupling and cat hams of a quarter horse. Stonehand was with his father and interpreted Sunheart's talk.

"He say yo' race," the boy announced. "His horse against yo' horse. Huh?"

"All right," Ray agreed. "I'll race him."

There was more talk through Stonehand. A distance was agreed upon and marked off. Sunheart, mounted on his bay, and Ray, on Ribbon, faced a mark. The whole camp, save

Black Wolf, the starter, gathered at the finish line. Black Wolf raised a yell and the horses leaped ahead.

The bay was fast; he ran like a scared wolf, low to the ground and flying. But Ribbon had that good hot blood of Mat Yoeman's studs back in his ancestry. Ribbon, left at the post by the bay, overtook him and went by and at the finish line was half a length ahead. Ray, grinning, breathing deeply from his ride, dropped down from the horse. Sunheart, too, dismounted. The Sioux's eyes were sullen, but he held out his rawhide reins toward Ray.

"What's this?" Ray demanded, looking at Stonehand.

"Yo' win," the boy said. "Yo' win horse too."

All around Ray the Sioux were silent. For the first time since he had joined them Ray felt that he was a stranger. He thought quickly and, happily, struck an answer to his problem. He did not refuse the bet that he had won. He did not know that he had bet Ribbon against the bay. Instead he took the rawhide reins and held them lightly for an instant before he thrust them out to Sunheart.

"Your father," he said, looking at Stonehand, "has given me many presents. My heart is glad that I can give him one."

For just an instant Stonehand paused. Then he spoke rapidly, and as he talked the sullen look left

Sunheart's eyes and he began to smile. He took the reins that Ray held out and said something to his son.

"He say," Stonehand interpreted, his face shining, "he will take this horse because yo' are his son."

With a yell Sunheart jumped to the bay's back and kicked with his heels. The bay flung into a run, circling the little group while the rider brandished his hand high overhead. Then, wheeling the horse, Sunheart came charging down, sliding the bay to a stop just before he reached his people. Dropping down from the horse again, he came up beside Ray, placed his hand on Ray's shoulder, and spoke.

"He say yo' have good heart," Stonehand announced. "He say now yo' be Sioux. Yo' like that, huh?"

"I'd like it fine," Ray answered.

Sunheart must have understood the tone if not the words, for he smiled, and his hand closed tight on Ray's shoulder. Beyond Sunheart, Ray could see the girl, Where the Lakes Meet. She met his eyes a moment and then looked away.

That night beside the fire while they ate Where the Lakes Meet brought Ray's food to him. Always before one of Sunheart's squaws had carried the cooking pot around the circle, but now the girl had it. Ray looked up at her and smiled before he speared his knife into the stewed rabbit in the pot and brought out a front leg. Where the Lakes Meet said: "No!" sharply and, removing the knife from Ray's hand, slid the foreleg back into the pot, delved with the knife, and brought out the saddle, the choicest piece of all.

Chapter 14

Sunheart's tepee was at the edge of the encampment, and by looking out the opening Ray could see the horse herd. His own two ponies, Ribbon and Brownie, were with the other horses, and he had long since ceased worrying about them. The Sioux were errant horse thieves, but a man who stole from his own people when they were camped together would be stripped of all his property and beaten out of camp. In this big encampment Ray was learning many things about the Sioux. A variety of different branches of the nation were represented: Brûlé, Miniconju, Ogallala, they were all there in Running Horse's camp, all headed down to the Nashota for the ration issue and a sun dance. The dog soldiers controlled the camp just as, before the buffalo were gone, they had controlled the hunt. In a way this was the annual buffalo hunt, for the beef issue would be turned out of the corrals to the Sioux once they had arrived at the Nashota Agency, and they would kill the steers and store the meat in the old, old manner.

Ray was concerned about the agency. There were one or two other white men in camp and a number of breeds, but he was new and an object of curiosity. Indians are inveterate gossips, and Ray's presence was sure to be reported to the agent at Nashota. It was about time that he leave the Sioux and go on over into Utah.

Sunheart pushed open the flap of the tepee and stepped in, Stonehand following him. Sunheart squatted down and began to talk, looking at Ray. Stonehand sat beside his father, waited for a break in the talk, and interpreted.

"Yo' got pony. Good horse. Better horse than my father's. You run race? Huh?"

"You want me to race Ribbon?" Ray asked.

"Yeah. We poor people. No chuck. Nothin'." Stonehand made the chopping sign which meant "cut off." "Yo' race Little Bull, huh?"

Ray had seen some Indian races since his arrival at camp. There were two kinds, one in which the racers ran to a tree, the first to touch it winning, and the other in which two strips of hide were staked on the ground and the ponies run to them. The horses were trained for this last race and, when they reached the first strip, jumped it, turned between the strips, and raced back to the starting point. To touch either strip disqualified the racer. He shook his head. "Ribbon can't race to a tree," he announced, "or to the hide strips. He isn't trained."

"W'ite man's race," Stonehand informed after a brief colloquy with his father. "Make two marks; race."

Ray's eyes narrowed. "I want to see the other horse," he said.

207

Stonehand interpreted, rose, and gestured. Sunheart also got up. "Yo' come," the boy instructed.

They left the tepee and walked through the bustling, active camp. Here a young buck and the girl of his choice sat, wrapped in one blanket, courting. Everyone could see them, but custom made a polite fiction of their being unnoticed and unwatched. A gang of small boys, naked as on their birthdays, each with a bow and a quiverful of arrows, were returning from a hunt, each one burdened with gophers, larks, the little curlews that frequented the Nashota bottoms, or other species of "small deer." In one tepee a group of squaws was engaged in gambling, the players using the bones of a bear's foot as implements in their game. An old squaw chaperoning a group of giggling girls came past, the girls casting sheep's eyes at Ray and at Stonehand and Sunheart. Sunheart was popular with the womenfolk and could easily have had more than the two squaws he already supported. Here a brave sat, almost asleep in the sun, his long lance, its head bright and with a decorative tuft below, thrust into the ground outside his tepee. Here was a buffalo-skin lodge, painted with many symbols, and here a young dandy combed and oiled his hair. There was dirt everywhere and dogs as ubiquitous as the dirt.

Little Bull's lodge was big, and Little Bull

himself, with several friends, sat in its shade. Beyond the lodge a horse was tied, bay, satin-skinned, beautiful, thoroughbred written in every line. At sight of the animal Ray's eyes widened.

"That horse?" he demanded.

Sunheart did not answer. He was glaring at Little Bull, who grinned craftily. "That not the horse he show!" Stonehand exploded. "He show other horse. He lie. He cheat."

Sunheart seemed to be of the same opinion, for he rasped words at Little Bull, who continued to grin. When Sunheart stopped Little Bull asked a question.

Face black with his anger, Sunheart flung a reply.

"He say, 'Yo' 'fraid?' Sunheart say, 'No 'fraid. We race.' We get beat." Stonehand's voice was doleful.

Sunheart then had been badgered and tricked into racing against the thoroughbred. Little Bull had outsmarted him and lied to him. But Sunheart could not back out. He must go through with the race or lose prestige. Carefully Ray ran his eyes over the thoroughbred horse, examining the clean barrel, the long coupling, the flat ribs, the body that spelled "run" in every line. He looked at the legs and caught his breath sharply. There, below the knees, were telltale bulges. Ray knew instantly how Little Bull came to have so valuable a horse.

"Will the race be the white man's way?" Ray asked deliberately.

Stonehand interpreted, and Ray saw Sunheart nod.

"Then," Ray drawled, "we'll race. But I must be there when the match is made." He saw the boy's questioning look and spoke again. "When the talk comes before the race I be there, huh?"

The boy spoke to his father, and Sunheart nodded gloomily once more. Little Bull was laughing, and Ray turned away.

"Where yo' go?" Stonehand demanded.

"To get my horse," Ray answered.

"I go too," the boy announced and set off with Ray. "We win race, huh?"

"Mebbe," Ray said cautiously. "We'll see." There was a way the race might be won, a way as tricky as the method that Little Bull had used in making the match.

That afternoon with Stonehand, Ray rode a circuit around the camp. Below the tepees he found a long stretch of wide ground, hard as rock. Ray's eyes glinted when he saw it. Here was the site for the race. Now if he could put his ideas to work . . . He gestured to the place and spoke to Stonehand and Sunheart, who accompanied him.

"We race here."

Turning, they rode back to the lodges. Little Bull's tepee was filled with braves when the three entered. Little Bull himself, tall, so dark as

210

to be almost black, was in the center of the tepee, and his friends were all around him. Man Who Walks and Black Wolf came in unobtrusively and squatted down. A bearded squaw man was close beside the door. Ray, seeing the squaw man, was pleased. Now he would have no trouble talking, for the squaw man could interpret much more accurately than Stonehand.

"How?" Little Bull grunted.

"How?" Ray answered and sat down.

There was a silence, and then Sunheart spoke at some length. Little Bull answered, and the squaw man said curiously: "Are you goin' to race that plug of yores against Little Bull's hawse?"

"I intend to," Ray answered. "What did they say?"

"Sunheart says he's willin' to race an' bet on it, an' Little Bull taken him up. Sunheart says yo're a white man, an' the race is goin' to be the white man's way. Little Bull says all right. Kid, that hawse of Little Bull's used to belong to an army officer at Fort Reno. He's a race hawse. You ain't got a chance."

"I've got a chance," Ray answered. "Tell 'em that white men race a long ways. Tell 'em a mile an' a quarter."

"This is yore own hard luck," the squaw man growled. "All right, I'll tell 'em." He spoke at length, stopped, and listened to what Little Bull, Sunheart, and half a dozen others had to say.

"Little Bull says his hawse is a white man's hawse an' that he'll race a mile an' a quarter," Ray's interpreter reported. "Whut else you got on yore chest?"

"I want to race on the flats below the camp," Ray answered, "an' I want to score three times before we start."

"How's that?"

"I want a runnin' start. I want to go out an' come back three times before the race really begins."

The squaw man frowned. "Why?" he demanded. "What's the use of wearin' yore hawse out before the race?"

"That's the way I want to do it," Ray answered curtly.

The interpreter shrugged and, turning to the interested warriors, spoke at length, emphasizing his words with gestures. When he finished Little Bull talked, apparently arguing the point, and then Sunheart, Man Who Walks, and Black Wolf had their say. Little Bull took another turn; two braves added their words; Sunheart grunted three short sentences, and there was silence.

"They don't see the use of the false starts," the interpreter announced.

"I don't race without 'em," Ray answered.

The interpreter spoke again. Little Bull consulted with his friends, turned, and said "Yes" in English.

"He's taken you up, kid," the interpreter drawled. "You goin' to bet on this race? If you are I'll just bet my squaw against yore saddle that you git beat."

"Make it two ponies," Ray answered, "an' I'll take you. I don't need a squaw."

The squaw man squinted at Ray. "You know somethin'," he challenged. "You got a scheme. You'll have to be smart as paint to outsmart the Sioux. They're hawse jockeys from away back."

"Do you want to bet?" Ray demanded.

The squaw man scratched his grizzled head. "Mebbe I'd better look at them hawses fust," he drawled.

As the sun sloped over into the west all of Running Horse's camp gathered on the flats. Running Horse himself was there, a fat, pleasant-faced man who grinned at Ray Verity and commented to the interpreter.

Ray, stripped to the waist, had put a surcingle on Ribbon. His beard curled and his long hair gleamed and his eyes were bright.

"Runnin' Hawse says he'd have to skin yore whole head to get yore scalp, kid," the interpreter drawled. "He wants to know if you want to bet."

"Tell him I'll bet my gun against three horses," Ray answered. "It might as well be whole hog or none."

"He says he'll do it," the squaw man announced. "Kid, what you got up yore sleeve?

213

I looked at them hawses, but I can't see where you got a chance. Yore hawse is nice enough, but that there hawse of Little Bull's is a runnin' fool."

"Did you bet on him?"

The squaw man shook his head. "Not yet I ain't," he said. "An' I guess I won't. The only ones bettin' on you are Sunheart an' his folks."

"Little Bull's horse is splinted," Ray said abruptly. "This is hard ground. We take three false starts and he'll have to stop every time, turn an' come back, stop an' start again. It won't do his splints any real good."

The squaw man's eyes gleamed. "Smart," he rasped. "It mought work. I'll just bet a little on you, kid."

"I've put up my saddle, my gun, everythin' I've got," Ray answered. "If it don't work I'm done. But I want you here to see that the start's good."

"I'll be yere," the interpreter assured and hurried away. Sunheart, face gloomy, came up. Stonehand, with his father, as always, said, "Yo' win, huh?"

"Mebbe," Ray returned.

The dog soldiers had cleared the crowd away from the starting line and ordered a lane along the flats. Away down below there was another crowd at the finish, marked by a big boulder and a cottonwood tree.

Ray squinted, saw the crowd, and glanced

toward the start. Running Horse was there, dignifying the race by acting as starter. Elk and Buffalo Horn, a subchief and a medicine chief, were the finish judges. Ray slid a leg over Ribbon and went up on the buckskin's back. Across from him he could see Little Bull on the thoroughbred. The thoroughbred was dancing, pounding the hard ground with his front feet.

They faced the start side by side, thoroughbred and quarter-bred, Little Bull and Ray Verity. The starting line was fifty feet away. Running Horse yelled a command, and the horses lunged ahead. Ray flashed past the starting line with Little Bull half a length ahead. Twenty yards beyond the line he brought Ribbon around. Beyond him Little Bull pulled the thoroughbred to a stop, the horse fighting his head and jolting hard on his front feet. Twice more they scored and then, both horses sweating, both full of run, came up to the line, jockeying for position. This was the start. Running Horse yelled; Ray kicked Ribbon and leaned forward, laying himself flat against the horse's back. Under him he could feel the powerful heave of the buckskin's quarters, driving them ahead. The bay thoroughbred crossed the line a nose in the lead, drew away, seemed to pull ahead with every stride.

"Come on, Ribbon," Ray yelled. "Come on!"

Ribbon came on. The thoroughbred no longer drew ahead but stayed in place. Little Bull was yelling, wild and high and victorious. Half a mile was past.

"Come on, Ribbon!"

Ribbon's black hoofs pounded iron-hard dirt. Ribbon's flaring nostrils came up a little almost to the bay's flank. Little Bull was using his whip, swinging the rawhide. A mile was gone. The wind brought tears to Ray's eyes. He was well forward on the horse, helping, getting all that he could from the buckskin powerhouse under him. The boulder and the cottonwood were close, and the savage crowd was yelling.

Ribbon, reaching, covering more than twenty feet at a stride, came on. The bay was running, too, doing the very best he could. But the bay faltered. That hard ground, those pounding stops and turns had hurt the bay horse. The splints hampered his action, hurt and slowed him. Ribbon's buckskin head came up and up, first to sweating bay flank, then to shining shoulder, to neck, to head. Side by side, like a well-matched team, buckskin and bay ran together, and then little by little the buckskin drew ahead. Ray felt a flash of fire across his shoulder as Little Bull struck him with the rawhide, felt Ribbon bound and almost break his stride as Little Bull's whip fell again. And then the boulder flashed past, and yells sounded shrill in his ears. He raised himself, looked back, saw Little Bull's scowling face, and eased Ribbon from his great racing stride down into a run, to a lope, to gentle canter, and to stop. Turning, he came trotting back to the finish line as, whooping and brandishing their arms, the men who had watched the start arrived.

The excitement carried over after the race. Bets were paid; Sunheart, Man Who Walks, Black Wolf, all were wildly exuberant, as were their families and those few friends who, taking a chance, had bet on Ray Verity.

The old squaw man came up to Ray's side and, grinning, winked broadly. "You made it," he chuckled, "but don't let Little Bull git you into another race. That stunt won't work twice. An' kind of watch him. He ain't what you'd call friendly."

Ray, looking at Little Bull's scowl, thought the words a miracle of understatement. Little Bull knew that he had been tricked and was mad all the way through.

Back at the tepees the plunder was divided. Ray had won five ponies, a blanket which he suspected of being lousy, and various other things. Sunheart, too, had recouped bis fortune, as had Man Who Walks and Black Wolf. They strutted, boasted, bragged, making themselves the heroes of the whole affair. Man Who Walks went into his tepee and began to bedeck himself, and the squaw man, who had accompanied Ray back to the lodges, said: "He's fixin' for a dance or somethin'. I reckon Sunheart might hold a scalp dance over this."

"A scalp dance? They haven't taken any scalps."

The squaw man grunted. "They don't need to take 'em to have a scalp dance. They'll have some old scalps, an' them'll do. What you goin' to do with the stuff you won, kid? Buy a woman?"

Ray shook his head.

"It ain't a bad idea." The grizzled oldster looked from under bushy brows at Ray. "A woman's mighty comfortin'."

Turning abruptly, Ray walked away from his questioner. Man Who Walks issued from his tepee, dressed in all his finery. Around his head a bright-colored shawl was wound turbanwise. He wore a shirt that dangled about his knees; his bare legs were bedecked with bracelets of hair; he was painted, and a mirror swung on a cord against his chest. Man Who Walks stopped so that all might admire his splendor, and Ray Verity, hastening to him, reached out impulsively for the mirror.

"Where did you get that?" he demanded. "Where did you get that shawl?"

The Sioux brave, not one to allow hands laid upon him, backed away from Ray and frowned, then, recalling the occasion for the celebration, changed the frown to a grin.

The squaw man hastened up. "Don't put yore

hands on him, sonny," he warned. "What's wrong?"

"Ask him where he got that mirror," Ray ordered. "Ask him where he got the shawl."

The squaw man spoke in guttural Sioux. Man Who Walks answered.

"Says he traded for 'em. Says he give a painted buffalo robe for 'em."

"Where?" Ray rasped. "Who did he trade?"

Again there was a colloquy in Sioux. "Back north." The squaw man waved his hand toward the Nashota. "Says he traded a man that had 'em up there."

"Who? What did he look like?"

Another question in Sioux. An answer. Man Who Walks parted his lips in a wide grin and touched his upper teeth. The meaning was unmistakable, and even before the squaw man turned and reported Ray knew the answer to his question.

"A feller that grins a lot an' has got two teeth that shine," the interpreter reported. "What's got into you, sonny?"

"I'll trade him for them." Ray managed to keep his voice level. "They strike me. I want 'em. I'll give him a pony for 'em."

"They ain't worth a pony."

"They are to me."

The squaw man shrugged and turned to Man Who Walks.

Man Who Walks sensed an advantage. There

was considerable haggling. Twice Ray raised his offer. Finally Man Who Walks succumbed. For two of the horses that Ray had won and for his hatchet Ray got the shawl and mirror. He carried them into Sunheart's tepee.

There is nothing noisier than an Indian camp at night when there are no enemies in the country. Ray, seeking some solitude and quiet beside the river, could hear the weird wailing of half a dozen flutes, rising and descending over their five-tone scale. A tom-tom thumped and a man yelled his exuberance. Children, precocious as are all Indian children, shrilled all together as they played at some game. There was a stir in the grass close by, and Stonehand appeared, sitting down beside his friend. Ray hardly heeded the boy. He held his mother's shawl and her mirror cradled in his hands.

"Beard," Stonehand said. That was Ray's name among the Sioux. Ray looked up.

"You got ponies," Stonehand said. "You fool for trade ponies, but you got 'nough left."

"Enough for what?"

"Where the Lakes Meet walks out of the tepee tonight," Stonehand said. "There will be many braves waiting. She yell when they take her. No yell if you take her. Three ponies buy Where the Lakes Meet. You got three ponies. Sunheart make room in lodge for you."

For just an instant Ray sat still. Then he turned to the boy. Ray knew the courting custom of the Sioux. A marriageable girl might walk out of her tepee and be seized by a suitor. If she offered the slightest resistance that brave must let her go. But if she did not resist, if she was quiet and did not scream, then he was the brave of her choice. Stonehand had put it to Ray plainly. Where the Lakes Meet would not scream or struggle if Ray seized her when she ventured forth.

"Tomorrow you tie pony to Sunheart's lance in front of tepee," Stonehand said. "Then you my brother."

In Ray Verity's mind a picture formed. Where the Lakes Meet was its center, the slight, graceful girl, beautiful for an Indian. Then that picture faded. Oddly he found himself thinking of another girl, a girl with blue indignant eyes and yellow hair. Hannie Koogler.

"You fool for trade Man Who Walks," Stonehand commented. "That stuff not worth two ponies. Not worth one pony." He gestured scornfully at the shawl and mirror in Ray's hands.

Decision hardened in Ray Verity. He had been planning, and now the plan suddenly crystallized. "If I don't watch out I'll not have any ponies," he said. "Help me get them from the herd, Stonehand. Somebody might steal them."

Stonehand said: "No steal. Bad medicine for steal in camp."

"I want them anyhow," Ray drawled. "I want Ribbon where I can watch him. My medicine says for me to get them."

That was the final, clinching argument. No Indian will go against the medicine of another, nor quarrel with it. Stonehand stood up. "We get 'em," he grunted.

Gradually the noise of the camp died. The fires flickered out, and quiet began to come. Ray Verity, sitting on the slope that led to the Nashota bottoms, looked through the gloom to where Ribbon and Brownie grazed with the three horses he had won from Running Horse. He had stolen his saddle from Sunheart's tepee, and it was beside him. He heard the muffled shriek of a girl and the grunt of a buck. Where the Lakes Meet had ventured out, had been seized, and had rejected her suitor.

Ray picked up the saddle and went down to the horses. Working quietly, he saddled Ribbon and put a lead rope on Brownie. Then, mounting, he rode west along the river, going cautiously, making no noise. The three horses that he left would go to Sunheart and, perhaps, pay him for the shelter and protection he had given. Where the Lakes Meet would find a brave, one of her own kind, that pleased her. Stonehand would mourn the absence of his friend, but that would pass.

The river gurgled shallowly over rocks, and

Ray turned to the crossing. The Sioux camp lay behind, and ahead were miles of country and a long, long road. At the end of the road was Smiley Colfax, a grinning man with two gold teeth who had traded a shawl and a mirror for a painted buffalo robe.

Chapter 15

When Mat Yoeman left Frank Arnold in the lobby of Gunhammer's hotel he went directly to the wagon yard beside the livery barn. He had been on the prod, ready to go on the warpath and tree the town, but Hannie had checked him. Mat found a pile of hay in one corner of the wagon shed, lay down, and, curling up, went to sleep. He slept all through the evening and night and in the morning wakened, sober and with the liquor he had drunk ringing bell-like in his head. A cup of coffee helped the ringing, and, returning to the barn, Mat sat on the bench beside the door.

Wagons, riders, all the people who had come to pay their last respects to Dutch Koogler, streamed out of Gunhammer. By noon the town seemed deserted, the streets depopulated.

Preacher Starke, coming down to get his team for the drive to Fort Neville, stopped beside Mat. Starke had some years before tried to buy a buggy team from the old man. Refusing payment, Mat had given the preacher the horses, saying that as he didn't go to church he ought to contribute.

"Well, Mat?" Starke said.

"Hello, Preacher," Mat answered. "You still drivin' them old plugs?"

"Still driving them." Starke laughed. "I still

owe you for them. Whenever you decide to get married come around and I'll perform the service gratis. I owe you that for the team."

This was a long-standing joke between the two. Mat chuckled. "I'll do that, Preacher. Don't drive them old ponies too fast."

"I won't," Starke promised and went on into the barn. Mat leaned back on the bench once more and basked in the sunlight.

He was still there when Frank Arnold arrived with Charlie Nerril. Arnold nodded briefly, said, "I thought you'd gone home, Mat," and resumed his talk with Nerril.

"I'll send you your commission as soon as I get back to the courthouse," he announced. "Don't pay any attention to Jorbet. He's no good. I'm not goin' to call in his commission because he's constable, but as far as I'm concerned, you'll handle the sheriff's business. I'll send you a bunch of notices as soon as I get them printed."

Nerril said, "All right, Frank," and the two went into the barn. Mat shifted position on the bench. Nerril and Arnold came out; Arnold mounted, shook hands with the liveryman, and rode off, and Nerril came back to the bench.

"So yo're goin' to be the deputy sheriff," Mat said.

Nerril nodded gloomily. "I guess so. As soon as I get my commission. I sure don't want the job."

Mat made no comment, and Nerril spoke again.

"There's a reward out for Verity. Five hundred dollars. The Stock Association is puttin' it up. Frank said that he'd send me a bunch of handbills on it. Dawggone the luck! Why can't they let a man alone to tend to his own business?"

"Five hundred dollars," Mat mused. "That's a lot of money to put on a kid. I didn't know Tenbow thought that much of Koogler. I reckon Dutch drew about seventy-five dollars a month for ramroddin' the 10 Bow, but now he's dead he's worth a lot."

"I know you think Ray didn't kill him," Nerril stated. "You got one idea, an' a lot of folks got another."

"What do you think?"

Nerril shrugged. "Ray could have killed Jorbet the night he was here in town," he drawled. "He didn't. An' there sure wasn't no reason for him to lay off Weathers. The kid went to Weathers for help, an' Weathers tried to take him into camp. I don't know if I'd of let Weathers go after that if I'd been in the kid's place."

Mat pensively scratched his head in front of one long braid. "You ain't a deputy yet?" he drawled.

"Not till I get my commission."

Mat got up deliberately and walked into the barn. "I'll get Bear Dance," he said over his shoulder. " 'Bout time for me to go home."

When he came out of the barn leading his black, Nerril had gone. Mat gave the hostler fifty cents, climbed Bear Dance, and rode down the street. At the Pastime Saloon he retrieved his six-shooter, left there during his sojourn in town, and, strapping it on, prepared to leave. For all the world like some rider who has forgotten a part of his errand, he wheeled Bear Dance in the street in front of the saloon, rode to Weathers' store, and, dismounting, went in.

Weathers was alone in the store, his clerk having gone home for dinner. "What is it for you, Yoeman?" Weathers asked, coming up to wait on Mat.

"I kind of disremember what I wanted to buy," Mat drawled. "While I'm thinkin' of it you might deal out a little information. You was here the night the Verity boys was killed, wasn't you?"

Weathers nodded.

"Just you an' Jorbet an' Tenbow an' Dutch, the way I heered it," Mat pursued.

"That's right."

"Ummm." Mat stroked his chin with his calloused fingers. "They'd been in yore warehouse before Jorbet started takin' 'em to Fort Neville. Say, did the Veritys owe you any money?"

"They owed a little bill. Wayne came in an' paid me that mornin', but he bought a little stuff that I charged after that."

"How much?" Mat produced a battered wallet. "I'm kind of tryin' to square up for 'em."

Weathers did not ask why Mat Yoeman was paying the Verity bills.

"Come on back to the office," he ordered, "an' I'll look it up."

Mat walked along the counter. He wanted Weathers back in the office, out of the store.

In the office Weathers examined an account book. "Doggone," he said. "I put that slip in here. Wayne an' Colfax an' Latiker were all here talkin', an' I made out that charge slip for Wayne. Let's see. Maybe I put it in with Latiker's. He bought some stuff." Weathers thumbed through the book.

"Wayne an' Colfax an' Latiker," Mat rumbled. "You know, it's always struck me funny that them Wagonwheel boys didn't he'p the Veritys that night. They was neighbors an' friends. Of course Smiley went with 'em an', I guess, done the best he could, but the others never taken it up. Seems kind of funny." Mat was enjoying this. Like a Sioux, he delighted to play with an enemy, and Weathers was certainly an enemy. Mat could adjudge him no other after Weathers' treatment of Ray.

"Not too funny," Weathers answered absently. "Wayne had kind of crossed the boys up. He told Latiker an' Colfax that he was goin' to close his west water hole. They didn't like it. Now where did I put that charge slip? It ain't in the Ls. Maybe I put it in the Cs."

"I don't think it's goin' to make any difference where you put it," Mat drawled. "I ain't goin' to pay it anyhow. So Wayne told Latiker an' Smiley he was goin' to close off his west water. That would kind of cramp their style, wouldn't it? An' yo're the jasper that was goin' to take Ray when he come in askin' for he'p! I'll jest pay you for that an' let the other go."

Mat's long left arm shot out and caught the surprised merchant by his little string bow tie. A savage jerk brought Weathers up from his chair, and Mat's right hand, swinging swiftly, cracked sharply against Weathers' cheek.

Clough Weathers was a big man but soft. Mat, hard as nails and angry, swung his right hand back and forth, first the palm, then the back splatting against Weathers' cheeks. Weathers struggled; he tried to fight back, and then he yelled while Mat slapped him remorselessly. The old man finished the chore he had set himself, swung one vicious final slap and, releasing his hold on the tie, sent Weathers staggering back into his desk.

"Now," he rasped, "call Jorbet an' have him try to arrest me. I'd like to talk to him some too."

Weathers cowered against his desk, and Mat, after a final scornful glance, padded out of the office, through the store, and to the hitch rail.

All the long way home Mat rode in silence, letting Bear Dance choose the pace. He covered the last twenty miles of his ride in darkness and, reaching the cabin, cared for his horse and then for himself. Squatting beside the fireplace, meat sizzling in his frying pan, he stared at the flames. "I'd ought to tell Frank," he mused. "He'd ought to know."

The meat spat angrily in the hot grease, and Mat turned it. "But I got to have more to go on," Mat rumbled. "That ain't quite enough. An' anyhow, how would it he'p Ray? Wayne's dead an' so are the twins, an' Koogler was camped on that water hole. Mebbe you'd better take to the hills, Mat. Mebbe you'd learn somethin' that would he'p the kid."

He wolfed down the hot meat and drank the scalding coffee and went to bed. In the morning, taking a little pack on Bear Dance, riding Custer, and with his long-barreled .38-.55 under his right fender, Mat Yoeman left his cabin, old Mat Yoeman who had lived in Crazy Horse's camp, who had scouted for Terry and Custer and shod Benteen's pack train. He rode west, over the hills and through the Notch, and, dropping down Notch Canyon into the roughs of the Wagonwheel, disappeared.

Hannie Koogler went back to the 10 Bow after her father's funeral. She had nowhere else to go. The 10 Bow had been home to her, and Miles Tenbow was her friend. He was thoughtful and considerate, and he had taken from Hannie all the burden of the funeral and its preparations.

For a day or two after returning to the ranch Hannie kept to herself in the foreman's house. Tenbow came to see her, inquiring gravely if she had everything she needed, and, being assured that she was well cared for, left her alone. Then, realizing that she could not simply sit idle, Hannie went back to work. When Dutch had been alive she had taken care of the foreman's house and the big house and cooked the meals for Tenbow, her father, and herself. Tenbow, coming in at night, found that the girl had prepared his supper. She served it to him and sat down at the table, just as she had always done.

"It's mighty good to have you lookin' after things again, Hannie," Tenbow said. "Mighty good."

"It was time that I went back to work," Hannie answered. "I'll have the house clean tomorrow, Mr. Tenbow." She paused a moment to nerve herself before proceeding. "I've been wondering what you wanted me to do. You'll want to put another man on as foreman now, and I suppose you'll want the house."

Tenbow gestured abruptly with his fork. "There's time to talk about that later on," he said. "Let it go for now, Hannie. I'll tell you this: You'll never want for anything or lack for a home as long as I'm alive."

Faint color stained Hannie's smooth cheeks.

"Thank you," she acknowledged. "You've been awfully good to me, Mr. Tenbow. And I haven't thanked you for—for looking after things for me."

Tenbow did not reply. He was watching Hannie. Under the steady scrutiny of his eyes the girl averted her gaze.

Miles Tenbow was a widower and childless. Since the death of his wife the 10 Bow had taken the place of a family, his whole life wrapped up in the ranch. Now as he looked at the girl sitting opposite him an idea crept into his mind. He was not old, not really old, even though his hair was white. He was strong and active. He had wealth in moderation, just as, at that time, all cowmen had wealth. He owned a lot of land and a lot of cattle and had a big mortgage at a Denver bank. Furtively Tenbow toyed with his idea.

"I do appreciate all the things you've done," Hannie said. "It's hard for me to tell you how much I appreciate them."

"Forget it, Hannie," Tenbow ordered gruffly. "Let's not talk about it."

Having begun to work again, Hannie took hold with a furor of activity. She cleaned the foreman's house, crying sometimes as she sorted Dutch's meager wardrobe or found some memento of him tucked away where he had put it. Then she attacked the big house, dragging out the carpets to beat them, hanging bedding on the line, washing windows, sweeping and scouring.

For a week or more she released her energy and then, with all the cleaning done and everything in perfect order, she found herself taskless.

Hannie had always loved to ride. Ranch-raised, almost brought up on a horse, she had spent many hours with Dutch. She was as good a cow hand as many of the riders on the flats and a better rider than most of them. She had her own horse, and now when the wrangler brought in the cavy he left Hannie's horse in the pen. Tenbow had not replaced Dutch and was covering a lot of country, rarely coming to headquarters at noon, and Hannie had almost all the day to herself. She spent the time on horseback. So for a full two weeks following her father's funeral she occupied herself, and then the blow fell.

She had cooked and served supper and eaten it with Miles Tenbow and was ready to clear the table when Tenbow spoke.

"Sit down a minute, Hannie. I want to talk to you." There was a seriousness in Tenbow's voice that alarmed the girl, and she seated herself, her rounded arms resting on the table as she looked at the man. Tenbow ran a finger over his sparse mustache and cleared his throat.

"I'm not an old man, Hannie," he began. "I've lived pretty hard an' worked hard, but I ain't old."

"Why—I've never thought that you were an old

233

man, Mr. Tenbow," Hannie said. "I never thought that either you or Dad was old."

Tenbow frowned. It did not suit his purpose to be put into the same class and age as Dutch Koogler. "I've done pretty well," he said, looking around the room. "I started out with two saddle horses an' about ten old cows. Now I've got the 10 Bow."

Hannie maintained a discreet silence.

"Hannie," Tenbow said, "how would you like to stay here at the 10 Bow always? How would you like to have this house for yores? How would you like to have accounts at the stores an' go into Denver an' buy what you want?"

"Why—" Hannie began, distress in her voice.

"Now wait a minute," Tenbow commanded. "I don't want to scare you. I think too much of you to scare you. I want you to take yore time an' think things over. But I want you to marry me, Hannie. I want you to be Mrs. Tenbow."

Caught utterly unprepared, surprised and startled, Hannie came to her feet. Her cheeks were red with her flush and her eyes large. "I—"

"Don't say anythin' yet," Tenbow interrupted quickly. "I want you to take yore time an' think it over. But I'd like for you to say yes, Hannie." There was something almost wistful in the man's voice as he spoke those final words and, rising, went to the door. He paused there briefly, looking at the girl, and then went on out, leaving

Hannie, sorely troubled, standing by the table.

In the days that followed Tenbow did not again refer to the subject, but it was plain that he thought of it. He dressed more carefully than was his wont and he did not leave the headquarters as early as was his custom, but waited until Hannie was up so that he could eat breakfast with her. Before, he had always eaten with the riders from the bunkhouse. Hannie was troubled. She liked and respected Miles Tenbow, but she did not love him. There was a streak of romance in the girl, deep down, that told her she must love the man she married and that no marriage of convenience would be enough. So it was with relief that she received the note that the rider from the Diamond Lake camp brought to headquarters one afternoon.

"Max Hinds brought it over yesterday evenin'," the rider informed. "Said he'd come past Marvin's place an' Miz Marvin give it to him. I had to come in today so I just brought it along."

"Thanks, Jake," Hannie said mechanically, glancing at the paper in her hands. "I'm ever so much obliged. There's a piece of pie in the kitchen."

While Jake ate pie Hannie read the note again, and when Miles Tenbow came in that night the girl went to him.

"Ruth Marvin wants me to come to stay with her awhile, Mr. Tenbow," Hannie said. "She's sick and she needs someone. I'm going over there in the morning."

Tenbow nodded. "All right, Hannie," he said gently. "You go ahead. I expect you'll be good for Mrs. Marvin. An', Hannie"—the girl paused and turned back to Tenbow—"while yo're over there you think about what I told you," Tenbow concluded.

The next morning Hannie packed her grip and was ready to go when Tenbow appeared. "I've had the buckboard hitched," he said. "I'll take you over to Marvin's, Hannie."

The days that followed were distressing for Hannie Koogler. Ruth Marvin was a shadow of her former self, worn out, run down by hard work, but more by worry. She had cause to be worried. Tom Marvin was a far different man from the bright-eyed young fellow that Ruth had married and that Hannie had danced with in Gunhammer. Unshaven, bleary-eyed, snarling, he was more animal than man. He drank constantly and snapped and growled at Ruth when she remonstrated with him. For a day or two after Hannie's arrival Marvin seemed to brace up but after that relapsed and was uglier than before, seeming to resent Hannie's presence.

They were branding at the Flying W, and Earl Latiker with the two Hinds brothers and Smiley Colfax had come to help out. It was only with the men that Tom Marvin made any pretext of civility, and Hannie wondered that they would tolerate his surliness. Colfax and Latiker and the Hinds brothers were pleasant to her and made things more bearable, but it was because of Ruth that she stayed at all. She felt that she was Ruth's last dependence, her last support, and that should she go the other woman would collapse.

Material things improved at the Flying W after Hannie arrived. She put the house in order, cooked for the men and for the children, patched young Tom's clothes and those of the two little girls, and generally set things to rights. She was glad when the Flying W calves were branded and Earl Latiker smilingly announced that they wouldn't trouble her any more.

"We'll miss yore cookin', Hannie, an' we'll sure hate to go," Latiker drawled. "But we've got to get my calves an' Smiley's marked. I reckon we'll pull out in the mornin'."

"Are you going, Tom?" Ruth Marvin asked.

Tom Marvin looked at her. "Of course I'm goin'," he snarled. "An' glad of it. Mebbe I won't have to listen to you whine for a while."

That was too much for Hannie. She had gradually filled up, and now she spilled over.

"And perhaps for a few days we won't have a drunken sot in the kitchen," she snapped. "And maybe little Tom won't run and hide whenever he hears a horse coming in. I've stood all that I intend to stand from you, Tom Marvin. I'll be here when you come back, and if you act like you have I'm going to do something about it. I'll go to Frank Arnold—that's what I'll do—and see if there isn't some way to make a man treat his wife decently!"

Marvin lumbered up out of his chair, murder in his bloodshot eyes. Latiker and Smiley Colfax closed in on him swiftly and dragged him, cursing and protesting, out of the kitchen.

"You shouldn't have said that, Hannie," Ruth protested. "I know that he's acting badly, but he's my husband."

"And you let him walk on you!" Hannie flared. "Ruth Marvin, if you don't show some spirit and stand up to him I'll—I'll go home; that's what I'll do!"

Ruth began to weep, and Hannie, instantly contrite, took the woman in her arms. But that night she lay awake planning and thinking. If Tom Marvin didn't straighten up, Hannie decided, she would do exactly as she had threatened.

The men left the next morning. Two hours after their departure Ruth called from the yard, urgency in her voice. Hurrying outside, Hannie saw three horses coming up the long slope that led to the Flying W. Three men were on the horses, and the two flanking riders supported the man in the center who slumped limply.

"It's Tom!" Ruth Marvin gasped.

It was Tom. Smiley Colfax, dismounting, supported Marvin until Earl Latiker could reach the ground. Then together they lifted Marvin from the saddle and carried him to the house.

"His horse fell," Latiker explained. "He jumped at somethin' an' stampeded. Tom had been fightin' him all mornin'. The saddle horn caught Tom when the horse rolled."

Tom Marvin lay on his bed, blood slowly seeping from his shirt. Ruth had dropped to the floor, kneeling beside her husband.

"You get him undressed," Hannie said practically, her prosaic words belying the fright she felt. "I'll bring hot water and bandages."

"That's the girl," Latiker praised.

They stripped Marvin of his clothing and washed away the blood. Hannie gasped at what she saw, and both Latiker and Colfax shook their heads. Marvin's ribs were crushed, and the steel horn of his saddle had punctured his body just below the breastbone. They bandaged the wound and stanched the flow of blood, and Ruth Marvin gently covered the unconscious man.

"There ain't a chance," Latiker pronounced, standing beside the door and speaking low-voiced to Hannie and Colfax. "He's finished."

"Can't you get a doctor?" Hannie asked.

Colfax shrugged, and Latiker answered: "The nearest is Fort Neville. He'd be gone before we could get a doctor here."

"We ought to do something!" Hannie urged. "Isn't there anything—anything at all?"

"Hannie." Ruth's call was low, intense with her suffering.

"I'll go to her," Hannie said. "You'll have to decide what to do right away. But I think somebody should go to Fort Neville for the doctor." She hurried back to Ruth.

Colfax jerked his head toward the door, and he and Latiker went out. Outside the house Colfax sat down on the stoop. Latiker, standing, looked down, and Colfax met his eyes.

"Well," he drawled, "are we goin' in to Fort Neville for the doc?"

Latiker shook his head. "No use."

There was silence between them, and then Colfax said: "Mebbe it's a good thing this happened, Earl. Mebbe it saves us some grief."

Latiker did not speak, and the smiling man amplified. "Tom was drinkin' all the time. An' he was a weak sister. Sooner or later he'd of let somethin' slip. We couldn't ride herd on him all the time."

"Yeah," Latiker agreed. "I've thought of that too. I was goin' to talk to you about that, Smiley. I'd been figurin' that we were goin' to have to do somethin' about Tom. Like you say, he'd of let somethin' slip, either about the Veritys or Koogler. This kind of saves us the trouble."

Again silence fell.

240

"Well," Latiker said finally, "I guess there ain't no need of ridin' for the doctor then. We both kind of feel the same way about it."

All through that day Tom Marvin lay in a coma. He breathed raspingly, but that was the only sign of life. Ruth stayed beside her husband while Hannie cared for the children. She fed them and, as dusk came, put them to bed. Twice she appealed to Latiker and Colfax, demanding that they ride for the doctor, and twice the men met her demands with shrugs and the statement that it was no use. Little Tom began to cry, and Hannie could not comfort him. He wanted his mother, and no one else would take her place. Going to the bedroom, Hannie called Ruth to her.

"You'll have to go to little Tom," she said. "He's crying and he wants you. I'll stay here."

Ruth Marvin's face was pale. "You'll call me, Hannie?" she asked. "If Tom . . . You'll call?"

"I'll call you," Hannie promised. Ruth went out, and Hannie crossed the room and seated herself beside the bed. She could hear Ruth murmuring to her boy, and Latiker's voice sounded in the kitchen as he spoke to Colfax. The lamp burned yellow on the table, and Tom Marvin stirred. Hannie sprang up, ready to call Ruth, and on the bed Marvin opened his eyes. The man's lips moved, and the girl bent down.

"What is it, Tom?" she asked softly. "What is it? Do you want Ruth?"

"Hannie?" Tom Marvin muttered. "Still here? I'm sorry, Hannie."

"You needn't be sorry, Tom. It's all right. I understand. You'd been drinking and you weren't responsible for what you said to me. It's all right."

"Not that!" The girl bent closer to hear the muttered words. Marvin's voice grew stronger as his eyes brightened. "Not that. It's Dutch. I didn't kill him, Hannie. I didn't. I stayed with the cattle. It was Smiley an' Earl. They killed him, not me."

Hannie could not move. Marvin's eyes closed, and the lucid interval was gone. His moving lips muttered fragments of words, "Ruth . . . Little Tom . . ." Hannie lifted her head. Smiley Colfax stood in the bedroom door, lips drawn back in his perpetual grin, gold teeth gleaming in the lamplight.

Hannie could feel the mad pounding of her heart. It seemed to rise in her chest and choke her. Had Colfax heard? Had he?

Chapter 16

Colfax came on into the room, stopping beside the bed. His eyes were hard as he looked at Hannie. "What's he been sayin'?" Colfax demanded. "I heard him talk."

Hannie could not look into Colfax' eyes. "He isn't conscious," she managed to answer. "He just says words."

"Ruth . . ." Tom Marvin muttered. "Where's little Tom?"

Latiker was at the door now, and Ruth Marvin called from beyond. "Hannie, what is it? Is Tom . . . ?" Her swift steps followed her call.

"He's ravin'," Colfax announced without taking his eyes from Hannie. "Don't let her in here, Earl."

Latiker barred the doorway, pushing Ruth Marvin back. Smiley Colfax continued to stare at Hannie. "He said somethin'," Colfax growled. "What was it?"

"Nothing," Hannie stammered. "He tried to talk. I was going to call Ruth."

For what seemed an age to the girl Colfax eyed her speculatively without speaking. Marvin moved and muttered again, and that apparently decided the man.

"You go on out with Ruth," he ordered. "Earl an' me'll look after Tom."

"Let me in! Let me in to my husband!" Ruth demanded. There was a brief struggle at the door.

"Go on out an' keep her quiet," Colfax rasped. "We don't want you in here."

Hannie skirted the end of the bed, cautiously passed Colfax, and reached the door. Latiker let her through, stepped in, and closed the door behind him. Ruth was in Hannie's arms, sobbing against her breast. "They won't let me in. Tom's dying and they won't let me in."

"Now, Ruth," Hannie comforted mechanically.

What should she do? There seemed to be no answer to the question. Hannie held the sobbing woman and stared unseeingly across the kitchen. From beyond the closed door of the bedroom where Tom Marvin lay voices sounded as Latiker and Colfax talked. They were debating some question, for she heard Colfax' voice rise in sharp query. She must get away. She must get out of here. But how? And how could she leave Ruth Marvin? Ruth was absolutely dependent on Hannie, alone, frightened, her husband dying. What should she do? What *could* she do? Little Tom whimpered, and through all her grief the mother heard the sound and stiffened in Hannie's arms.

"You'll have to go to little Tom," Hannie said.

"You'll have to go to your children, Ruth. They need you."

Little Tom lay on a pallet in the lean-to behind the kitchen. He looked up as the woman entered, and his arms went out to his mother. Ruth knelt beside her boy, seizing the child possessively. The two small girls were asleep, and as Ruth comforted him little Tom gradually quieted.

"Ruth," Hannie said quietly.

Ruth looked up.

"I've got to go." Hannie kept her voice low. "I must get away, Ruth."

"No!" There was pleading in Ruth's voice. "You can't leave me, Hannie. Please!"

Hannie knelt beside the woman. "I must, Ruth," she said earnestly. "You know I wouldn't go unless I had to."

From the kitchen came the sound of a door opening. Colfax' voice rasped: "Hannie?"

"Yes?" Hannie answered, hiding her fear, keeping her voice level. "Do you want me?"

"No," Colfax answered. "Not now."

The words were simple enough, nothing in them to cause alarm, and yet the tone was freighted with some sinister meaning. Hannie caught it, and Ruth Marvin, almost blinded by her grief, caught it too. Her eyes were wide as she stared at her companion, and little Tom, somehow alarmed, renewed his sobbing.

"What is it, Hannie?" Ruth whispered.

Hannie's eyes were wide and her face white. "I heard—I'll not tell you, Ruth. If they thought you knew they'd—We must get out of here, both of us, and we must take the children."

"And leave Tom? No, Hannie! What is it? What happened?"

The women crouched together, their arms about each other. Little Tom whimpered.

"They killed my father," Hannie whispered. "Tom told me. I feel sure Colfax heard him. Oh, Ruth, what will we do? What will we do?"

In the bedroom Smiley Colfax glared at Earl Latiker and asked the same question. "What'll we do, Earl?"

Latiker looked at the man on the bed and then turned his eyes to Colfax. "You heard him?" he demanded. "Are you sure, Smiley?"

"Of course I'm sure. I heard him tell her."

Silence came to the men. Colfax stepped to the door and called. "Hannie?"

"Yes?" the answer came. "Do you want me?"

"No. Not now."

"What was the idea of that?" Latiker rasped.

"To see if she was there."

"An' where," Latiker snarled, "would she go? Tell me that, Smiley."

Colfax shrugged. "No place, I guess. Well, Earl?"

"She'll have told Marvin's wife too," Latiker

mused. "Damn it! We ought not to of left her in here. We ought to of stayed with Tom ourselves an' kept the women out. Who'd of thought he'd ever get to where he could talk? Why—"

"It ain't what we'd ought to of done," Colfax interrupted bluntly. "It's what are we goin' to do? I ain't goin' to have my head put in a noose by no damned woman."

"She knows we killed her dad," Latiker growled, "an' she'll have told the other one. It looks like there's just one thing for it, Smiley."

"You mean . . . ?" Colfax rasped.

Latiker nodded.

"How? We've got to fix it right, Earl."

"There's goin' to be a fire," Latiker said slowly. "That's the only way that I can see, Smiley. A fire that'll catch the whole outfit while they're asleep."

"The kids too?"

Latiker shrugged. "The kids too."

Colfax shook his head. "There's Max an' Shorty," he reminded. "They'll be comin' back to look for us when we don't show up. They'll know somethin' happened."

"Damn them," Latiker growled. "I wish that they'd been with us when we settled with Koogler."

"But they wasn't," Colfax rasped. "They got cold feet after that Verity business."

"We've got to be with Max an' Shorty when

the fire breaks out," Latiker said. "We'll have to tell 'em that Tom got hurt an' that we took him home. We'll say that he wasn't hurt very bad. We'll bring 'em up here to see Tom, an' the fire's got to be burnin' when we get here. It's got to be foolproof."

"I thought the other was foolproof," Colfax growled. "It got blamed on Ray Verity all right. An' then this damned fool"—he jerked his hand toward the bed—"got to drinkin' an' got hurt. An' then"—there was utter venom in Colfax' voice—"he had to talk!"

On the bed Tom Marvin's hand fluttered. There was a long rasping breath and then quiet. Colfax walked over and looked down.

"Anyhow," he snarled, "he ain't goin' to talk any more. I don't like this, Earl. I think what we'd better do is pull out. We can leave the country, an' they'll never catch us. Let the girl talk if she's a mind to."

"An' leave everythin' I've got?" Latiker demanded. "Not me! We'll have to plan this. We'll have to do it quick. It's got to—What's that?" He jerked the door open and stood staring out into the empty kitchen.

"Hannie?" Latiker called.

"She's gone out," Ruth Marvin answered. "She'll be back in a minute. Can I see Tom now?"

"Come on, Smiley," Latiker rasped. "Where'd she go, Ruth?"

"She went out for a minute. Can I see Tom? Please let me come in." Ruth came out of the lean-to into the kitchen.

"See him if you want to," Latiker rasped callously. "He's dead."

Ruth screamed and ran across the room. Latiker stepped aside to let her pass and went on into the kitchen. Colfax joined him. They could hear Ruth sobbing in the bedroom.

"That damned Hannie Koogler," Latiker rasped. "I don't like her goin' out. I don't like it at all. Why'd she have to be here anyhow?"

"She'll be back in a minute," Smiley comforted. He crossed the kitchen and pulled open the outer door. The night was dark, only the stars giving light. At the corral a horse snorted his fright and moved swiftly.

"By God!" Colfax' voice blared. "She's at the corral. She's tryin' to get away!"

Hannie heard the shout. It had taken much whispered consultation, much gathering of courage for her to make this attempt. Ruth was adamant in refusing to leave her home. Not even the possible peril of her children swerved her. She would not leave her husband. The only course, the only thing that could be done was for Hannie to go for help. They knew that they were in danger. Neither woman underrated Latiker and Colfax, for these men had killed once and would kill again to protect their safety. With Ruth urging and helping her, Hannie slipped out of the window in the lean-to. She stepped on and overturned a tub as she descended, and that was the noise that Latiker heard.

Crouched beside the tub, Hannie heard Latiker call and Ruth's answer. Close to the ground as she was, she could see the corral against the sky line and the heads of the horses in the pen. The men, after carrying Tom Marvin to the house and attending to him, had put up their horses, but they had not unsaddled. Hannie slipped toward the corral. If she could get a horse out and turn the others loose the mad scheme that she and Ruth Marvin had concocted might succeed, otherwise the chances were slim enough. The Flying W was twelve miles deep in the Wagonwheel, and the nearest help was the 10 Bow camp at Diamond Lake, which lay eighteen miles or more beyond the gap. Hannie knew that she must be mounted, for on foot she was helpless. As she put her hand on the corral gate and fumbled for the latch light streamed out of the kitchen door, and she heard Colfax yell: "By God! She's at the corral! She's tryin' to get away!"

It was no use. Hannie turned and ran blindly from the corral, across the little open space behind the Flying W house, and downhill. Squawberry grew in a thick clump to her left, but she did not see it. She could hear Latiker and Colfax calling behind her, and the voices were a spur that increased her speed. Then underfoot a treacherous rock rolled and she went down. She crawled, not trying to rise, but like an injured, frightened animal seeking escape. The squawberry, sturdy-stemmed and prickly, tore at her as she reached it, but the thicket promised concealment. Regardless of the branches that fought her passage, she forced a way in and then, prone upon the ground, lay still.

Sharp to her left, Earl Latiker spoke. "You sure she come this way?"

At a distance Colfax answered: "She run behind the house."

"I don't hear her," Latiker snapped petulantly. "She didn't get a horse, did she?"

"No."

The man moved on a step or two while Hannie held her breath. It seemed to her that surely he must hear the pounding of her heart.

"She's hidin'," Colfax rasped as he came up to join Latiker. "She can't get away. She ain't got a horse. We'll find her."

"Somethin' movin' over to the left," Latiker snarled. "Damn her! We waited too long. You should have killed her, Smiley, back there in the house."

The men moved away, their voices drifting back. "We'll find her," Colfax assured his companion. "Come light we'll find her sure. She can't get away."

Latiker's answer was lost. Hannie lay quiet. After what seemed hours she raised herself cautiously and crawled again. It took a long time to get through the squawberry. When a branch snapped or when the leaves rustled she stopped, waiting, listening. Latiker and Colfax were working along beside the house. A light danced and moved. The squawberry thicket ended, and Hannie stopped at its edge. Then, rising, she ran again, not heeding direction, not seeing the Whetrocks looming to the left or the closer landmarks that might have helped her. Instinctively, blindly, wild with her fright, she ran, sometimes tripping, sometimes falling, until at last she could run no more and was forced to stop. She stood a moment, catching her breath in great sobs, and then blindly, as she had run, began to walk toward the south.

How long she traveled she did not know. Always there was darkness about her. Underfoot were rocks or grass or sandy earth. Once she came to a little stream and, floundering in the mud, almost went down. Somehow she escaped the mud. The ground sloped up, an endless, rising hill. When she caught her breath she ran, and when breath was gone she stopped, only to start again. Gradually her panic left her and weariness engulfed her. Her legs were numb and her shoes were in tatters, and ahead of her there was a lighter space in the dark rim below the sky, a giant unevenness. She heard something move. A horse snorted surprise and alarm. A gaunt skeleton, an upright that held a crossbeam, loomed against the sky. The horse snorted again, and out of the dark a voice rasped:

"Stop right there! I've got you covered!"

With a little moan Hannie Koogler sank down to the ground and crouched there, cowering against the earth.

All the way north from the Nashota, Ray Verity made time. Distance that Sunheart's Sioux had covered in a day was a matter of hours for the man alone. Ribbon carried him, and when Ribbon tired Brownie had a turn. He traveled, as the saying is, "from can to can't," from the time he could see until he couldn't, and he covered country. There was a new wariness about him, a new alertness. He begrudged the hours that perforce he spent in resting his horses and letting them graze, knowing all the while that he depended upon them and that they must eat and rest. Hunger scarcely bothered him. With the Sioux he had learned that many things disdained by the whites were good to eat. A prairie dog gave him a meal now, or a rabbit shot at morning or evening dusk. Two days north of the Nashota he first glimpsed the Whetrocks rising out of the flats and felt his heart quicken a beat. The mountains marched along the sky, and ride as he might, did not seem to come closer.

On the evening of the day he saw the hills he reached the railroad. The telegraph wires swung their undulating ribbons from pole to pole along the track, and as Ray approached for a crossing he found a road. Ribbon struck into it, and Ray gave him his head. On a pole close beside the crossing a notice, glaring white, attracted the boy's attention. He stopped to read.

$500 REWARD

The undersigned will pay $500 for the Apprehension and Arrest of

RAY VERITY

Wanted for Murder

Description: About five feet ten inches tall. Blue eyes. Brown hair. When last seen was wearing a full beard. Has small scar below right eye. Riding a horse branded Ace of Spades on left hip. Is armed with double action .38-caliber Colt, gold inlayed and engraved.

WARNING: This man is dangerous.

Signed:

FRANK N. ARNOLD, *Sheriff*

WANTED: DEAD OR ALIVE!

Ray reined Ribbon away from the post. So it had come to that! What had he done, he wondered, that warranted such a notice and reward? "Wanted for Murder," the poster said. Whom had he killed? Surely not Virgil Jorbet. Jorbet's yells had been too loud and full of fear to come from a dying man.

Ray rode on. There was a hardness about him now, and the glitter had returned to his eyes. "$500 Reward. Dead or Alive." Well then, the man who took that money would earn it. When the reward was paid Ray Verity would be dead.

Until now in his traveling Ray had avoided all settlements, had skirted around ranches and camps, and hidden from the few riders that he saw. Now as evening came he rode boldly into a little crossroads store and, dismounting, put Ribbon's reins over the hitch rail and walked inside. There were two men in the store, the merchant and a lanky rider buying tobacco. Ray waited until the merchant came to him.

"I want," he said, "some crackers and sardines. Give me a couple of cans of salmon too."

"You want these in a sack?" the storekeeper asked.

"Yeah. In a gunny sack so I can carry 'em. I want about four cans of tomatoes. An' put in a dollar's worth of candy."

The merchant filled the order. "Anythin' else?" he asked as he put the loaded gunny sack on the counter.

Ray's eyes were hard as he grinned. "Yeah," he drawled. "Charge 'em to Colonel Colt." Clough

255

Weathers' fancy gun slid out into his hand and glinted knowingly at the storekeeper and the rider as Ray backed toward the door. "Don't come out," Ray warned as he reached the opening. "Stay put an' stay healthy."

He was gone. The merchant took a long breath, and the rider started toward the door. "Stay put, Clem," the storekeeper warned, using Ray's own words. "You heard him."

Outside there was a rattle of hoofs and a derisive yell.

"You know who that was?" Clem demanded. "That was—"

"Of course I know. That was Ray Verity. Look, Clem. You fork yore horse an' head for the ranch. Get some boys together. We'll git that jasper. There's five hundred dollars on him, dead or alive!"

Clem started for the door and stopped. "Nope," he said, turning back. "I ain't goin' to do it. Come to think of it, I ain't broke. Did you see the way he looked at me? I don't need five hundred bucks. Not *thut* bad."

"Then you damned coward," the storekeeper flared, "git on yore horse an' go to Fort Neville. Tell the sheriff—"

Lanky Clem shook his head. "Not me," he interrupted. "We're brandin'. I got work to do."

For two more days Ray rode toward the north. With the provisions he had stolen there was no need to hunt. He changed horses as they tired and stretched his days until they reached into the night, and then, as dusk came, he found the Whetrocks to his right and behind him and rode down a gentle slope. To the north the gap stretched away, Verity Gap, and to the south were the flats. One post and the crossbar of what had been a door arose from blackened, weed-grown ruins.

Ray stopped Brownie and sat looking at the site. Then deliberately he dismounted. An odd whimsy had struck him, a fancy that he would satisfy. For one more time he would sleep in the Verity cabin, for one more time he would occupy these ruins that had been his home. He unsaddled, stripped the meager pack from Ribbon, and staked the horses out to graze.

Carrying saddle and limp gunny sack, he walked across what had been the door. The ruins of the living-room fireplace, the chimney still standing, mocked him. He gathered wood, blackened pieces of what had been wall logs, and built a fire in the fireplace. Squatting before it, he ate sardines and crackers and then, leaving the ruins, went to the spring and drank.

Returning, he watched the fire die out and then stretched himself upon the earth and lay there looking at the stars. He could hear Brownie and Ribbon moving as they grazed, and somewhere close by a cricket sang a courting song. Sleep would not come for the thoughts that filled his head. One of the horses stamped. Then there was a snort of alarm. Ray sat up, drew the Colt from his holster. Something was moving, someone was coming up the hill. The horse snorted again.

"Stop right there!" Ray snarled. "I've got you covered!"

He gained his feet. Below, outside the ruins, there was a sudden flurry of motion. He heard a little moan and, Colt ready, ran forward, caught roughly at a shoulder, and checked his pull. The flesh he gripped was soft, smooth, not the hard shoulder of a man.

"Who are you?" Ray demanded hoarsely. "Who—?"

"Hannie. I'm Hannie Koogler."

"My good God!" Ray exclaimed. "Hannie!"

Chapter 17

When Mat Yoeman rode into the Wagonwheel he followed a definite idea. To prove Ray Verity innocent of Dutch Koogler's murder he must prove someone else guilty. He had several candidates for the position. Mat began his reasoning with the cause of Koogler's death. Dutch had been put into the gap to prevent rustling. Dutch was dead. Therefore, as Mat saw it, Dutch had spotted someone moving stolen cattle, and as a result Dutch had been killed. The community in general jumped to conclusions and tabbed Ray Verity as the murderer, but Mat, sure of his friend's innocence, set about proving it.

He worked all through the Wagonwheel looking at cattle, staying out of sight, and using the infinite cunning and patience that he had learned among the Sioux. His search was unsuccessful, but at its end he was just as determined as when he began. He found no 10 Bow cattle, no Drag 9s, no Bar Ks. All the brands he saw were legitimate and belonged where he found them, but Mat was not stopped. The search of the Wagonwheel was just a beginning.

That portion of his investigation finished, he went on north, as persistent as a heel fly in summer. There was a northern exit to the roughs, and beyond it was a great expanse of country, some towns and a railroad. Thirty miles north of the Wagonwheel, stabling his horses in a little railroad shipping point, Mat made his first contact.

"I see yo're ridin' an Ace of Spades horse," the liveryman commented. "You must be from down south of here."

Mat nodded agreement.

"Don't see many of them southern brands up here," the hostler continued. "I bought one from a feller last fall. Pretty good horse."

"I raise 'em," Mat drawled. "That's my brand. I'd like to see the horse."

Accommodating Mat's wish, the barn man took him back along the stalls and presently stopped. Mat, looking at the horse, recognized a bay that he had sold to Max Hinds.

"Feller that had him was in here with a bunch of cattle," the barn man said. "We got to dickerin' around, an' I traded him out of the horse."

"Remember what brand was on the cattle?" Mat drawled. "I can't seem to place the feller that bought this horse."

"They had a Walkin' V, I think," the barn man answered. "You might ask Jack Walker. He buys some cattle out of that country."

"Whereabouts," Mat drawled, "would I find Mr. Walker?"

"Downtown. Likely at the Dollar Saloon. He hangs out there."

Mat went to town.

Walker was a shifty-eyed individual who proved reticent until Mat mentioned Max Hinds. Walker cautiously admitted knowing Max. A little more talk, the implication that he, Mat Yoeman, was looking for a cow buyer who wasn't too particular, a lot of whisky consumed over the bar, and Walker loosened up.

"I could," Mat suggested, "put around fifty head of steers in here pretty easy if I had a market for 'em. I know where I can get holt of that many."

"You can't ship from here no more," Walker warned. "The Stock Association has an inspector here now. I got to have a bill of sale for any that I ship."

"A bill of sale ain't hard to write," Mat suggested.

"The brands have got to match it. I had some trouble with that bunch I shipped a month ago."

Mat hazarded a question. "Did Hinds bring a bunch up?"

Walker shook his head. "No. It was Marvin an' a couple of fellers. They—Say, yo're kind of curious, ain't you?"

Mat saw that he had gone too far. "They're all friends of mine," he answered expansively. "What say we have another drink?"

Walker took the drink, but it had no effect. He closed up, clamlike, and for all his subtle maneuvering, Mat could get no more information. Still he had what he wanted, one name: Tom Marvin. He put the drunken Walker to bed that night and early the next morning was trailing back toward the Wagonwheel. Three days after his conversation with Jack Walker he rode up to Tom Marvin's Flying W.

The door of the house stood open, and no one answered Mat's call. He called again, waited, and, still hearing no answer, went in. The deserted kitchen showed nothing, and Mat prowled. He saw the pallets of the children in the lean-to and in the bedroom found a sheet-covered body. Mat pulled back the sheet. Tom Marvin lay there, and Mat's first glance told him that he would never ask Marvin any questions concerning a bunch of cattle sold to Jack Walker.

Puzzled because Ruth Marvin and the children were not present, Mat left the house. He scouted around it carefully, cutting sign that he could not accurately read. He saw where horses had gone out of the corral, found other tracks showing that two men had ridden up, entered the house, come out, and ridden off. He found, too, where a woman had run across the yard behind the house, but the tracks that were most plain and that intrigued him led from the kitchen door across the yard and south toward the gap. Mat followed these, riding slowly along on Bear Dance and leading Custer, keeping his eyes on the ground where a woman had walked, two children with her. Ruth Marvin, carrying one child, and the other two older youngsters walking with her had come this way.

Twice Mat lost the trail and was forced to dismount and cut for it. The second time he saw that Ruth had gone sharply to the east. Two sets of horse tracks coming from the north might or might not account for this sudden departure from the line. Mat followed in the new direction, came to a small creek where alders grew thick, and stopped. The tracks went into the alders.

"Miz Marvin!" he called cautiously. "Miz Marvin!"

For a long time there was no answer to the call. Then in the alder thicket a little tousled head appeared. Like a small frightened wild thing Tom Marvin looked at Mat. Mat did not move. His deep voice rumbled as kind and gentle as Mat could make it.

"Hello, sonny."

The boy poised, ready for flight. Mat stayed still. Finally little Tom advanced a step, coming into the open.

"Where's yore mama, sonny?" Mat asked gently.

"In there," said little Tom and gestured to the thicket.

Mat dismounted. The boy was ready to run.

Mat flipped his long yellow braids. "Playin' Injun?" he drawled. "Reckon I'll have to watch out for my scalp. Whereabouts is Mama?"

Little Tom ducked back into the alders and Mat followed.

He found Ruth Marvin, utterly exhausted, cowering beside her two small girls. Mat asked no questions. He went back, got Custer and Bear Dance, and, leading them close, took a little flask of whisky from his pack and coerced Ruth to drink. Then, squatting, he waited for the whisky to take effect.

A little color came to Ruth Marvin's cheeks. "Tom . . ." she began.

"No need to tell me," Mat broke in. "I was there. Do you reckon you could ride, Miz Marvin? I could put you an' mebbe two of the kids on Custer an' take the other on my saddle. I'll get you to town."

"I've got to hide," Ruth said desperately. "I've got to. They'll hunt for me. They're hunting for Hannie now."

Mat checked his preparations. "I reckon you'd better talk first," he said sharply. "Who're 'they'?"

"Earl Latiker and Smiley Colfax," Ruth answered, her voice showing how nearly she had reached a breaking point. "They killed Mr. Koogler."

Mat held out the flask. "You take another little

drink," he commanded. "Git some stren'th an' tell me."

Ruth took the flask, choked on a swallow of the liquor, gasped, and began to talk. She had hardly spoken two sentences before Mat was back, working on Custer's pack, making it ready so that the horse could be ridden.

"You can tell me while we ride," he rasped, glancing at the sun which climbed above the Whetrocks. "We ain't got much time, I reckon."

Finished with the pack, Mat helped Ruth Marvin mount, put the smallest girl in her arms and little Tom up behind where he could hold to her waist, and himself took the other little girl on Bear Dance. Then side by side Mat and Ruth Marvin left the alders and rode south across the Wagonwheel.

Other riders were abroad that morning. Frank Arnold, appraised by an angry storekeeper that Ray Verity was in the country, had struck for Mat Yoeman's cabin in the hills. Finding it deserted, he was now engaged in making a long swing up through the Notch and down Notch Canyon, even though he believed his search useless.

Miles Tenbow, too, was moving. Patience had ceased to be a virtue with Tenbow. Hannie had stayed long enough at the Flying W. It was time that she came home, time and past time that he had his answer. Tenbow drove his buckboard toward the gap.

Smiley Colfax and Earl Latiker also rode toward the gap. Leaving the Flying W at daylight, they warned Ruth Marvin not to move, not to stir from the place, and made certain of her obeying their orders by driving off the horses that came in to water at the tank. The two men departed on their search, fully realizing that theirs was a desperate mission. They must find Hannie Koogler. The girl knew them for murderers and silencing her was imperative. They rode in long wide sweeps, seeking sign and, finding it, they followed the trail. The country was dry and the trail faint. Time and again they lost it and, because it wandered, they could not be sure of one true direction. But of grim necessity they stuck to their task.

Behind Colfax and Latiker, as they came south, were Max and Shorty Hinds. When they were not joined by Latiker, Colfax, and Marvin, the Hinds boys became alarmed. They had helped brand Marvin's calves, and the agreement was that all five should work together until the branding on each place was finished. Leaving their ranch early in the morning, they rode back to the Flying W, finding a deserted house, a dead man, and horse tracks that led south. Latiker and Colfax had gone to the gap, no doubt, taking Ruth Marvin and the children. This seemed reasonable to Max and Shorty, for doubtless the men were taking the women and the children to town. But the Hinds

266

boys were puzzled. Why had not Earl and Smiley loaded Marvin's body in a wagon and taken it along? They rode to find out.

So it was that from south and north and east men converged on Verity Gap, and in the gap, at the ruins of the Verity cabin, were Ray Verity and Hannie Koogler.

When Ray found Hannie there in the night he was first speechless with astonishment. Hannie, relief overwhelming her, threw her arms about Ray and sobbed against his chest. Ray held her tight, the surprise draining from him, leaving a fierce desire to find the person responsible for her plight. Who had frightened this girl so that she trembled and sobbed uncontrollably? And why was she out alone at night in the range country? Ray had no answer to either question.

Gradually the first sharp paroxysms of weeping diminished, and Ray, sensing that now she might respond, spoke to her soothingly.

"Don't, Hannie. You're safe now. Don't cry, girl."

At first the words had no effect. Then as realization came to the girl that here was security, she quieted further but clung to him as though fearful of being alone again. His arm still around her shoulders, Ray led the girl back toward the ruins of the fireplace. Hannie, scarcely able to walk, limped beside him, and, picking her up, Ray carried her the rest of the way in his arms.

He put her down beside the fireplace and busied himself. A match flamed briefly, and the first tiny glow of a fire began to flicker. Hannie's fear was roused again by the light.

"Don't," she choked. "They might see. They might find me."

"It makes no difference if they do," Ray answered, and there was a timbre in his voice which reassured the girl. "We got to have a little light."

The fire grew, expanding its circle of light, and Ray looked down at Hannie's tattered shoes. There was blood on one shoe, and Ray's rasping exclamation made the girl look at his face. What she saw there reassured her more than words. In the ruddy glow of the fire Ray's eyes were blue and hard, and under his curling beard the clean line of his jaw was strong. His hair, worn in braids, glistened in the light, and his clothing was worn, tattered, and stained, all save the buckskin shirt. Noting his face, the wide shoulders, the corded throat that glimpsed bronze at the V of the neck, reading those blue eyes, Hannie felt relief and security. The last sob died in her throat. She choked upon it and then began to laugh, quietly at first, and then with a rising hysteria. Alarmed, Ray jumped up and came to her. The laughter was uncontrollable now, more alarming than the sobs had been.

Ray caught the girl's shoulders and shook her

roughly. "Hannie!" he rasped. "Stop it!" He shook the girl again.

Hannie fought herself, battled the hysteria, and gradually won control of her shattered nerves. Ray released her shoulders and squatted down. "That's better," he commended. "We'll see what we can do about those feet." The big knife in his hand caught the light and glinted as its sharp edge slit the torn leather of her shoes.

Ray winced when he saw the condition of Hannie's feet. With no word he went out into the darkness and picked up a wash pan which had escaped the fire. Filling the vessel at the spring, he brought it back.

"Soak your feet in that," Ray ordered.

As bidden, Hannie put her feet in the basin. The water was deliciously cold and soothing. Ray's eyes were narrow as he watched the girl.

"Can you talk now?" he demanded.

Hannie nodded.

"Then tell me: What are you doin' out here at night?"

The question brought back all Hannie's terror. Ray must have seen it in her eyes for he spoke again quickly. "Steady, girl. You're safe enough."

Hannie shuddered. "They're looking for me," she said. "The men who killed my father."

"Who?"

"Earl Latiker and Smiley Colfax."

Silence for a moment, and then Ray spoke

again. "Go on, Hannie," he said quietly. "Tell me the rest of it."

"They killed him," Hannie said. "Tom told me."

The tale she told was disjointed at first, the events not in sequence, and Ray was forced to prompt with questions, then kept his silence as Hannie ordered her thoughts. The girl's voice murmured there beside the ruined fireplace, and out in the dark the cricket resumed his love song and the horses moved from time to time. Halfway through her story Hannie reached out her hand and Ray took it, holding it tightly in his big palm.

"And so I got away," Hannie completed. "I was trying to get to Diamond Lake and then I fell, and you—" She stopped. Turning her head, she looked at the man beside her.

Ray was staring at the fire. His eyes were thin slits, dark steel glinting behind the half-closed lids. Ray's right hand lay lax upon his knee, and as Hannie watched the fingers closed, tightening into a fist.

"An' they had it blamed on me," Ray said quietly. He was silent then until Hannie ventured a question.

"Where have you been, Ray? Why did you come back?"

"South with the Sioux," Ray answered briefly. "I came back because I found my mother's shawl. Colfax had traded it to Man Who Walks when the Sioux came through the Wagonwheel." He released Hannie's hand and abruptly got to his feet.

"I'll take you wherever you want to go in the mornin'," he announced. "I've got two horses. You'd better lie down an' rest now."

"I can't," Hannie answered. "I couldn't sleep."

"Lie down anyhow. I'll be up an' around, Hannie. You got to rest if yo're goin' to travel tomorrow."

Hannie removed her feet from the wash pan and lay down upon the saddle blanket that Ray brought. By turning her head she could see Ray standing looking down at the dying fire. He was immovable, motionless as a rock jutting up from a plain. For a long time Hannie watched him, and then despite her protestations of a moment before, her heavy lids closed down and she slept, utterly exhausted.

Her sleep was troubled. In her dreams Latiker's dark face haunted her; she could see Smiley Colfax' mirthless grin. In the dream Colfax advanced on her slowly, an evilly gleaming knife raised. She fought against the dream, rising with a long, terrible scream. Ray was beside her instantly, caught her hands as they struck at him, and shook her gently.

"Hannie, wake up! It's Ray!"

The dream faded. Arms, hard as iron, were around her and there was safety in them. Simply as a child Hannie turned to the man who held her.

"Ray," she murmured, "I dreamed that they were here. I saw them. Don't go away, Ray."

"I won't go," Ray promised gravely. "It was just a dream, Hannie."

He tried to free the girl, but Hannie clung to him, feeling the safety in his hard young arms. Ray lifted the girl and carried her to the fireplace and there, with his back against the rough stone, he seated himself, cradling Hannie against his side.

"Yo're all right," he comforted. "Rest easy, Hannie."

The tension drained out of the girl and she relaxed, leaning against Ray. Her breathing became soft and regular, and he reached out cautiously for his saddle blanket and the deerskin that he used for a bed and covered her with them. Hannie stirred and murmured: "Ray."

"Right here, Hannie."

"I knew that it wasn't you," the dreamy voice whispered. "I knew."

Ray's arm closed a little tighter around the girl who believed in him. Hannie stirred, snuggling closer, sighed, and relaxed. Ray Verity sat there, staring off into the night, looking up at the stars. Hannie's hair was soft and fragrant; her body was rounded, smooth, made to fit into the curve of his arm. With night-accustomed eyes he could see the soft curve of her cheek where it rested against his shoulder. A new tenderness, a new sense of responsibility filled the man.

The stars paled and the dawn wind rippled across the grass. Light touched the horizon and Ray, looking down, could see Hannie's long lashes drooped against her cheek and the sweet sweep of her lips. She was like a child lying there, but she was not a child. Possessiveness welled up in him and with it something else, a wild, fierce longing that he had never experienced. He bent his head and brushed the smooth cheek with his lips. Surprisingly Hannie turned her face toward him. She had not been asleep. Her lips were raised, and Ray Verity bent his head again while Hannie's arm stole up around his neck.

For a long moment neither moved. Then awkwardly Ray raised his head and freed his arm. The sun was coming over the top of the Whetrocks, sending the long shadows of the peaks amarch.

"You got to dreamin'," Ray said hoarsely. "It scared you. I brought you over here an'—"

"I remember, Ray." Hannie was smiling tremulously.

Ray scrambled up. "I'll get somethin' to eat," he stammered. "I got some canned stuff. An' I'll fix yore feet so we can travel. Where do you want me to take you, Hannie?"

"Wherever you say, Ray."

There was no escaping Hannie's eyes. Tender

273

and luminous, they would not let Ray go. He dropped to his knees beside the girl, and his voice was hoarse as he asked: "Did you mean that, Hannie? Did you?"

For just an instant he waited, and then Hannie gave her answer. "I meant it, Ray."

"It wasn't because you're scared or because you're sorry for me?"

"No, Ray."

A small pause. The girl spoke again. "And you, Ray. Did you mean it too?"

"You know I did, Hannie!" The man's voice was suddenly fierce. "You know it!"

The sun cleared the top of the Whetrocks.

Chapter 18

Water from the spring, a can of salmon, and the last of the crackers comprised their breakfast. Ray waited on Hannie, carrying the food to her. "Don't try to walk," he ordered almost gruffly. "I'll fix somethin' for yore feet. I'll make some moccasins."

Hannie laughed shyly at the idea of Ray making moccasins. They were so filled with this new thing, this sense of possession that had come to them both, that thoughts of their plight were far from their minds. Hannie would not meet Ray's bold look, and her cheeks were red with the rich blood under her golden tan. For the moment they were engrossed with each other and all else was forgotten.

With breakfast done Ray made two buckskin sacks, using his knife for a tool. Both laughed at the footgear, but Hannie's eyes were tender as she put them on and tied the buckskin strings. They were the first things that Ray had ever given her.

"A squaw wouldn't be seen dead carryin' those moccasins," Ray announced, eying his handicraft. "I—" He stopped short. The word he used brought reality to them. "Dead." It put the period to any lightness.

Ray left Hannie then and went to the horses,

leading Ribbon and Brownie back. "I'll put the saddle on Brownie," he announced. "You'll ride him. I'm goin' to take you to Gunhammer. That's closest."

"Can you take me there, Ray?" Hannie asked. "Is it safe for you?"

"As safe as anyplace." Ray busied himself rubbing dirt from Brownie's back.

"Ray."

Ray turned.

"What are you going to do after we go to Gunhammer?"

Studied concentration filled Ray's face. "I'm comin' back here."

Hannie said nothing.

"I've got to come back." Ray argued against her silence, justifying himself. "It was Latiker an' Colfax all the way through, Hannie. I found my mother's shawl an' her old mirror clear down on the Nashota. A Sioux buck had traded Smiley for 'em. There's just one way he could of got those things. He took 'em out of the cabin before he burned it."

Hannie would not meet Ray's eyes, and anger flared in him. "They killed your dad!" he rasped. "Why wouldn't I jump 'em?"

"Ray," Hannie said, "I'm afraid."

"You'll be safe enough in Gunhammer."

"Not for myself. For you. Must you come back, Ray? Couldn't we go to the sheriff? If I told him what Tom said, wouldn't that be enough?"

There was a heavy silence for a moment. Then Ray said hoarsely: "I guess not, Hannie. If they killed yore dad, why wasn't it them instead of Tenbow that killed Wayne an' the twins? I've got to know, Hannie. They're goin' to tell me."

It was no use. Hannie, looking at blue eyes that were like chips of polished flint, sensed the futility of argument. Still she tried once more. "Not even for me, Ray?"

"Not even for you." Under his beard Ray's face twisted. He turned to Brownie again, putting the blanket in place, smoothing it, swinging up the heavy saddle.

"I'll take you to Gunhammer now," he said flatly as he finished. "It's time we started."

Hannie got up. Ribbon, black-tipped ears cocked and grass protruding from the corners of his mouth, was looking off toward the north. The buckskin snorted softly, clearing his nostrils.

"Look, Ray!" There was alarm in Hannie's voice.

There to the north, beyond the sagging fence of the hoosegow pasture, two riders came down a long slope. "It's them! It's Smiley Colfax and Earl Latiker!"

Too late for Gunhammer now. Too late to run. Ray's eyes searched the foreground. "I'll have to hide you," he rasped. "Come on, Hannie."

Beyond the ruins of the cabin, near the burned

corrals, there was a mound of dirt, an old root cellar. Ray led the way, hurrying the girl, pulling her along. He heaved on the heavy plank door and threw it back, exposing the cobwebbed, dirt-filled steps.

"Down there," Ray rasped, his hands on Hannie's shoulders. "You'll be safe enough."

Hannie resisted the pressure. "You won't—" she began.

"Get down an' hide!" A push sent her almost falling down the steps. "Stay there until I call you!"

The plank door swung down, settling into place with a groan from rusty hinges. Sunlight streaming through the cracks of the planking shot golden motes of brilliance. Crouched on the bottom step, Hannie heard Ray's hurried departure. She waited—endlessly.

Ray ran back to his horses. He did not believe that either he or Hannie had been seen. The riders were a quarter of a mile away. A hasty plan in mind, Ray mounted Brownie. He would meet these men and stop them before they came up the slope to the ruined cabin. Ray sent Brownie along toward the fence corner.

The two riders had noted his approach. They stopped just at the lower fence. Brownie minced along, head low. The best cutting horse the Walking V had ever owned, Brownie never roused until it was necessary, then it took a man to ride him, for the old horse was quick as a cat and could turn in less than his own length. What were Colfax and Latiker waiting for? Ray asked himself. Why didn't they come on?

The question was soon answered. Two more horsemen had come over the rise and, spurring, rode down toward the fence. Ray recognized the horses. These new arrivals were Max and Shorty Hinds. They, too, pulled up, joining Latiker and Colfax. Now what? For an instant Brownie checked as Ray lifted the reins. Then the old brown horse walked on. He could not, Ray thought, afford to rouse suspicion. He must ride up to these men and greet them as he had always done.

Down at the lower fence Smiley Colfax spoke to his companion. "That's Ray Verity, Earl. I know that old brown horse."

"That's Verity all right," Latiker corroborated. His eyes were sharp as he looked at Colfax. "Do you suppose he's found her?"

Smiley shrugged. "What if he has?" he rasped. "There's a five-hundred-dollar reward on Verity, dead or alive, an' no questions asked."

"He's ridin' down to meet us," Latiker drawled. "Smiley—"

From behind the two men came a faint yell, and both turned. Two riders were on the ridge, spurring down toward them.

"Max an' Shorty, damn it!" Colfax snapped.

Here was an unexpected and unwelcome addition to their forces. "What'll we do with them?"

Latiker shook his head. "I don't know yet," he growled.

The Hinds boys came pounding up and pulled their horses to a halt. "We figgered somethin' was wrong," Shorty announced. "We come back to Marvin's. How'd Tom get killed? Where's Ruth an' the kids? We—"

"Never mind that now!" Latiker rasped. "There's Ray Verity comin'."

"What about it?" Max Hinds was a slow thinker, slower than his brother.

"There's a five-hundred-dollar reward on Verity!" Shorty answered. "That's what about it."

"He's comin' right on," Colfax growled. "Just like he owned the place."

"Let him come!" Latiker snapped. "Let him ride right up to us."

"Are we goin'—?" Max began.

"We're goin' to shoot!" Latiker snarled. "It's a damned sight easier to pack a dead man than a live one. Act friendly. Here he comes!"

Ray brought Brownie around the lower corner of the sagging fence. Brownie shambled along as though half asleep. "Hello, Earl," Ray called. "How are you boys?"

"Fine," Latiker gave answer. "How are you, Ray? When'd you get back?"

Brownie stopped fifteen feet away from the

other horses. Almost mechanically the riders swung in line to face Ray Verity. "Well," Ray said, "what about it, boys?"

The question was like a stone dropped into the flat surface of a lake. It was unexpected, as unexpected as the gesture that placed Ray's hand on the butt of the double-action Colt. Earl Latiker and Smiley Colfax and the two Hinds brothers found themselves looking into a pair of rock-hard blue eyes.

"What about what?" Latiker asked. "What are you on the prod about, Ray?"

Ray estimated chances. There were four men against him, men that he knew well. Latiker and Colfax were the hard ones; the Hinds boys were not so tough. Hannie was back there hidden in the root cellar, and he had to think about Hannie. He could, perhaps, account for one, perhaps two, of the men who faced him. It was a temptation. His hand was on his gun. All that he needed to do was pull the weapon and shoot. He would not come out of it, but what of that? What counted was Hannie's safety. Ray's eyes surveyed the men speculatively. Latiker and Colfax were nearest the fence, Colfax' horse almost against the sagging wire, and the Hinds boys were on the outside, first Shorty, then Max. Max was riding a young horse. Ray's back was to the sun, and the others looked into it.

"What about what?" Latiker repeated.

This was not a simple thing at all. The Ray Verity who faced Latiker and these others was not the pin-feathered kid who had juned around Verity Gap and the Wagonwheel. This was a man, iron-hard, seasoned, tough as an old boot top, and he had his hand on his gun. It was not going to be easy.

"About a lot of things," Ray drawled. He had come to the end of the road. He knew, sitting there on Brownie, that he was finished, that there was just one difference between Ray Verity and a dead man: he could still account for at least one of these men before he went. He was going to do just that, but first he must do that other thing that he had planned. He would throw his accusation into the faces of these men.

"About killin' Wayne an' the twins," Ray's voice went on. "About burnin' my place an' stealin' my cattle. About killin' Dutch Koogler. That's what about."

He saw, with eyes that encompassed all the men who faced him, that the last words were a shock. Max Hinds looked startled, and Shorty half lifted his hand.

"We never," Shorty blurted. "*You* killed Dutch!"

"Did I?" Ray drawled. "Then why don't you collect that reward?"

He closed his legs on Brownie as he spoke, and the old horse came alive, head up and alert. "You dirty murderin' devils!" Ray Verity flared and jumped Brownie at Max Hinds' young horse.

The bronc spooked, shied, and fouled Shorty's horse. Latiker had gone for his gun when Ray snarled his challenge, and Colfax, only a fraction slower, also had his weapon out. It was like playing tenpins. Max's horse bumped Shorty's; Shorty's hit Latiker's, and Earl Latiker's horse, whirling, bumped Colfax' big sorrel into the fence. The sorrel got a leg across the sagging wire and, panic-stricken, kicked and bucked, further fouling and cutting himself. Ray had gone past, set Brownie down, and cut him back so swiftly that the old horse spun almost like a top. The fancy Colt was in Ray's hand, the hammer back, and the first shot spewing from it followed Latiker's by a fraction of a second. "It ain't the first shot that counts; it's the first shot that hits." Ray could almost hear old Mat Yoeman's voice. Latiker's lead buzzed past, and Latiker, hit full in the chest, went back against his cantle as his horse jumped, toppled to one side, and, foot caught in the stirrup, was dragged into the fence by the frightened animal. Ray did not see that. He was attending to Smiley Colfax, letting the Hinds boys go.

Shorty was shooting now, but Max, his green horse still frantically bucking, fought the maddened animal. He was too slow-witted to drop off and, from the ground, put a finish to all this action. Shorty was shooting wild, but Smiley Colfax was doing well for himself.

Quick-witted and dangerous as a wolverine, Smiley had quit his horse when the animal went into the wire. He ran, the fence between himself and the others, crouched on one knee, and, leveling his Colt, sent three quick shots at Ray. One shot cut a lock from Brownie's mane; a second thudded into the cantle of Ray's saddle, cutting through a fold of his buckskin shirt to get there, and the third burned along Ray's ribs. Colfax' fourth shot missed, for Ray sent Brownie straight at him, the old horse running like a frightened wolf. Just before Brownie reached the fence Ray cut him sharp to the left and set him down. Brownie squatted and slid to a stop, and from that almost motionless platform Ray fired twice, his first aim good and his second better. Smiley Colfax, hit low in the belly, pitched forward just in time to receive the second bullet through his snarling mouth. He was done.

Ray, too, was almost done. Shorty Hinds had a full bead drawn on him, and Max, on the ground at last, was leveling off with his six-shooter when, from the north, a rifle chanted two quick notes. Shorty dropped his gun and spun in his tracks, falling face down, head toward the north. Max squawked his hurt and fright, dropped his gun, and tried to run. His leg buckled and he fell. Ray, wheeling Brownie, Colt raised to chop down for another shot, checked the motion. There were four men on the ground. Colfax lay inside the fence, unmoving; Latiker was just at the fence where his foot had pulled free of the stirrup; Shorty Hinds lay to the north, and Max was sitting up. Ray brought the Colt down to point it at Max, and the slow-witted Hinds boy raised his hands. Brownie, the action over, stood alert, ready for what might come next.

Slowly, like an old man, Ray came down from the saddle. His ribs burned like fire, and there was a bullet gash across his thigh that he had not noticed before. Dropping Brownie's reins, he walked toward Max, and for the first time he heard his name. "Ray! Ray!"

He half turned. Hannie Koogler was running from the burned cabin, following the lane along the fence. Beyond her Ray could see a buckboard, its team running.

"Don't, Ray! Don't shoot!" Max pleaded and, turning to him, Ray realized that he had kept his gun leveled at the man. He lowered it, momentarily indecisive, and then returned it to his holster and halted, his hand still on the gun butt. Horses' hoofs were pounding and, looking up, Ray saw big black Bear Dance coming in from the north, Mat Yoeman astride and riding like an Indian, the old .38-.55 brandished above his head. Ray dropped his hand away from the Colt. Behind him Brownie shook himself until all the leather on the saddle cracked and rattled. Bear Dance slid to a stop, and Mat flung himself down, took three quick steps, and was beside Ray.

"Are you hurt, Ray?" he rasped.

Ray's eyes were dazed as he looked at his friend. "How did you get here?" he queried.

Mat did not answer. He had put down the rifle, and his hands were going over Ray, swift and rough. "You ain't hurt," Mat rasped. "You danged young fool. I seen the whole thing. I—"

What Mat might have further said was lost. Hannie, arriving, threw herself upon Ray, her arms around his neck, her body pressed close to him, her voice an agony of fear.

"Ray . . . Ray . . ." Ray's arms went up around the girl, and he held her close. For an instant Mat looked at the two of them, then snorted, turned on his heel, and strode off to Max Hinds.

"Ray," Hannie sobbed against Ray's chest, "I heard the guns. I thought . . . I thought . . ."

Such was the scene that Miles Tenbow, pulling his buckboard to a halt, encountered. The team stopped, and Tenbow jumped down almost before the wheels stopped turning. He ran forward, shouted: "Hannie!" and then stopped. Ray lifted his head and saw the ranchman. Hannie, perhaps hearing her name spoken, perhaps feeling the stiffening of Ray's body, released one arm and turned. Side by side the two faced Tenbow.

"Shucks," Mat Yoeman growled, bending over Max Hinds. "In the leg. I ought to of done better than that."

For a full minute no other word was spoken. Then Hannie, one arm around Ray, Ray's left arm circling her slender waist, said: "They killed Dad, Mr. Tenbow."

"They?" Tenbow said as though he did not understand.

"Smiley Colfax and Earl Latiker."

Tenbow's face was gray. "Colfax an' Latiker?" Still it seemed that he did not comprehend.

"Yeah, Colfax an' Latiker!" Mat Yoeman had left Max Hinds and gone over to the fence. He was kneeling beside Latiker. "Come here, Tenbow. Leave them kids alone. Latiker ain't dead—yet."

With an effort Tenbow took his eyes from Hannie and her man. He turned slowly. Mat was staring past him.

"By glory," Mat rasped, "here's Frank."

Frank Arnold, carrying a small girl on his saddlebow, was riding up toward the fence. Behind the sheriff came big sorrel Custer, carrying Ruth Marvin. Little Tom peeped from behind his mother, and Ruth had a child in her arms. Arnold stopped his horse and looked from one to another, from the men on the ground to those who still stood upright.

"Well," he said slowly, "anyhow I *heard* the

287

shootin'. Stay back, Ruth. You don't want the kids to see this!"

Hannie, with a little cry, freed herself from Ray and ran toward Ruth, and Arnold, his arm crooked about the baby he carried, freed his right foot and swung down heavily to the ground.

"Somebody take this kid," he commanded, "an' tell me what happened."

Chapter 19

The sheriff's office occupied a room in the northeast corner of Fort Neville's courthouse, and Mat Yoeman, disdaining a chair, squatted by the window where he could look out into the street and enjoy the sunshine. Frank Arnold occupied a swivel chair beside his desk, and Charlie Nerril, newly arrived from Gunhammer, had another chair. There was about the three men a sort of relaxation. They lounged companionably as men do when they have finished one job and have no other in immediate prospect. Mat was talking, his voice a drawling rumble.

"I got plenty of time. Miz Starke's cuttin' Ray's hair, an' after that Ray's goin' to borrow the preacher's razor. Hannie says she wants to see the man she's marryin', an' Ray's harvestin' his crop."

"Hannie," Nerril predicted, "will run her brand on that boy good an' strong. He won't be a maverick no more."

There was quiet in the office while each man digested Nerril's statement. Mat said: "I dunno. Hannie mought handle him all right, but there was a time or two when I knowed I couldn't. Ray was just crazy for a while after I got him."

"He wasn't what you'd call gentle up there in the gap," Arnold rasped. "If ever there was a fool stunt . . ." The sheriff let the words die away.

"It was crazy all right," Mat seconded. "There he was with four of 'em waitin' to take him. I seen the whole thing, remember. He set his horse an' figgered it out just as cool as a cucumber. Got things the way he wanted 'em an' then jumped the gun."

"He shot Colfax first, didn't he?" Nerril asked curiously. The Gunhammer deputy had received a secondhand account of the happenings in the gap and was not satisfied with it.

"Nope." Mat shook his head. "Latiker was first. Ray jumped his horse into Max Hinds an' kind of went from there. I talked to him about it. He said that he knew Latiker an' Colfax was the dangerous ones. They was the ones that had killed Dutch an' they was lookin' for Hannie. I tried to pump Ray, but he wouldn't say much. The way I figger it, he just didn't care. He was goin' to look after Hannie an' he didn't give a good cuss what happened to him. He cut down on Latiker an' then taken Colfax for a ride. That's the way it happened."

"An' the Hinds boys shootin' at him all the time!" Nerril marveled.

"Max was tryin' to ride a buckin' horse part of the time," Mat said dryly. "Max ain't what you'd call smart. How's his leg comin', Frank?"

Arnold grunted. "Good enough. Max is a damned sight better off than his brother."

"I was shootin' for keeps when I pulled down on Shorty," Mat drawled complacently. "He was goin' to do Ray's business for him. I taken my time on that shot, but I kind of hurried with Max."

"You did all right," Arnold commented. "Max is satisfied with yore shootin'." All three men chuckled grimly. Max Hinds, reposing now in the Fort Neville jail, should be well satisfied with Mat's shooting. Of four men, Max was the only one alive.

"I don't know quite what to do with Max," Arnold continued. "He wasn't in on the deal when Dutch was killed. He didn't even know about it. An' he says that it was Latiker an' Colfax that rigged up the whole thing when Wayne an' the twins were killed. Says he was just along."

Again there was a silence in the office. Nerril cleared his throat preparatory to speech, but Mat forestalled him. "We kind of owe Max at that," Mat drawled. "If he hadn't told us we'd never knowed just how the Veritys got killed. Latiker wouldn't talk none. I'll say this for Earl: He was tough right to the last minute."

Again the talk ceased while the men thought. Mat and the sheriff were remembering a hard-faced man who, dying, had cursed them.

"I reckon," Mat ruminated, "that Earl was kind of the ramrod. You know, boys, this was a pretty big stink over a kind of little thing. Here's seven men dead an' what about? Nothin' except maverickin' a few cattle or mebbe stealin' a few. Wayne an' the twins would be alive today if it hadn't been that Tenbow blackballed the Wagonwheel. An' Latiker an' Colfax an' Shorty would be livin' if they hadn't bucked when Wayne closed the gap to 'em." Mat shook his head. "Just a few cattle. I dunno. Mebbe it'll stop with this."

"It won't stop," Arnold said quietly. "It'll get worse. Times are changin', but there's some men that won't change with 'em. Things will get worse an' worse until there's finally a blowup." The sheriff spoke prophetically, looking far ahead. Within short years his prophecy was to come true, and a cattlemen's war would flare in Wyoming.

"Mebbe," Mat drawled. "Anyhow, we can say it's stopped for now."

He pushed himself around so that he could better see out of the window. Nerril cleared his throat again. "What's Mrs. Marvin goin' to do?" he asked.

"She's goin' over to the 10 Bow," Arnold answered. "Hannie gettin' married this way leaves Tenbow without a housekeeper. He's goin' to take Mrs. Marvin an' the kids an' keep 'em at the ranch."

"You know"—Mat glanced from the window to the sheriff—"I don't think Hannie's marryin' Ray sets too good with Tenbow. I think he's kind of sweet on Hannie hisse'f."

"What's Verity goin' to do after he's married?" Arnold asked, changing the subject abruptly. "Go back to the gap?"

Mat shook his head. "He don't want to, an' Hannie don't neither. They had too many things happen to 'em to go back there. They're goin' up an' hold down my place for a couple of weeks an' then they're goin' to pull out. I know a place over in Utah that's just built for 'em. I'm goin' to give the kids a little bunch of mares an' a stud, an' they're goin' down an' raise some horses."

"Where are you goin', Mat?" Nerril asked.

Mat grinned. "Down to Nashota. They're issuin' rations there, an' the Sioux will have a sun dance an' a big powwow. I'm goin' to take it in."

"There's still a warrant out for Verity," Arnold said slowly. "That old warrant that Weathers swore out."

"There's a reward out for him too," Mat announced with asperity. "I call it a fine thing, after the way the kid was choused around, to keep that old warrant alive."

"Weathers has made a complaint against you too, Mat," Nerril broke in. "Yo're goin' to have to pay the J.P. ten dollars for disturbin' the peace the next time you come to Gunhammer. You shouldn't of slapped Weathers."

A contented grin broke across Mat's face. "It

was wuth it to me," he drawled. "Dawggone. Ten dollars. I reckon I'm goin' to have to sell a horse. I'll need about twenty bucks."

"What's the other ten for?"

Mat got up. "I never like to leave no strings danglin'," he answered. "I'll owe the other ten after I get through slappin' Jorbet. Frank, speakin' of rewards an' such, Ray's broke."

Arnold frowned. "I don't know what I can do about that, Mat," he said. "I can't line up who got the Walkin' V cattle or where the money went. Marvin got some of it, I guess, but Mrs. Marvin—"

"Ray wouldn't take a dime from Miz Marvin," Mat interrupted. "Now lookit here, Frank." He crossed to the sheriff's desk and, pulling a gun from his waistband, placed it in front of the officer. Bright and glittering with engraving, Clough Weathers' double-action Colt winked up at the sheriff.

"Ray's gun," Mat announced.

"An' what about it?" Arnold asked, looking from the gun to Mat.

Mat was grinning. "That there's a outlaw's weapon," he announced. "You know danged good an' well nobody could ever take that gun off Ray unless he was dead. Now there's yore reward notice. See it?" He pointed to the bulletin board on the office wall.

Nerril and Arnold looked at the board. Big

and bold in black type the words flared out on a poster: "$500 REWARD."

"You got that money in yore safe, Frank," Mat drawled. "The Stock Association give it to you."

"So?" Arnold's eyes were quizzical.

"So there's Ray's gun. He had to be dead for me to git it. How about payin' me the reward?"

Arnold hesitated.

"They owe it to him." Mat's voice was suddenly savage. "Cattle gone. Land gone. Run all over the country. They owe it to him."

Arnold got up from his chair and, crossing to his safe, squatted in front of it and fumbled in its interior. Then, returning, he held out a sheaf of bills to Mat Yoeman.

"Thanks, Frank," Mat said quietly. "Yo're square, you are." He stuffed the bills into his pocket, and his voice was happy as he spoke again.

"It's just time for the weddin'. Are you boys comin' down to Preacher Starke's?"

Nerril looked questioningly at the sheriff. Arnold stared at Mat and slowly shook his gray head while a grin broke across his face.

"Give the kid my best, Mat," he drawled. "Wish him good luck an' kiss the bride for me. I won't be down to the weddin'. It wouldn't look right. You see"—the sheriff hesitated—"I've done paid that reward. As far as this sheriff's office is concerned, Ray Verity is dead."